A Novel by
EJ Thornton

**Books To Believe In
A Division of Thornton Publishing, Inc
Copyright 1998**

Cover art by Mark J. Robertson

A Books To Believe In Publication
All Rights Reserved
Copyright 2004 by EJ Thornton

Proudly Published in the USA by
Books To Believe In
a Division of Thornton Publishing, Inc
17011 Lincoln Ave. #408
Parker, CO 80134
Phone: (303) 794-8888   Fax: (720) 863-2013

GreatAngelBooks.com
BooksToBelieveIn.com

Second Edition: ISBN: 1-932344-76-4
Library of Congress Catalog Card Number: 99-90315

First Edition: ISBN: 0-9670242-0-X Copyright 1998

This book is dedicated to God,
my family, my friends
and all our angels...
thanks to their love,
I have everything.

When you show hospitality
to strangers, you might just
have entertained angels unawares.
-Hebrews 13:2 (paraphrased)

"If you knew who walked beside you at all times,
you could never experience fear again."
-A Course in Miracles

❖   ❖   ❖

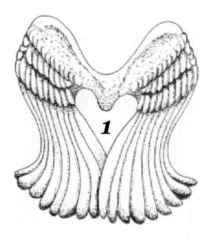

It all started the night I died.

I was in bed asleep, or so I thought.

Then the most wonderful voice in the world whispered, "Dad, get up. It's time to go." That was the voice of my daughter Sheila. She had died tragically of cancer a couple of months before, at the age of thirty-six. I often saw her in my dreams, wonderful, wonderful dreams, vivid and real.

"Sheila!" I whispered and smiled.

"I'm here, too." A man's voice came from behind her. It was a familiar voice. I opened my eyes. I swore I'd seen him somewhere before.

"Who are you?" I asked, still somewhat groggy.

Sheila giggled. They were both very excited.

"My name is George," he replied. I needed more than merely his first name to connect to that one useful memory just out of my reach.

"Okay, what's going on here?" I hesitantly asked Sheila, who grinned from ear to ear, positively giddy.

"It's time for us to be together, Dad."

"I know. I love these dreams. All the pain of your death melts away. It's like you're really here with me," I told her, then I sighed. "But it's hard when I wake up and realize it was just a dream."

"There's a reason for that, Dad," Sheila started to explain, "but time it is different. Dad, you had a heart attack and died peacefully in your sleep. Now we're here to escort you into Heaven." I paused for a moment and looked her in the eyes. Her eyes held steady.

"Okay, I want to wake up now!"

"I'm sorry, Martin, but that's just impossible."

Sheila and George stood over me, lovingly smiling.

"Give me your hand, Dad," Sheila sweetly said, extending her arm to me.

I flailed for a minute to try to wake myself up. I should have been able to feel my heart racing. I tossed myself hard, then harder, but my body stayed still. This was too weird. Eventually, I gave Sheila my hand. She helped me sit up and then stand up.

"Look." George pointed back at the bed. I looked back and I saw myself still lying there, with a strained look on my face.

"I'd really like to wake up now."

"Stubborn as ever," George chuckled, shaking his head.

"I'm sorry, who are you again?"

"I'm George. I was your great-grandfather. I died a few years before you were born. But for all your seventy-two years, I've been your guardian angel and you've been my charge, the one I was assigned to protect and guide."

"I've seen you before," I pointed at him trying hard to place any memory that would make sense.

"Yes, in old photographs."

"And maybe a couple of other places over the years." Sheila nudged him and he smiled slyly.

Shaking that off, I got back to the issue at hand determined to reason my way back to familiar ground. "If I'm dead, who is going to take care of my precious Glory? You know how much she needs me. If I'm dead, who's going to lead the elder's meeting at church in the morning? Then there's Sarah. I promised her a road trip this weekend. I have too much to do. I have to go back." I turned away from them to try and figure out how to get back inside my own skin.

George quickly put his hand on my shoulder, turned me back toward him and looked me straight in the eyes. "Your work will continue, Martin. I merely have to teach you how to do it as an angel. That's all."

I looked straight back into his eyes, with a plea to go back to the world, but all I saw was genuine concern and love. I stared into his eyes and peace fell over me like a waterfall.

"And Mama will be taken care of, by more people and angels than you could ever imagine," Sheila said, putting her hand on my other shoulder.

A beautiful, bright, white light appeared. It came from behind George and encompassed us completely. I stopped protesting. Heaven was calling me and it was my time to go. George turned and led us toward the light. I held Sheila's hand tightly and followed my guides into Heaven.

On the walk through the bright light, scenes of my life surrounded me; important events and turning points. I saw scenes from my childhood. I saw my mother's anguished face right after my father passed away. I saw myself with my brothers, playing hard when we were young and fighting even harder as we grew older. I saw images, both happy and sad. I saw the people from the town where I grew up. I saw the time I was caught stealing a piece of candy by old Mr. Wannabaker. Then I saw the smile on his face, as he cheered me winning the pumpkin-carving contest during the Harvest picnic that same year. There was the widow Dunberry, our next door neighbor, who I'd always helped with household chores. She always patted me on the head, until I outgrew her. There were images from the civil rights marches and riots of the sixties. We broke across many a lunch counter barrier, until we were either served or arrested.

I saw my ordination as a minister. There were images of the people of my congregations and the countless marriages, baptisms and funerals I'd presided over. Among the many faces in my congregation, one stood out, as it always had in my life, that of my lovely bride, Glory. Glory, I called her, because the day she told me she loved me, I knew I'd found the Promised Land! I saw my marriage and the birth of each of my four children, Jeremiah, Sheila, Peter and Sarah. I saw their smiling faces as they grew up. I relived the relationship struggles as they grew into adults. I felt again the death of my mother and the illness and death of my daughter. Finally, I saw the last time I kissed my Glory goodnight on my last night on earth and now here I was.

As we emerged on the other side of the light passage, figures walked toward us. A familiar voice called out my name. She smiled joyously. "Martin, my son. Come to me."

We embraced. The amount of pure love and joy I felt overwhelmed me.

"Mother," was all I could say.

"Son," a strong voice said. I looked up and my father stood right beside me. He'd died when I was twelve. "I'm proud of you, son and the man you have become." He put his hand on my shoulder. His strength and love flowed all through me.

Then George said, "We have a lot to do. You will be back with these lovely angels very soon. But we need to keep going."

"But I just got here. I need more time." I looked at Mother and Dad's faces and they encouraged me to continue on with George. So I went on.

We entered a garden filled with the most spectacular flowers and most beautiful scents I could've imagined. There was perfection in every petal, leaf, and stem. This place was the definition of serenity.

We sat on an intricately carved, curved marble bench. George began to explain my situation. "Martin, you lived a good life, a productive life for God, and you will be rewarded greatly in Heaven. There are choices regarding your future that you need to make soon. I will explain all the options, of course, and using your wisdom and my guidance, we will choose your path for you."

"My path?"

"It will all become clear to you soon, but now we have to go back. It's time to think about your earthly family. They're unaware you're gone. Only a few seconds have actually passed on Earth. We need to help them with this transition. You'll be there and be affecting your loved ones in very profound ways."

"I get to go back and be with them?" I asked eagerly. "I really get to go back and see them all again?"

"You're an angel now, Martin," he told me in a soft, strong voice, "and you're free from the constraints of the physical world. You have new capabilities, although you need to be trained in how to use them. After you choose your path, you'll develop new powers. It all will become clear, very soon. But for now, let's go help the family through this."

I nodded and the instant our eyes met, they locked. When I looked around again, we were back in my bedroom in the world.

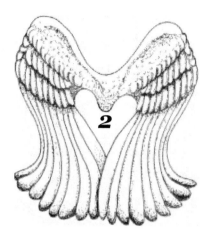

"How did you do that?" I asked, as I tried to regain my bearings.

"It's very simple. As an angel, all you have to do is think of being someplace or with someone and when you desire it, you're there with them. It's one of the best parts of being an angel," George explained.

So there I was. I looked down on my lovely wife, fast asleep, my still, lifeless body was right next to her.

"George, is she going to wake up and find me there, all alone like this?"

"Is that how you want it?"

"I think that would be too hard on her."

"Then, how would you like it to happen?"

"What do you mean?"

"If you could have your way, how would you like to be found? How would you like her to find out you've died?"

"Well, someone should be with her."

"Who would you like it to be?"

It came to me immediately. "Sarah. Sarah is who needs to be with her." My youngest daughter Sarah still lived at home, while she attended college. She was in the room right down the hall.

"Okay then, let's go wake up Sarah and get her to come in here."

"How do we do that?"

"Think back, Martin. I know there were times in your life when you felt compelled to be somewhere and you only understood the reason after you got there?"

"Yes. Lots of times."

"Most of those times, I led you or let some other angel lead you where you needed to go. It happens all the time. That's what an angel does, guides you where you need to be. I'll show you how you do it. First, think about being with Sarah."

So I closed my eyes and when I opened them, we were in Sarah's room. "Whoa!" I said. "That was fast."

"Time and space are different for you now, Martin. The main concept you need to grasp is that time *can only go forward*. Going backwards in it is impossible. Stopping it is impossible. But you can slow it down as much as you need to to accomplish the task at hand. Sometimes people report that during an accident, it felt like they were going in slow motion." I nodded. "Angels!"

"Okay, but how does that help us wake up Sarah?" I looked down at my sweet sleeping daughter. "How are we going to get her from here to there before her mama wakes up?"

"First, we need to summon Sarah's angel. While our charges are sleeping, if they're completely safe, the angels get to handle other business or visit other people. Wait until you see who this is." George rubbed his hands together quickly and grinned with anticipation. "Emma," he whispered.

If it were still possible, I'd have fainted. Emma was my mother's mother. She looked at me and smiled. "Welcome to Heaven, Baby." She gave me the sweetest kiss on the cheek, just like when she was on earth.

"Grandmama!" I paused while I absorbed what I saw. "How?" She died so many years before Sarah was born.

"I waited for this one, my first grandchild's baby girl. I wanted this one." She looked at Sarah and her face beamed with light and love. "This is going to be hard for her. We knew it was coming, so I tried to prepare her." Then she looked at George. "How are we doing this?"

George paused, then said, "Martin, imagine a beautiful, large, white feather."

I closed my eyes and did just that.

"Open your eyes," George said.

There in my hands was the feather, just the way I imagined it. I almost dropped it. "Settle down, Martin, it's just a feather." George and Grandmama laughed at me.

"Now, go tickle her nose with it," Grandmama instructed.

"Can she see any of this?" I asked.

"Oh no," Grandmama said. "She's really sensitive to what we say to her and our interactions with her, but she's oblivious to us. People rely on their ears for hearing when in reality their souls hear much more reliably, really."

I went over to her and very gently passed the feather under her nose--it twitched and I jumped. Grandmama and George laughed again and looked at each other with an understanding that surpassed me at this point. I did it again. Sarah scratched her nose. I looked at the angels and they nodded that I needed to keep on. I did it again. She rolled over and put her arm up to protect her face from the annoyance.

"Talk to her. Tell her what you want her to do," Grandmama said.

"Sarah," I whispered. "Wake up. Wake up Baby."

"Tell her why," George instructed.

"Sarah, it's Dad. Honey, wake up, your mama needs you. Baby, I died in my sleep tonight," I explained.

"Huh?" She bolted up in bed, shaking and breathing hard. She looked around frantically.

"What did I do wrong?"

"Nothing. You're doing great. Tell her to calm down, then to go check on Glory."

"Shhh, Sarah, shhh," I said. Sarah took a deep breath. She shook her head and looked around again. "Sarah, go check on Mama. Go Baby, she needs you." Sarah got out of bed, put on her robe and walked quietly down the hallway to Glory's bedroom. We all walked there with her.

She knocked quietly on the door, only loud enough to hear if someone was already awake. Silence... She slowly turned the knob and opened the door. It was dark in the room, so she turned on the desk lamp to its first dim setting and walked over to my side of the bed. She could see that I was gone. She gasped for air, but covered her mouth, so that her mama would keep sleeping. Tears welled up in her eyes. She sat down for a moment on the chair by the desk and tried to compose herself, tears rolling down her cheeks. She gathered her strength and took a couple of deep breaths, then went to wake her mother.

Sarah knelt by the side of the bed, took her mama's hand and laid her head on it.

Glory stirred. "Sarah? Sarah, honey, what's the matter?" She sat up in bed, all her attention on Sarah. Sarah looked up at her. Glory saw her tears. "What is it, Baby?" She gently wiped her daughter's cheek.

Sarah pointed her head in the direction of my body. Glory put her hand on my shoulder as if to wake me up, because it looked to her like Sarah wanted both of us for her problem. But as she touched my body and looked over, Glory realized what Sarah's problem was. Glory felt my cheek and cried out. Then she looked back at Sarah and took her in her arms. They held each other close and cried.

"What can I do to help them take away this pain?" I asked George.

"By going over and holding them. Wrap your arms around them and tell them how much you'll always love them. Tell them you are close by and that you are just fine. And that you know for a fact that they will be all right because that's what the angels are telling you. Tell them anything else you want. They'll hear you with their souls. Just try it."

I went and knelt by the bed next to Sarah and put my arms around both of them. "I'm right here. I'm still with you. I'm all right. I wish I could comfort you more. I'd do anything to make it stop hurting. It really will be all right." I kissed them both, then moved to where I could watch them better, to see what was going to happen.

Sarah looked up, wiped the tears on her face and tried to comfort her mother. "You know, I bet he's watching us right now, telling us 'quit yer cryin'.'" She sniffed a little and looked around. "Where do you think he is, Mama? You know he's here."

"Yeah, Baby, I know," Glory said through her tears. "I bet he's watching us from the doorway, like always." Sarah looked over right at me. That's exactly where I was.

George created a soft breeze over the desk and the papers ruffled very slightly.

Sarah sighed, "You're right, Mama. You're right." She blew a kiss in the direction of the door. I felt her breath as I caught the kiss in my hand the way I always did.

Sarah held her tight as Glory cried. Sarah tried to comfort her. "He's with Sheila now. They're both in Heaven together."

Right on queue, Sheila appeared by my side and took my hand. I looked at her and at George bewildered. It was all strange, sad and wonderful.

"This is the hardest part, Dad," Sheila said. "So we have to be closer than ever for a while. They'll be fine; we'll take care of them." All the angels circled around them. We all joined hands and prayed for their faith to give them an abundance of strength, courage and compassion during this time of transition.

After a bit, Glory and Sarah did the things that needed to be done. They went down to the living room and called the police to report the death. George made sure that my cousin Terrance received the call at the station. He came right over and handled it all, to make it easier on her.

I watched as Sheila played games with her sister Sarah and tried to make her smile. Sheila went over to Sarah and whispered in her ear to watch Terrance. Sheila made Terrance's pen slip out of his hand. It looked like he dropped it. She helped the pen on the way to the floor, instead of letting it fall on the floor, she tucked it into the cuff of his pants.

"Where did that thing go?" Terrance turned around to see where it had dropped. He turned around again and again quickly and lost his balance. He fell back over the arm of the recliner. He just sat there, with his legs in the air, as the pen stared him in the face. "Hmmm. There it is," he announced and got up without missing a beat.

Sarah covered her mouth trying to hold in a laugh determined to come out. Terrance scratched his head and looked at her. She quickly looked high at the ceiling. The lightness of that moment helped for a moment.

Sheila flew back over to me. She brushed Terrance's neck on the way by. "What'dya think of that?" Sheila asked, while Terrance rubbed his neck.

"What are you doing?" I sounded like I was going to punish her for something she had pulled, like she was twelve again.

"I'm getting their minds off this for a second or two. Wanna try?"

It felt like this was a Saturday afternoon long past and she had just run back to the house after discovering another one of her many treasures, excited to share it with everyone in the family.

"What do I do?" I asked.

She looked around. I looked around. All the angels in the room were smiling, watching us spend time together again.

"First, figure out who you want to touch. Pick Sarah, she's lost in a daze right now and she's alone. Now think, what would be special, that's just between the two of you?"

I looked around the room for something that was a special connection between Sarah and me. There was the macramé hanger that she had made for Glory and me for our last wedding anniversary and in it, the plant she had rooted from a cutting from one of her mother's plants. That was it. I went over to it. "This," I said to Sheila.

"Nice choice," she said and smiled. "Now, very subtly, softly and slowly, swing it. But first, let me get her attention focused on it." She sat next to Sarah and put her arm around her sister. "Dad's over by the plant you gave him. He wants to let you know he's all right." Sheila stared at the plant and a light from her eyes encompassed the plant, making it crystal clear, but everything else around it fuzzy. Soon all I could see was the plant. "Okay, Dad, now go."

"I love you, Sarah," I said as I pushed on the pot. It swung back and forth for a few seconds. Sarah's dazed eyes came into sharp focus around the plant and she shifted in her chair. She looked around again and then relaxed back into the couch.

"I love you too, Dad," she whispered and rubbed the chill bumps that had just raised on her arms. She sighed slightly and soon after that she dozed off to brief sleep.

I was fixated on the plant.

Sheila joined me. "That was nice," she kissed me on the cheek.

"Yeah." I stood there and admired my sleeping daughter, while I held tight to her sister.

"Angel Light," Sheila said. "I used Angel Light."

"Angel Light," George said and came to join us by the plant. "If there's something we want someone to see, we stand by them and stare at it until it's all that we can see. A glow comes over it and we call that glow Angel Light."

Terrance left momentarily to call in the details of the situation from his patrol car. Glory stood at the bay window in the living room and stared into space. Her arms were folded in front of her and she rubbed them like she was cold. The sun peeked over the distant mountains on the horizon.

"Let's paint the sunrise, Dad," Sheila said.

"How do we do that?" I asked.

"Imagine the sky is a painter's canvas," Sheila said. "Mama loves pinks. Let's give it lots of pinks." Sheila waved her hand slowly up in the air towards the horizon and the hues over and all around it gradually turned into beautiful shades of pink.

I followed her lead, "Lots of thin, whispy clouds." I imagined the clouds and waved my hands as Sheila had and to my amazement, the clouds gradually formed just as I had imagined them. They reflected the pinks vibrantly.

"Mama will like this," she said.

I walked over to Glory and put my arms around her, like I always did when we'd look out the window together. "We did that for you, do you like it?" I whispered in her ear.

"What a beautiful sunrise," she said and sighed. "I wish you could see it, Martin."

"I can," I said softly.

"I know you can. You're probably seeing lots of people and things right now." Another tear streamed down her cheek.

"I'll be here for you forever. I'm right here now and I'll always love you." I wanted to stay until I was sure she had heard me.

Sheila interrupted us. "Dad, it's time to go now."

Glory's angel took over for me at the window.

"Martin, we need to get her some more help," George said.

"Of course, Vivian!" I said. I instantly knew who he meant!

Vivian was Glory's best friend in the world; Glory needed her here. Quicker than a heartbeat, we were in Vivian's bedroom. The angel network was already at work. Vivian was wide-awake. She paced up and down her bedroom floor.

"She knows there's something wrong with Glory, but she's afraid to call because it's so early and she's hoping she's imagining things," Vivian's angel, Goldie, explained.

Viv looked so worried. She paced back and forth with her arms folded, just like Glory. It was as if she could feel what Glory felt.

"Just go over there," Viv's husband softly said. "If there's something wrong, you'll know. If all is well then, just take her out for a cup of coffee; you know she's always up with the sun."

"You're right, you're right," she said to her husband and started to get dressed.

I must've looked puzzled, because George then explained, "Close friends have an unspoken bond. Their angels are as close as the friends themselves. It enhances the beauty of the friendship."

"So Vivian knows something is wrong because she can sense what Glory feels?"

"That, and her angel told her that she needs to go to Glory. Between those two things, she woke up worried, tense, almost frantic. She's confused about where these feelings are coming from, so she doubts the validity of them."

"So she knows what it is?" I was in awe!

"No, she only knows how upset she feels and that it must be something big. She can only guess at possibilities. If she just trusted in her intuition, she'd zero right in on what's wrong."

Vivian dressed hurriedly, put her hair in a scarf and kissed her husband and said, "I'll call you in a little bit."

"Viv, she's all right," he said, trying to comfort her.

"Let's hope so," she said and raced out of the room, down to the garage, started the car and drove off to see Glory.

We followed her. As Viv drove up to the house, she saw the police car outside. "I knew it!" She stopped and jumped out of the car. She left her purse and everything inside. She ran up to the house and knocked hard on the door.

Glory came to the door, her face tear-stained. "It's Martin," she said. "He's gone." With that Mama fell onto her friend and the tears exploded anew. Vivian stood there, held Glory tight and cried, too. All the angels in the house gathered around them and prayed for their continued faith, strength and courage.

"It hurts to see her in such pain," I told George.

"You've done a good job getting her the help she needed."

"I want to do more. I wish I could show her that I'm okay. I wish I could tell her all about seeing Mother and Dad and Sheila again. I wish I could make her understand how close I really am and how wonderful this all is."

"I know."

"But you know what I wish most?" I asked him. He listened intently. "I wish I'd have known how close you were to me when I was alive on earth. Angels! Angels are everywhere, all the time. I thought they were God's messengers on extraordinary occasions, but I was so wrong. Being a minister all those years, you'd think I'd have known better. I have so much to learn."

"We all do," George agreed.

"You hear the stories of the incredible events in people's lives and you know that the Lord and his angels were hard at work. But you, you were there every day? You had to have been! You were there every day of my life."

"I never left you unprotected."

"You know what? I want to look in on the rest of my family, before they hear about my death. I want to catch them one last time, without them knowing. Is that possible?"

"All things are possible, Martin." He looked to Heaven and smiled.

I thought of my youngest son, Peter. Instantly, we were in his house, with him and his family. To them, it was the beginning of a normal day. The children got ready for school. The baby was at the table with his breakfast. My son helped his daughters gather their schoolbooks by the front door. Angels were everywhere, helping everyone with everything. The one around my grandson made faces and blew kisses. There seemed to be actual interaction.

"Can the baby see his angel?" I asked.

"The angel is distracting him. The baby leaned over too far in the high chair. He would have fallen. But his angel showed himself to him, caught his attention and saved him from falling. He's only visible to the baby. Even so, he'll be invisible again when someone comes back into the room. The angel probably quit doing that when he's old enough to speak, but while he's this little, it happens frequently. Angels love to play with babies and babies love to play with angels. Look over there." George motioned at my granddaughter. "She's looking for her other shoe. Her angel knows where it is. Let's see how long it takes her to listen."

I watched as her angel whispered in her ear, "It's under your bed. It's under your bed." Her mom asked where she'd left it, when she'd seen it last. Poor darling had trouble thinking straight under all that Hurry-up-you're-late-for-school pressure. My granddaughter finally sat down on the stairs, put her face in her hands, rocked, and started to softly cry. Her mother threw her hands up about the whole issue and went to get the baby out of the high chair. When it was all quiet for the girl, her angel said again, "It's under your bed."

Like it was her own idea, my granddaughter got up, went into her room, looked under her bed and found the shoe, then ran out of the room and yelled, "I found it!"

"Praise the Lord!" her mother said. The angel nodded in recognition of what was said, smiled and went out the door to school with her charge.

I wanted Peter to know how much I loved him. I went over to my son and sat next to him on the couch. "I love you so much. I'm so proud of you and if I had to do it all over again, the only thing I'd change is to love you more."

He sighed and sat back, looking out into space and gave a slight smile. Just then, the phone rang.

"Who's that this early?" he asked his wife, who shrugged her shoulders.

Peter answered the phone. "Hello?" There was a pause. His knees buckled. His wife, Melinda, ran over to him and he put his arm around her. She held him tight.

"Is Mama all right? . . . We'll be there as soon as we can . . . Okay . . . Okay . . . I love you, too. Take care of Mama until we get there. Bye."

He hung up the phone and all of us angels gathered around them and prayed for their strength as he told his wife of my death.

"I was just thinking about him too," he said. "How coincidental is that?" Their eyes met and stayed. "Yeah, I know," he bit his lower lip. "Dad, wherever you are. I hope you know how much I love you. I'll make sure Mama is okay." Then he broke down, buried his head on his wife's shoulder and cried.

After a few minutes, he suddenly jerked his head up, panic-stricken. "I've got to find Jeremi! Did he come home last night?" My other son, Jeremi--short for Jeremiah--lived with Peter and his wife, but unfortunately, he drank far too much. "Jeremi, where would you be about now? Hmmm."

Peter thought for a moment, then he rushed out the door.

"Where is Jeremi?" I asked George.

"Just think about him and you'll find him," he replied. So I did. The next thing I knew, we were in a stranger's house. But, sure enough, there was right Jeremi, passed out on the couch, snoring, with a half-full beer bottle about to spill on his lap and a cigarette butt that had burned out in his hand.

"Holy cow!" I exclaimed. George gave a disappointed look of recognition. Jeremi's angel was there, his great Uncle Henry, on my father's side. Henry was glad to see us.

"Martin!" We embraced, then he looked back at Jeremi.

Henry turned somber. "He's drinking more now than ever. I'm so frustrated with the way he ignores all my help. Getting through to him now will be a challenge and it'll probably take a little while or else some intervention. What do you want to do?"

I looked at George for guidance. "We need to get Peter over here." George left.

This was the first time since I'd died that George had left my side. I looked over at Henry.

Henry looked tired. He was the first sad angel I'd ever seen. "How long has he been like this?" I asked him, referring to Jeremi's condition.

"Well, tonight, about two hours, but you know this has been going on for years. He's getting worse and worse. The alcohol has won him away from me." He looked at Jeremi and shook his head in despair and frustration.

I looked around the room. There were a lot of tired angels in this room. Then I realized that there were many more people in this room than there were angels. Puzzled by this, I looked to Henry.

"Some of their angels have quit."

"Quit? Angels can quit?" I was astounded.

"If your charge does something that offends the very nature of your soul, you have the angelic prerogative of quitting. It's a monumental step and angel rarely do it, but when an angel has lost all positive effectiveness, they need to move on to some other charge, whose life they can effect in a positive way. For example, someone who's committed murder or someone who hates indiscriminately and teaches others to hate for arbitrary reasons, they lose their angels. Things like that. It can be that dramatic or sometimes, they just slip slowly away . . . I hope you understand what I mean."

A knock on the door interrupted our conversation. George, Peter, and his angel, William, were back with us. Some young lady got up, stumbled to the door, squinted enough to see Peter. She let him in and pointed to the couch where Jeremi was, then stumbled back to the chair she'd been in and went back to sleep.

Peter went over to Jeremi and shook his shoulder. "Jeremi, bro, come on, wake up man, it's important!" Jeremi's snoring ceased briefly, but then it started back up again. "Jeremi!" Peter said louder. That accidentally woke up a couple of the other sleepers around him. They grumbled back "Shhhh!" and held their heads. Peter ignored them and shook Jeremi by the shoulders a little harder - nothing. Peter took the beer away and pulled the cigarette butt out of his hand, put Jeremi's arm over his shoulder, dragged him out of the house and laid him out on the front lawn. We all went with him.

"He needs some help," Henry said.

Almost immediately, a spray from the neighbor's sprinkler got caught on Henry's breath--or a surprise gust of wind, depending on perspective. The water landed right in Jeremi's face. He woke up, mumbled, cussed and tried to figure out where he was.

Henry came back and said curtly, "He needed that."

George, William and I laughed so loud I thought for a moment Peter heard us. Peter laughed a little bit, too. He looked to the sky and said, "Thanks!"

Henry replied emphatically, "You are welcome!"

"Wake up, bro, it's important! Are you with me, man?" Peter insisted.

"What do you want?" Jeremi was indignant and held his head to protect his hangover.

"Jeremi, it's important. Look at me."

I could tell Jeremi heard the seriousness of Peter's tone and likely remembered the same tone when we lost Sheila. Jeremi's indignant behavior turned somber and he looked at Peter. "What is it?"

"Dad passed," Peter sat on the grass next to him.

"Oh God! Oh God!" Jeremi yelled, and stared at Peter in disbelief.

Peter put his hand on his brother's shoulder. "He died peacefully in his sleep last night. Sarah just called. She and Viv are with Mama right now. They want us to get there as soon as possible."

Jeremi nodded, then held his head, as much to hide his tears as to protect his hangover. "We just lost Sheila, now Dad too. It's too soon. This is too much." He swallowed hard. "I need a drink."

I was overwhelmed! He'd always put on an act for me. I knew it was an act, but this reality was far worse than I'd imagined. I turned to Henry. "He's in bad shape." Henry nodded in agreement. My heart sank. "Is there anything we can do?"

"What would you do?"

I thought for a moment, shook my head, shrugged my shoulders, turned away from Henry and went to go hold my sons.

"C'mon, man, we gotta clean you up before Mama sees you."

I walked between them so that I could put my arms on both my boys' shoulders. I walked with them back to Peter's car and rode with them back to the house. Jeremi buried his face in his hands the whole way. Peter drove silently, occasionally putting his arm around his brother.

I was the lone angel in the car with them. George, Henry and William were somewhere else. This time alone with them was nice. I sat between them with my arms around both of them. I whispered, "I love you both." It was the only time Jeremi looked up, then he sighed and buried his head again. Peter sighed and a tear rolled down his cheek.

Finally, we were back at Peter's house. Jeremi went to his room and collapsed on his bed, and stared blankly and was asleep again a few minutes later.

I watched him and tried to figure out what I could do to make a difference. My lectures about drinking had fallen on deaf ears when I was alive.

"They'd fall on deaf ears now, too, even if he could hear you." George had rejoined me and read my thoughts. We both watched over him.

Soon after, Henry joined us, too. "Peter took him in, but he rarely sleeps here--he's usually at some after-hours party and then he sleeps the day away. Then he goes back to work in the pub and the pattern repeats itself. He avoids having any responsibilities to anyone or anything. So he's living an irresponsible lifestyle and nothing is challenging him."

"Then he needs some responsibility! That'll help him grow up and straighten out." I sounded more like an angry father than a brand new angel.

"There is a plan," George said, "that will hopefully get Jeremi back on the 'straight and narrow.' You figure very highly in the plan. We need to discuss it, to see if you're willing to take on the responsibilities to make it work."

"What's the plan?" I was anxious to hear it. I'd do anything, if it would help Jeremi come back to the land of the living. "How can I help? What do I do?"

"What Jeremi needs most of all is to get away from the angelless people who have been surrounding him. Then he needs to get back around his family and associate with other people who have their lives and minds focused on God, people who'll stand up to his faults and make him confront them and help him overcome them. It'll be hard. But God does have a plan; we just have to help Him carry it out."

I nodded to George that I understood, then I looked back at Jeremi. "Could you help me get through to him now?"

"Sleep is a special time," he said. "It's one of my favorite times. On special occasions, when we really need to communicate, we can visit them in their dreams. I enjoy doing it because it's really the only time we can converse outright. But it's such a vivid experience for them that we only do it occasionally. Too many interactions overwhelm them. But now might be a good time for you to go talk to Jeremi."

"How do I visit him in his dream?"

"First, set the stage: Whisper to him about a special, serene place you both like. Choose some place like the stream where you used to take him fishing, or his favorite mountain meadow or your old study where you both spent a lot of time--wherever is special to both of you. Then hold his hand and ask him to join you there. As soon as it takes over his dream, he'll be with you there. Then just talk. He'll have a million questions. Talk, you'll enjoy it." He motioned for me to begin.

I sat on the bed next to Jeremi. I leaned over to whisper in his ear. I tried to think of the most beautiful place we had ever been together. I remembered the pristine beaches on the coast, near where we used to live. There was one special beach where we used to go when he was little. I wondered if he would remember.

"Jeremi, it's me, Dad. I want to talk to you. Let's take a walk on the beach--remember that beach where we used to go clam-digging? I'll take your hand and take you there." I closed my eyes and remembered the most beautiful beach I'd ever seen. The waves pounded the massive rocks, the spray went up incredibly high and a fine, cool mist followed. The seagulls screeched in the background. When I opened my eyes, I was there and on the beach. Jeremi was very close to me, but still asleep. I went over to him and called his name. He stirred and woke.

He noticed his surroundings before he saw me. He watched as a wave smashed against the nearby rock, then put his face up to catch the spray. When it did, he smiled. Then he saw me. He got up, rushed over to me and we embraced. "Dad!"

"Jeremi, son, I love you. I want you to know I'm still here with you."

"I love you, too, Dad. Are you dead?" Jeremi was understandably confused.

"Yes, son, I am."

"Am I?"

"Relax, Jeremi, I've come to you in a dream. That's all" Good question, though. I had to appreciate how he might interpret this and help him stay calm. "You're just dreaming. I'm here to visit you. Do you remember this beach? We used to come here when you were little."

"Oh yes, I loved coming here. The clams we got here were screamin'. I loved to watch the waves roll in. The power of it always put things in perspective for me. "

I liked this Jeremi. This was Jeremi - his spirit, in its true form. George was right, this was very special.

Jeremi's reflective mood turned mournful. "Dad, what am I going to do without you? I already miss you so much."

"At first, I tried to fight it, son, but I had to go. It was my time to go and there's nothing wrong with that. The only hard part about this whole thing is how much it hurts my family and friends. If they only knew how close I really am, I think they'd feel a little better. Sheila and I painted a sunrise this morning for your Mama, then I held her as we both admired it. She could feel I was there with her, I know she could."

"How is Sheila? I miss her so much. Is she here on this beach with us? Can she be?"

"This is just us. Sheila's doing great. She's more beautiful than any angel I ever imagined when I was alive. It's wonderful to be with her again." We walked along the beach. "Jeremi, I'm worried about you."

"I know, Dad. I know." He sighed. "It's just hard, you know."

"What is so hard for you?"

"Going on. Living from day to day. Finding a reason. I was so messed up when Sheila died, I lost so much time I could've spent with her. I'll never forgive myself for screwing up so badly. I watched her suffer, and then I got drunk to forget. I tried to drown the pain. I wasted so much time trying to deny how sick she was. I left just when she needed me most. I let her down, Dad. Then I let my wife down and she left, then I know I let you and Mama down. It's just easier to hide than to face any of that. Now you're gone and I wasted that time with you." We sat down on the beach and he held his head in his hands again and cried.

"Jeremi. I love you, son," I said softly. "I love you!" I reiterated. "Sheila loves you, too. She knows how hard her illness was on everyone and especially for you, her 'big brother.' You had to come face to face with a lot of hard realities. But you've got to face them. If you run from them, you'll run forever. Love is all about forgiveness. I know she knows how you feel. She can see you and she can hear you. But you and I both know she'd wear you out if you used her death as your excuse to stay drunk all the time. You need to face your problems. Turn to God. Go back to church. Ask for help. Jeremi, you're such a wonderful person, but you're drinking your life, your talents, and your dreams away."

"I told you, it's so hard." He sighed again.

"It's harder to live with a life of wasted dreams than of wasted time. You remember that. I'll always be with you. I'll give you a sign only you'll know. When you need someone who loves you, unconditionally, I'll let you know I'm there. I'll make sure Sheila will too, okay?" He nodded. "I'll leave you with this: If you try hard to get better, I promise you I'll be there with you every step of the way. You can do it. Focus on how to live, try to enjoy feeling alive again. Will you do that, for me, for your sister, for Mama?"

"Dad, I hope we can meet again like this soon."

"Me, too." I held him again, kissed him on the forehead, "I love you." I closed my eyes and we were back in his room and Jeremi in his bed.

Henry and George waited for us. "Was it nice?" George asked.

"Very nice," I said. "Can I do this very often or do we have to save it for special need occasions?"

"We can do it as often as we think they can handle it," Henry explained. "Both fortunately and unfortunately, it is such a vivid experience they remember every detail of it. But it also frightens them because they're afraid they're crazy. After all, they're talking to a dead person. Just watch what happens when he wakes up now. Then watch the drama when he tells someone about it."

Jeremi rolled over and woke up, startled. "Huh?" He shook his head, tried to wake himself up further, then realized he still had a hangover. "Ow, ow, ow." He sat up in bed, enough to lean up against the headboard. Frightened, breathing rapidly and definitely still disoriented, he pulled the covers up around him and stared out into space. "Whoa, what a trip!"

"I see," I said to George sadly.

"That's one of the reasons. It's a very traumatic experience. I wish it was easier for them."

"Me, too."

Jeremi decided he needed to get up and pack for the trip.

"Okay, Martin. It's time to let their angels watch over them for a while. We've got some important things to discuss. Let's go." He looked me in the eyes and they locked. When they unlocked, we were back in the garden in Heaven.

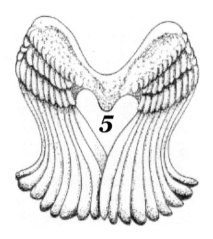

5

"What do you want to discuss?" I asked him.

"Your future. What do you want to do, now that you're here? You have a lot of choices and a lot of decisions to make."

"Decisions?"

"When you were alive, you served God, right?" I nodded. "You're an angel now. Do you want to still serve God?"

"Of course I do!"

"Then you need to learn the capacities in which you now can do that. That's what we're here to discuss." He paused. "There are all kinds of angels, Martin. There are the kind who live in Heaven and only venture out when the Lord sends them on special assignments; they stay here and serve God and the other angels in many ways until they are called. They go visit their families when they want, but with very little interaction. But a great and glorious honor goes to those who choose and are chosen to be Guardian Angels. When you agree to become a Guardian, you are a teacher, a protector, a guide and a major influence in your charge's life. It's a tough job, but it is rewarding beyond words. Guardians usually choose to guard someone special in their families, although there are rules governing certain circumstances."

"Rules?"

"First of all, males guard males and females guard females. There are several reasons for that rule, but the main one is that it's better for male angels to guard male humans. They understand their minds better."

"Okay." That rule was easy to understand.

"Secondly, you're encouraged to go back to your family, to the next child born in your family. You usually choose that anyway because you're closer to all the members of your family and that helps you with this transition as well."

"Sounds right."

"If there are special circumstances, then you can take the place of an angel who's already been assigned. When the mother of a young child dies, if she has been faithful, she is rewarded with the choice of becoming a Guardian Angel for her own child; she can take the place of the angel charged with the child. Both angels will stay until the mother angel is confident in her new role. Most mothers choose this; fathers, too. If the mother only has boys, then she can only assist the other angels. The parent who can will usually choose the youngest because the older children feel the same need to watch over the little ones. They all work together, just in different ways."

"Is that what Sheila did?" I asked.

"Yes, she's still assisting the baby's angel. So she's more free to float for the moment, but soon she'll take her place and the baby's angel will be given a new charge to guard."

"What about me, then?" All my children, at least my boys, were grown. "If I were to become a Guardian Angel, who would be my charge? Do you know?"

He nodded. "If you agree, that is."

"Who?"

"Your grandson," he replied.

"Which grandson?" I asked. I had more than one.

"The one that will be born in about nine months!"

My heart leaped for joy; a new baby, how wonderful. "Whose baby will he be?"

"Jeremi's."

"Wait a minute! Stop right there. He's single and you know he's in a lot of trouble. What are you thinking? Besides, you know he tried to have babies with his ex-wife, but they never did. She already had a son. That means Jeremi was the one with the problem having kids."

"There're several things going on here, Martin. First, all things are possible. Second, Jeremi's just fine in this regard. It was his wife's problem. After her son was born, there was an injury. We made sure she just never knew about it."

"Oh brother, he thinks it's his problem. That's going to spell T-R-O-U-B-L-E." I shook my head in disbelief. "Will he get back with his ex-wife?" I asked, still trying to recover from the shock.

"No. It's much more complicated than that," George continued. "Jeremi is having a lot of problems. He's lost his focus on anything and everything. He's just floundering around in life. He's going down into a hole and unless something is done to save him, we're all going to lose him. You saw how tired Henry was. Jeremi's lost to Henry. But your faithful Father in Heaven has listened to yours, Glory's, Peter's, and his sister's prayers and is answering them by giving Jeremi a son. A beautiful son, who will be talented and gifted. Someone Jeremi, hopefully, will want to turn his life around for."

"How's he supposed to support a baby? He's living with Peter! He works at a pub. Have we really considered all this?"

"Selecting the baby's mother was done carefully. She needs to be strong enough to stand up to Jeremi's faults. Also compassionate enough to see how special he is, even though he's tried to hide it from the world. Vulnerable enough that he feels the desire to take care of her. She has to be someone who's already established herself as a faithful, diligent and responsible mother. Someone who can take care of the baby in a good home with or without Jeremi present. Someone who will accept the baby unconditionally, love him forever and also be of good enough heart to share him with your family, regardless of Jeremi's commitment to her."

"Have you found someone like that? That seems like a pretty tall order to fill."

"Jeremi has."

"He found her? Who is she?"

"Her name is Jeannie. She's the mother of two young, beautiful girls. One is five. The little one is two. She's in the process of ending a lonely marriage. All she wants to do is continue to be able to provide for her girls. She's a very devoted mother."

"How did they meet?"

"At the pub where Jeremi works, she and he karaoke together."

"They met at the pub? Yikes, was that such a good idea?"

"She had to meet him where he was - he's always in a bar." George knew what I thought. Unfortunately, I had to agree with him on that score.

I inquired further about this Jeannie. "Is she a singer?" Jeremi sang professionally, years before, but the band had split up. He still kept himself near music as much as he could, though.

"She sings well - but she needs to keep her day job! Jeremi and Peter have the gift but Jeannie uses singing as therapy to help her through the hard times in her life. She sings the songs for the way she feels. It's an emotional release and also a temporary phase. She'll only be in the bar scene for a little while. But she's there long enough to meet and get involved with Jeremi."

"Is she . . .?" I stumbled for the right word.

"Black?"

"No. I was going to ask if she was spiritual."

"Of course," he answered.

"But since you brought it up. Is she?" He'd aroused my curiosity.

"She's white." He paused. I must've looked a little shocked. "Is that a problem?"

"You should know better than to ask me that! But there're so many more issues in an interracial relationship. Are they ready to handle that, too?"

"You're right, Martin. But they've already learned those lessons in life. You raised your kids right and so did Jeannie's folks. Jeannie and Jeremi both have an innate ability to look beyond skin color, to meet the person on the other side. To them, it's just plain natural."

My eyes sought out his and I stared at them intently. The warmth and sincerity in them assured me more than words ever could have.

"Would you like to meet her?" George asked.

"Absolutely."

The next moment, we were in an office with three women, all diligently pounding away on their computer keyboards. The first one was very serious and straight-laced, everything on her desk was in a neat little pile. Jeremi liked things orderly. Even still... I could tell the next one loved music. There were musical knickknack's everywhere there was room on her desk, sprinkled in between several heaps that once were piles. There were pictures of grown children on her desk, a boy and a girl, however George described little girls. Then there was the third woman in the room. All around her were pictures of little girls and kindergarten-style artwork. Tacked in between were inspirational quotes, which apparently reminded her to be positive about life and to take control of her own situation. She positioned herself to face the other two ladies in the room. I watched her for a little while.

"I see you found her, Martin." George told me.

After a couple seconds, Jeannie looked up from her computer and looked around for something.

"She's pretty sensitive to us," a woman's voice came from behind me.

"George, this is Pearl. She's Jeannie's guardian." Pearl was very strong and vibrant.

"I'm glad to meet you. Do I know you?" I asked because there was something very familiar about her.

"You've only known me through George. He talked about Jeannie and me to you when you were alive. You only know us through those talks," Pearl explained.

"Does Jeannie know we're here?"

"She's very sensitive to what she thinks are changes in energy. She's tried to reason it out in her mind, but she has trouble overcoming the lack of a logical explanation. She's a computer programmer and things need to make logical sense for her. So she denies what she's experiencing. She's getting wiser, but she's a little scared."

Jeannie went back to work on the computer. Obviously intent on her objective, it looked like she could tune everything out if she wanted to. I wanted to see what she was working on, so I went behind her and looked over her shoulder. Jeannie stopped working and got chill bumps.

"Wait! Martin! Stop!" Pearl commanded. "Get out from behind her now! She hates that!"

I quickly flew back in front of her. I moved so quickly that I accidentally stirred some of the artwork on her wall. Jeannie whipped around quickly enough to see her artwork move. She got really tense.

"I'm sorry," I told her. "I wanted to see what she was doing."

"It's okay. Jeannie absolutely hates anyone behind her, human or angel. See how she's arranged her space? She has it so nobody can sneak up on her and get behind her."

"Hey ya, Judie," Jeannie said, while still turned around, trying to figure out where the breeze came from. "It's break time. Wanna take a walk?"

Judie, the one who had all the music trinkets on her desk, looked over at Jeannie, then at her watch. "Sure."

Jeannie got up quickly from behind her desk. She leaned against a wall to wait for Judie to change from high heels into slip-on flats for their walk. Pearl, George, and I tagged along.

They worked downtown, but near an old residential neighborhood, with old trees and pretty gardens--a nice break from the office.

"Okay, so what happened this weekend?" Judie asked with great anticipation, once they got out of everyone's earshot.

Jeannie seemed to forget about everything that just happened and began to explain. She took a deep breath and smiled. "Well, I got a sitter on Friday and I went to the pub with Anne. Jeremi was there, running the Karaoke. I sang 'When Will Anyone Ever Really Love Me?' and 'I Need A Hero In My Life.' That felt really good! You get all that anger out, singing really loud like that. Everybody claps and tells you how great it sounded. It's so cathartic. I love it. Then I finally got Anne up there. She was quiet at first, but she got into it. She sang a slow song. It was nice."

"Where was Jeremi?"

"He came over to see me, so I'd have company while Anne was singing."

"You mean to keep anyone else from coming over and talking to you while Anne was singing." Judie smiled slyly.

Jeannie blushed, smiled and said sarcastically, "That's what you think."

"That is what I think!" Their eyes met and Jeannie looked away quickly. Judie enjoyed teasing Jeannie.

"Where was I?" a flustered Jeannie asked.

"He was keeping you all to himself," Judie answered.

"Quit it! After Anne sang, he got up and sang this duet, where he sings both parts--guy and girl--it was amazing. Everybody loved it. Then he got all these requests for him to sing these really bizarre songs. People asked if they could sing with him and stuff. The place was really rocking. It was fun."

"Sounds like it."

"Then this young guy nobody'd ever seen before comes in and sings 'Amazing Grace.' The whole place got quiet. I'll tell you it was something. In a bar, 'Amazing Grace,' and everyone loved it. It was awesome." Jeannie drifted back in memory for a moment, lost in her own world daydreaming.

They walked for a bit in silence, then Judie said, "So, did you see him later?"

"Huh? Oh. Only when I was on exile, we went to a park by the river."

"Exile?" I asked Pearl.

"It's when her ex-husband has the girls at her apartment. She has to leave. He lives in a really bad environment. So she lets him come over to her apartment to see them. It is for the best! She calls it 'Exile.'" She usually takes a book and goes up to the pub or to a movie. It's a lonely time for her. So she tries to go where there are people she can talk to."

I nodded that I understood well enough.

"So what happened?" Judie prodded.

"Well . . ." Jeannie acted like she was going to tell all. Then she decided to keep her friend guessing. "I just went home."

"Right!" Judie said. Their eyes met and Jeannie looked quickly away. "I knew it!" Judie said.

"Oh, hush up," Jeannie blushed. They arrived back at the office again and needed to get back to work-type conversation.

"You working late today?" Jeannie asked.

"Yes, the deadline is coming up and the users keep changing their minds about what they want. You know," Judie answered.

"Yeah, I know," Jeannie said, using the same tone as Judie had. They both laughed and went back into their office building, back to their desks and back to work.

Pearl turned to me. "Well, Martin, now you know as much about Jeremi and Jeannie as she's willing to let anyone in on. She's growing closer to him, but they're also both erecting walls to keep from getting too serious. They both feel something very strong for each other, but it scares them."

"It looks like she has good friends," I said.

"Soon, they're both going to find out who their real friends are," Pearl said.

George sighed in agreement.

"So, she's going to be the mother of my next grandson. I like her. Is she really up to this?"

"We're going to be there to help her through. She'll be all right," George assured me.

"That's an awful lot to ask someone to do for someone else. Is this going to disrupt her life? What about her family? What about her girls? What about her job?"

Pearl said. "There's more going on here than merely hoping Jeremi will come around." I looked at her perplexed, so she went on. "Ever since Jeannie was a little girl, she always wanted three children. Under different circumstance maybe, but this way it's better. There are a lot of things this experience is going to teach her, things that she needs to learn to grow spiritually. Tests she needs to go through so that her faith will grow and she can get back on track, too. She's more on track than Jeremi, but she needs a wake up call too. This baby will be a great reward for her, her girls, and her family. There are several specific lessons that are going to play out here, for her and her extended family. The baby's presence is for Jeremi and for his side of the family, but Jeannie's family is going to be greatly blessed, too."

That was the first moment I caught a glimpse of how perfect God's plan for us really was. He took so many complex situations and blended them together to make each piece fit perfectly. This was going to be interesting to watch.

George motioned that it was time for us to go.

"Good-bye, Martin," Pearl whispered, "I'll see you soon."

She smiled. I waved good-bye. The next thing I knew, George and I were back in Heaven.

I sat quietly beside a crystal sea and tried to absorb everything that I had learned in the past few hours. It seemed like much longer than that, but on Earth, I had been gone less than a day.

"Time's increments are now meaningless to you. You only feel like time passes when you're down on Earth and right next to your living loved ones. You can make it seem as fast or as slow as you want to while you're in the world," George told me.

"I just want to sit still for a minute or an eternity--whichever applies." There was so much to absorb, so much to think about.

George smiled, "Just reflect, Martin. Think about what you've learned and reflect on what you're going to do. Do you want to be alone or do you want to talk to someone special?"

"Another dream?"

"No, other angels," he replied quickly. "Sheila and your parents want to see you."

I got a second wind! I wanted to see them, too. Before I could say "Yes" there they were.

"How are you doing, son?" Dad asked.

"I've been busy," I said and he smiled knowingly. "It's all so overwhelming. Who our angels are and what they're doing. I'm completely amazed and awestruck."

"It only gets better, Dad," Sheila said.

"That's right, you're with your babies!"

She positively glowed when she acknowledged her new assignment. "I'll see them grow up and get to help them when they need it. It will be special. Of course, I'd like them to feel how close I am, but I'll keep letting them know through ways they'll understand." Sheila smiled broadly.

"So, Dad, after you died, did you guard one of us boys?" I asked.

He shook his head. "I respected all your angels. I was allowed to guard the whole family with them and that's what I did."

"Even after mother remarried?" He nodded. "Was that hard for you?" I thought that it might have been difficult for him to watch her with someone else.

"I love your mother so much, I had to find a way to help her bear the burden of raising you kids without me. So, I found the best man I knew. I very much approved of who she remarried; in fact, I was the one who made sure they met. The rest was up to them, but I got them together. When you look at the greater good, which is Heaven's perspective, selfish feelings like jealousy melt away. They are replaced by concern and respect. That's how it is in Heaven and should be on Earth."

I missed these talks with my dad so much. He'd always made so much sense. I used his example in countless sermons to illustrate righteousness and goodness. I loved listening to him all over again. I drew it all in and sighed contently. He picked my stepfather; I could believe that. We joked about that from time to time. It's great to know we were actually right about it. Mother squeezed my hand and looked into my eyes and smiled. I did the same. Words were unnecessary. It was just love so strong you could almost see it flow between us.

"Dad," Sheila whispered, "we ought to get back to Mama."

"I want to stay a little longer, this feels so good to be back with you," I said.

"Oh, we're going with you," my mother said. "When families come together, it's a reunion for angels, too." She patted my hand and we were in the house, back in Glory's bedroom. She sat in my recliner, leaned forward, held her arms tight around herself again, just like this morning. The sweetest sight, however, was her angel, Naomi. Glory thought she was sitting on the chair, but Naomi was underneath her in the chair, rocking back and forth like a rocking chair. She held my Glory tight. Naomi rocked Glory back and forth on the chair. Poor Glory was so lost in her grief, it broke my heart.

"Do you want to take over?" Naomi asked me.

"Yes," I said. She got up and I quickly slipped in where she had been. Glory felt the change and readjusted herself with me and I rocked her.

"I'm Naomi," her angel told me. "I'm the cousin who had the accident when I was ten. I was able to grow up with her and then take over as her angel when I was ready."

"She talked about you a lot," I reminisced. "She loved you very much."

"And I love her. We're going to get her through this, trust me. She really will be all right."

"I believe you." I rested my head on Glory's back. Her back relaxed a little and I gently rocked her for several minutes.

There was a soft knock at the door. It was Vivian. "Are you all right, honey?"

"I was just sitting here, imagining all the times he sat in this chair, hoping somehow I could feel him still in it," Glory replied.

"Does it help?" Viv asked.

"Oh, yes. I can still feel him here. I can still smell his cologne and hair cream that rubbed off on this old chair. I like sitting here, it helps." Tears welled up in her eyes again and I stroked her cheek. Her hand went up to her cheek right after I did that.

"Can I get you anything?" Vivian took her hand.

"Who was that on the phone a little while ago?"

"Peter. He and the family will be here tomorrow morning."

"Jeremi?" Glory asked with an added quality of concern in her voice. Viv nodded. "Jeremi, too."

"Martin was so worried about that boy."

If she only knew. I was glad she was pleasantly ignorant of it - at least for the moment.

"Do you feel like being around people? Sarah's doing her best to keep up with everyone who's arriving, but there're an awful lot of people and it's getting a little out of hand." Viv held out her hand to help Glory up.

Glory wiped the tears from her cheek and took a deep breath, nodded. "Yeah, let's go."

So we all went to the living room. George stopped us all before we went down, saying, "Let's give them some room." With that, all the angels got very small and flew. He said in my ear, "It's easier to maneuver when you're little when there're lots of people. It's a new perspective." He smiled. "Try it."

"How?" I asked.

"Just imagine it and it'll happen," he answered.

So I did and I was small and it felt really strange, everything so big, but I could easily fly wherever I wanted. We all went to the living room. My mother had already seen Sarah's angel, my grandmother, her mother. It was like one of the reunions when they were alive; hugs and kisses, smiles and laughter. It warmed my heart so much.

This explained why there was always so much love any place the family all got together. There were loving reunions on all levels, earthly and angelic. The angels were right, this did keep getting better and better.

So much was going on in the house, it was hard to keep track of it all. Sheila's children, some of my cousins and their children were there. Terrance was there again. People gathered in small groups and retold stories of our adventures. They laughed and cried at the same time.

All the young children played together, my grandchildren and some nephews and nieces. The highest concentration of angels was around them. I zoomed down around the children. They played on the kitchen floor, a combination of blocks and towers. Terrance stood there, watched them and drank a glass of water. From time to time, he instructed them on which move to make next. There were six children there, ages nine years (Sheila's oldest) to six months (one of my grandnephews). The baby was trying to chew the blocks. The baby's angel played peek-a-boo with him. The angel swooped in close and around his charge and back. It made the baby giggle.

The other children were confused, wondering what could possibily be making him so happy.

"He's just a happy baby," his seven-year-old sister said, when all the kids gave the baby a peculiar look.

Then they went back to their game. A couple of the other children's angels got in on the fun and followed every move the baby's angel did and that made him laugh harder. Sheila's oldest child looked at him, like he was crazy and said, "There's something wrong with that child." That statement upset her angel slightly, so her angel took a dive into Terrance's water and threw the splash right on the top of Sheila's daughter's head. All the other children laughed.

"That's what you get for saying that." Terrance laughed and made a quick move to avert the slap she aimed at him. She gave him an eyeful of attitude as he left. He just laughed. She shook it off, wiped it off and played with the kids again. Terrance told the story to the next person he saw, pointed and laughed.

Glory heard the baby laugh and came into the doorway to watch.

"See, Grandma, see?" Sheila's oldest said and pointed at the baby. "Something's wrong with that child!"

"Hush, let the baby play with the angels," she chided her granddaughter. Then she just stood there. I believe she tried to imagine what the baby saw. The more she watched and imagined, the more peaceful her expression grew.

George was the only angel left beside me now. I asked him, "Can she see what is really happening?"

"Glory is a wise woman, Martin," he assured me. "She knows, without a doubt, that the angels are all around her. She's watching for signs. She sees this one and it gives her comfort."

I watched Glory. The more she watched, the more peaceful she got. The more peaceful she got, the more fatigue took her over. Thankfully Naomi was holding her up, because nothing else was.

George went and buzzed around Vivian's ear. She was sitting down talking to several people about the day's events. As George buzzed, she swatted at the disturbance like a fly, but her head turned enough to see Glory. Vivian realized what was happening. She got up immediately, excused herself from the conversation and went over to Glory, put her arms around her and Glory leaned on her friend and they both went over to the couch. A couple of the men came closer to see if they could assist, but the women insisted they were fine.

"Do you want to go to bed?" Vivian asked.

"I'm fine, honey. I'd like to stay right here with everybody." Glory patted her hand to assure her friend that all was well.

"Whatever you want, dear." Viv kept hold of her hand.

The conversation Vivian had been involved in picked up where it left off. I watched Glory as she slowly sank back into the couch cushions. There, surrounded by all of her friends, family and angels, she drifted peacefully off to sleep. Vivian watched this progress. As soon as Viv was sure Glory was asleep, she shooed people out the door. They all looked at Glory and blew her a kiss as they left. They told Vivian and Sarah to call them anytime for anything. Viv and Sarah promised they would.

After everyone was gone, Sarah went to Vivian and hugged her tightly. Vivian held her like a mother. She loved her like a daughter. When Sarah regained her composure, they cleaned up the living room and kitchen very quietly. The angels helped where they could.

Naomi sat with Glory, Naomi had closed her eyes.

"Is she sleeping?" I asked George.

"No. She's reflecting on the day. When you see a brighter glow, then she's praying. When our charges are sleeping, it's our free time. If our charges are safely tucked in their beds and if all is safe, one of the family's angels can watch over the house. That way we can be notified if trouble begins while we're gone from them. It's our time to visit other people we love, living and angel. It's a time of great learning for us. It's a time of great discussion and wonderful fellowship. It's your choice; you can go anywhere and be with anybody."

"Can I just stay here?" I asked.

"Yes. But I hope you'll understand if I leave for a while. Just call my name if you need me, I'll be right back here with you."

"I just want to be here tonight, with her." I referred to Glory, of course.

"I know," George replied. "You always put her first. You were a good husband."

"Thanks," I said. George disappeared. I sat on the other side of Glory and held her hand. She stirred a little. I kissed her goodnight.

"I'm so sorry you're going through all of this," I whispered in her ear. I bowed my head in prayer. "Dear Lord. You have received me into your Heaven and for that I am truly thankful. I pray now for my family, for my wife, for my children, for my children in trouble and their future children. I pray that you'll always love them, comfort them and guide them in your ways, sending your messengers to help you help them. I love them and I love you and I thank you Lord for a wonderful life. All Praise and Glory to you. In the name of Jesus, I pray. Amen."

I spent the rest of the night there. I sat by Glory. I immensely enjoyed just being by her side. I wished I had appreciated each moment more, but I appreciated each moment now and I treasured it unlike anything I ever had before.

I reflected on the day and wondered about the future for the family. I was confident, through all I'd experienced so far, that they were going to be all right and that they were well taken care of.

I had fun in the night testing my "Angel light" to see if I could get Sarah or Vivian to notice things. It amazed me how easy it was. I got Sarah to stare at the family picture and I lit up my face, to let her know how proud I was of her. I got Vivian to notice that the lights were left on in the guest bathroom and she got up and turned them off. Then I drew a fanciful pattern in the ceiling with the different paint textures. By the time I was finished lighting the different pattern, it looked like a beautiful flower. Viv recognized it right away and she said, "That's pretty, Martin. You know how I love columbines. I'm sure going to miss you." Soon after that, she brought a blanket out and covered Glory up. Then she went to sleep in the recliner.

The predicament with Jeremi kept troubling me. The thought of him having a little boy at this stage in his life, was both fun and frightening at the same time. I knew what kind of person he was, when he was sober. Until we got him straightened out, however, I worried what kind of influence he'd be on his new son. I found peace when I trusted in the Lord's wisdom. I prayed for strength for Jeremi in his struggle. I prayed Jeannie would look past his flaws and see him for his potential and I prayed for her girls and their future son.

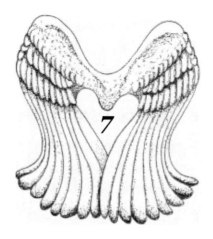

George showed up near dawn. "Did you have a good night?"

"Yes, I had a very nice night."

"Well, are you ready to face the adventures of another day?"

"Where do we get to go?"

"How about going to go meet your future grandson's sisters and their angels and help get them ready for the day?" I looked at Glory as she began to stir a little on the couch. George reassured me, "Relax Martin, we'll be back soon."

"Okay," I agreed.

Suddenly, we were in a small, two-bedroom apartment. An alarm clock buzzed. There was Jeannie in between two small girls in her bed; they had both snuggled up so close to her that she had trouble maneuvering to hit the snooze button. She turned to see the time, then snuggled back down in the bed with her girls, who slept soundly through all of it.

"It'll be a couple of minutes before they get out of bed. Do you want to look around?" George asked.

Like her office, Jeannie's apartment had inspirational quotes about self-confidence and her inner spiritual self everywhere: posted on the refrigerator, tacked on the wall of the bathroom, her bedroom, and in the hallways. She had dozens of photographs as well of people all over her walls. Most of them were pictures of the girls with other people who looked enough like the girls to assume they were their relatives.

"Good morning, Martin. Good morning, George," Pearl's voice came from behind us. "Come to get to know your new family, I see." She smiled. "Well, let me give you the official tour. You've met Jeannie, she's thirty-one. The oldest girl is Carole; she's five. The youngest girl is Lynne; she's two and a half. They're both very smart, happy and well-adjusted children, but different as night and day. Their angels will be back as soon as they wake up. You'll like them. You'll see what a challenge being the guardian angel of a small child really is."

"They've lived here for a few months. Soon after the girls' father left, they moved here from their house, which was for the best. Jeannie wanted out of that lonely house. This apartment will work for now, but we'll need something bigger when the baby comes."

I looked around and had to agree. This was small, but it looked ample for them at the moment.

"These pictures are all of family. She's the youngest of five children. There's a ten-year span from oldest to youngest. She has three brothers and one sister. They all live far away. She's on her own for all that she's going through now and what's coming. She's definitely going to learn what being self-reliant is all about, but that's part of what this is supposed to teach her," Pearl explained.

"Part?" I asked.

"There are so many lessons coming in a short period of time for her. It'll be a hard road, but she'll come out shining on the other side. We'll do our best to make sure of that. It takes a lot of pressure to make a diamond."

"Is she being punished? Having this all happen this way?" I asked. I still was a bit muddled about the reason she was chosen.

"Punished? Heavens, no!" Pearl laughed a little. "The timing of this is more critical to Jeremi's predicament. However, it plays in her favor to a great extent."

"How?"

"Jeannie needs to get a little of her own medicine. She needs the shoe to be on the other foot and learn that God is the only judge that matters." She paused and I looked her a question. "A little family history is in order here. Jeannie and her first husband were married, then two years later Carole comes along. Well, that's all well and good and the way that things should happen, but she was full of herself with that fact and when she met people who got that order reversed, she was secretly judgmental and proud. So she judged and now others will judge her for the same reason. That's why the timing for her. She's doing some penance for those sins now, to teach her a larger lesson. She's going to develop such compassion for women in this predicament, that after this, hopefully she'll be inspired to do great things. The reason for the baby, among other reasons, is that she was always destined to have three children, so, here comes number three and a boy to boot. It always amazes me how perfect the Father's plan is when so many things are accomplished at one time and for so many people. Only God could be so wise."

We made eye contact with that statement and both sighed. There was going to be a lot of work to do to get them through all the trials life was about to throw them.

The alarm went off again. We all went back into the bedroom. Jeannie slipped out of bed without waking the girls and stumbled one eye still closed, the other squinting, into the bathroom. She closed the door behind her. Pearl disappeared, too.

George and I stayed with the girls. Their angels appeared beside each of them. The one by Carole said, "Hello, Martin."

The one by Lynne said, "Hi." Both smiled broadly.

"This is Marie." Carole's angel gracefully nodded. "And this is Edwina." Lynne's angel gave a little wave. "They're the girls' angels. Pearl has told them about you."

"I'm delighted to meet you both. You have beautiful charges," I said referring to the sleeping children beside them.

They both smiled, nodded in agreement and Marie graciously said, "Thank you."

I watched as Marie stroked Carole's cheek gently enough to make her stir. Carole woke up enough to see that her mother had already gotten up. She got up and walked blear-eyed to the bathroom, just like her mother had and Marie went with her. I had to laugh. It was so cute.

"When the little one wakes up, will she do the same thing?" I asked.

"Runs in the family," Edwina admitted. We all chuckled.

We heard Carole and her mother talk in the bathroom. Shortly thereafter both emerged in their bathrobes. Jeannie instructed Carole on what outfit to wear and what accessories to bring, so she could help her dress.

During the next half hour or so, I witnessed the most spectacular display of angel/people interaction that I'd seen so far. When one of them was looking for something, her angel shined her angel light on it until it was found. Jeannie yelled out commands and the girls' angels repeated them to the children until whatever it was, was accomplished.

Little Lynne was out in the kitchen and reached up to the top of the counter. She was in danger of pulling stuff off the counter onto her head, but Edwina pushed the pile of papers back out of her reach.

I informed George anxiously, "Jeannie will notice that! She moved that whole stack of papers!"

"Just watch," he smiled.

Lynne walked into the family room and proceeded to get into more things. Edwina, always one step ahead, pushed things out of her way. It was a game with them. The smiles on their faces matched perfectly. Sometimes I wondered if the baby could really see Edwina.

When Jeannie came out to the kitchen, she walked past the stack of papers that had been moved. She looked back over her shoulder to do a double take, said, "Hmmm, how'd those get there?" She shrugged her shoulders and turned back around (because Pearl had shouted at her) with barely enough time to dodge the door jamb she was about to walk into.

Pearl sighed. "That was close."

The incident with the door jamb apparently wiped any thoughts of the misplaced stack of papers right out of Jeannie's thoughts. She went on with getting herself and the girls ready for the day.

George explained, "If your charge is going to get hurt, you, as their angel, have to make snap decisions as to the best way to protect them. Moving a stack of papers or inanimate objects away from little children will receive little notice from others in the house, so that's done routinely. Sometimes, like you saw, it's a game the angels play with the children to keep them occupied until someone is physically in the room with them. We only play those games when they're really little. When the parent comes out and sees some things moved around, they just assume the little one did it. It all works out. When they get a little older, it can scare them, so we change how we play with them."

When I saw this, I thought back to when I was alive. I had fun imagining what the angels were doing. I tried to apply what I had seen this morning, to every morning when I grew up and my children grew up. The echoes of my mother's commands in my ear was George making sure I'd remember something important she'd told me to do. All the times I'd walked past stacks of papers wondering how they had ended up where they were, I just dismissed it as the children getting into them. The more I thought about it, it occurred to me that the incidence of papers moving in my life decreased as my children got older and started happening again when my grandchildren were born. It all fit. It became incredibly clear. They were always there, always doing things with us. I never understood or appreciated how much they actually took care of us from minute to minute, every day of our lives, crisis situations and peaceful situations alike. Angels were with us routinely, daily, every moment. It was absolutely astounding to consider.

The more I watched, the more I was amazed and the more I wanted to do this. I definitely wanted to be the new baby's Guardian Angel. I smiled knowingly at George.

"I bet you've made your decision," he said.

"Yes. I want to do it."

"Well then, let's start preparing Jeannie and Jeremi. Tell her the good news."

Jeannie came into the family room and looked at her watch. She began a last-minute flurry to gather up the children, Carole's backpack, Lynne's diaper bag and her work folder. So I got close to her and as I stumbled for words to say, she whizzed right back out of the room.

"Let's wait until she's alone and can hear us," George said.

She whizzed by again and grabbed more things as she went by. She picked up Lynne, too. As she loaded up her car, Marie whispered something to Carole. Carole yelled, "Mommy, my snacks!"

Without missing a beat, Jeannie nodded, rattling the keys she was holding in her mouth. She finished buckling up Lynne, closed the door, ran back into the house, got a sack out of the refrigerator, ran back to the car, gave the treats to Carole and drove away, checking her watch and shaking her head in disgust.

"Is it always this frantic in the morning?" I asked Pearl. She nodded, shrugged her shoulders and smiled.

Jeannie dropped the girls off at the daycare. When she got back to the car, she took a second for herself. She put her hands together on the steering wheel and put her head down on them. "I need to get more sleep!" She glanced at her watch and shook her head in disgust again.

"Is now a good time?" I asked.

"Let's set the stage with some music," Pearl said. Jeannie pushed a tape in the tape player, a song about destiny. "You came in and I discovered that my life would never be the same. You are my destiny, you are my one and only. You're the one God sent to me. I'm so glad He chose you, for me, for love, forever."

"Give me a break, destiny, ha!" Jeannie said out loud and pushed the tape out.

George counted on his fingers, one, two, three. "Jeremi is your destiny!" George and Pearl said together.

I could tell those words hit her like a blast of wind because her head jolted back against the seat and she stared up at the ceiling with her eyes open really wide.

She blinked hard and shook her head. Then she started her car and drove away, muttering to herself. "I wonder what Jeremi is doing right now? He said he'd call last night - hmmm. Oh well, I'll see him after work tonight. Geez, what made me suddenly think of him? Oh yeah, that song. Destiny, schmestiny, Jeannie, you're imagining things. Get a grip."

She made it to work, walked into the building, dropped her purse off at her desk and grabbed her coffee cup and headed off to the lunchroom. Pearl said, "Watch this. Every day, like clockwork, she reads her horoscope. Wait until you see what hers is today." Jeannie, true to form, opened up the paper to her horoscope, which read "Today is a day of great beginnings. Black is a significant color for you."

Jeannie read that and choked on the coffee.

Judie walked in behind her and patted her on the back. "Are you all right?" she asked.

Jeannie shook her head and pointed to the horoscope. After Judie read it and looked at Jeannie, she laughed and said, "Somebody knows about you, huh?" She patted Jeannie on the back one more time after filling up her cup with coffee, left the lunchroom and chuckled to herself all the way back to her desk.

As Jeannie left the lunchroom, she shook her head and muttered, "Significant color! Destiny, schmestiny. Get your mind on your work and off Jeremi!" When she got back to her desk, Judie took one look at her and laughed all over again. Jeannie tried-unsuccessfully--to keep her laugher to herself. They both gave each other one last knowing glance and smile and went to work at their computers.

"Pearl, how'd you do that?" I asked.

"Nothing to it. We're trying to get a message across to her, right? So we need to put it in front of her any chance we get. We can use any means at our disposal. It's actually very simple. The only question is, is she listening?" she responded.

"Is that everybody's horoscope today?" I asked.

"Nope. But it'll be in any paper she looks at." She smiled. They laughed. After watching the pleasure they took in doing the jobs they were sent to do, I caught their enthusiasm and drank it in. I enjoyed watching these Guardian Angels at work.

Once we got Jeannie to work successfully, my thoughts returned to Glory. George read my mind or maybe he just knew everything about me and sensed this. He nodded at me and we were back with Glory. Sarah made Glory breakfast. Both of them picked at their food.

The doorbell rang. Peter's face appeared in the window. He, his family and Jeremi had arrived.

"Good timing," I told George.

"I know." From the look on his face, I think he planned it. I shook my head and simply smiled.

Sarah ran to the door and opened it up. Everyone gave her a big hug at the door and then came into the kitchen to greet Glory separately. Once everyone got in, they congregated in the kitchen and stood in one massive group hug. Their angels held hands around them all, in a circle of safety. Sheila showed up and grabbed my hand. George and I joined into the circle, too.

"Keep them from crying Martin, say something," George said.

All the angels looked at me.

"It is so hard to see them cry. I want them to be happy. They're all together. I love seeing them like this," I explained.

Sheila whispered in Peter's ear. Peter had his arm around Sarah. He slowly moved his hand up her side, right up to her underarm and tickled her. Sarah knew that everyone was really serious and sad. She tried hard to resist reacting, so Peter did it again. Sarah gave in to the pressure and she snorted. Everyone looked at her, most of them wiped their eyes, in time to see her punch Peter in the arm. It was like they were kids again. Glory laughed through her tears. Peter and Sarah's eyes met and they started to crack up, too. Sarah snorted again.

Melinda appeared perturbed by her husband's juvenile behavior. She asked, "What do you need us to do for you, Mama?"

Right on queue, Vivian walked into the kitchen and said, "Give an old friend a hug!" as she joined the group. Gradually, each one broke from the group and separated into their own conversations.

Vivian and Sarah briefed Peter and Melinda on the funeral arrangements. Jeremi and Glory went off into the dining room, so I went with them. "Mama, Dad came to me yesterday. I met him in a dream. We were at our favorite beach on the coast. We talked. We had a great talk! He said he was with Sheila and that she was the most beautiful angel he had ever seen. He said they painted the sunrise just for you yesterday."

Glory got chillbumps and took Jeremi's hand. "There was the most spectacular sunrise, yesterday."

Jeremi shivered. He got reassurance that what he had experienced was real. They gave each other a hug. "What else did he say?" Glory asked.

Jeremi looked away from his mama and was quiet for a bit, I guess he was replaying the dream quickly in his head. He looked back at her. "Just that he loved everybody and that he was closer than we could ever imagine." They both looked around the house, staring hard at places that I used to frequent. If I was alive and I saw this, I'd go and goose one of them. They would've jumped a mile. Instead, I breezed past between them. As soon as they felt it, they squeezed each other's hands and smiled.

"He's here, Mama," Jeremi said.

"I know," Glory acknowledged and gave his hand another squeeze. After a few seconds, she kissed Jeremi on the cheek and said, "I'm so glad you're here." She let go of his hand and went to greet Peter and Melinda privately.

Jeremi realized that nobody was looking, so he went out to the garage. He opened the spare refrigerator and started to root around. He quickly found what he was looking for, a beer. He checked around again to make sure he was alone. He opened the beer and gulped several swallows. Then he let out a big "Ahhhh."

"Dad would've put that out in the garage," I heard Peter say, as he opened up the door. Jeremi stashed the beer can in the door of the refrigerator and pretended to be looking for something else. "What you're looking for is already opened and in the door of the fridge, Jeremi."

"There you go again, jumping to conclusions. I just needed something to steady my nerves. We're back here, at another funeral, give me a break - please." Jeremi tried to divert attention away from himself.

Peter got right in his face and said, "Mama needs us more than she ever has in her life. Your drinking has to stop - especially now! Even if she had the strength to deal with it right now, I'd make you get a grip on yourself and think of someone else for a change."

"Damn, it's just a beer! Like you never took a drink," Jeremi defended himself, the way he usually did by attacking someone else.

"At nine in the morning?" Peter turned his back on Jeremi, to find what he had come in for. He grabbed a book off the bookcase, gave Jeremi one last warning glare, took a deep breath, shook his head and went back inside the house.

Then, as if to spite him, Jeremi picked up the beer and chugged the rest of it down. He put the empty can in the garbage can under a potato chip bag that was on top. He pulled a breath mint out of his pocket, chewed it up quickly, tested his breath and went back inside, too.

"What are we going to do with him?" I asked George.

"This is going to be tough on you. But things you have to work hard for, you appreciate more," he reassured me. I nodded and we went back inside.

The rest of the morning flew by. The visitors unpacked. Phone calls from friends came into the house, one after the other. The callers all wanted to know what they could do for the family. People from the church dropped by with casseroles or vegetable trays. Each wished it was more. They hugged Glory and told her how wonderful I was. They'd usually pass along a special story we shared. They laughed and cried and left, then the next one came. Each person visiting Glory had an angel who visited with me. They talked to me about their relationship to their charge. Then they told me about a time that they got George to influence me in some way. Some were the sermon topics I picked, that spoke right to the heart of a problem their charges had. Some were Bible verses to quote, hymns to sing or calls to make because the angels were making their charges weigh heavily on my heart.

I wish I had paid more attention to the little things that happened all around me everyday; I might've been able to appreciate these angels at work. It's funny, too, I remembered perfectly every detail these angels described. If I'd been alive, the details would have been fuzzy. As an angel, my memory was perfectly clear. It was a wondrous gift to have all that back.

Early in the afternoon, Vivian, Glory and Peter left to make the funeral arrangements. That left Sarah, Jeremi, Melinda and the children home to take care of things there. I went with Glory and her party to meet with my associate pastor Brother Hamilton at the funeral home. I watched as Glory and Peter picked out my casket. It was dignified, with a white satin lining. Then they picked my favorite hymns to sing, "Blest Be the Tie That Binds" and "How Great Thou Art." Peter would give the eulogy. They planned the nicest service. It comforted me to know how well they knew what I wanted. On the way out, Peter and Vivian helped a crying Glory to the car. I'm sure she was very grateful to have Peter's strong arm to lean on and a faithful friend she could always count on. Their angels flew above them in a circle of protection.

George and I went ahead of them, back to the house, where Jeremi and Sarah visited and the kids watched TV.

"How did you meet her?" Sarah asked.

"At the pub. She comes in to sing a couple times a week."

"Does she sing very well?"

Jeremi thought for a moment, with an impish grin. "She sings these 'I hate men' songs, and she really gets into them."

"Is she any good?" Sarah rephrased the question.

Jeremi nodded. "If she's rehearsed, yeah. If it's the first time she's sung it, I go outside for a cigarette."

"Can you smoke in the bar?"

"Yup," Jeremi answered, giving her a look like, 'You know what I'm saying?'

"Oh, that's cold!" Sarah went over to him and smacked him on the shoulder. "So, if she hates men so much, why is she seeing you?"

"She's just beginning a divorce from this guy she was married to for eight years. She said he never appreciated her singing in the house, so she quit singing for all those years and she's getting all her frustrations out by singing them out now. You should see her face when she does it, though." He shivered and made this really odd face, where he stuck his lip out awkwardly. "Lord have mercy!" he said and they both laughed.

"Kids?" Sarah asked.

"Yeah, two great kids, little girls. They're cute. The baby calls me 'Emi.' I've only seen them a couple of times, but they are really sweet little girls." Jeremi got a distant look in his eyes. "Oh man! I've got to call her."

"You left town without calling her? You dog!" Sarah slapped him on the shoulder again.

"Where's the phone?" He looked around in a panic.

"Where it always is," Sarah said.

Jeremi went out to the living room and dialed the phone. "Hey, baby," he said quietly. "I meant to call you last night. Something's happened; I'm at my parents house . . . Yes. My father had a heart attack and died." He started to choke up a little. Then he swallowed hard. "Thanks. . . I know. . . Yeah, I'll be fine. Everybody's here. . . Yeah, I flew in with them. . . This morning. . . I'm fine, really. Listen, I had this dream, it was incredible. I'll tell you about it later. . . A few days at least. . . Okay, I'll call you then. . . I've got to go now. . . You, too. Give the girls a kiss for me. g'bye."

"You in trouble?" Sarah asked her brother after he got off the phone.

"It's okay, she understood."

"Let's figure something to do with all this food for dinner tonight," Sarah changed the subject on him. They looked over the casseroles and picked three of their favorites and popped them in the oven to warm. Jeremi combined a couple of the vegetable and cheese trays into a pretty centerpiece on the table.

They cleaned up the kitchen and I smiled wide as I heard Sarah recite the old table-setting poem we taught her when she was about five. "'Fork' has four letters and it goes left of the plate. 'Left' has four letters, that's why this is great! 'Right' has five letters. So does 'knife' and 'spoon' too! God named the silverware to make it easy for you!" Before she could say it three times, the table was set for a beautiful family dinner.

Glory and Peter were still gone. Apparently, they'd stopped to take Vivian home.

By the time they made it back, dinner was about ready. Glory came into the kitchen, hugged Sarah and Jeremi and said, "Thank you."

Sarah asked, "Are you all right, Mama?"

"Yeah, yeah, I'm all right," she answered, sounding anything but.

Sarah and Melinda rounded everyone up for dinner. The kids washed their hands and the adults came in to help serve. Jeremi ushered his mama to her seat at the right of the head of the table. As everyone sat down, all the seats were taken, except for the head of the table, my seat. Nobody wanted to sit there at this meal, so I did. It was beautiful to look around the table and see all my family together, even though their faces were strained.

Glory asked Peter to say the blessing, in which he thanked God that they were all together, loving and supporting one another in this time of mourning. To which everyone said, "Amen!" or "Yes, Lord!"

Since it was crowded, the angels went small and each took a position on or near their charge. Sheila came, too. She worked hard to get Sarah's attention. As soon as she did, she flitted from one person to the next and gave them a kiss and whispered, "I love you" in their ears. Each person reacted by either itching the cheek she kissed or brushing their hair back away from their ears. Sarah watched everyone down the line, all around the table, react in rapid succession, like a drill team doing a staggered maneuver. By the time the fourth person did something peculiar, her eyes were big. By the fifth, her jaw dropped, where it stayed until Sheila made her way around the table to her. When Sarah's hand went to her own cheek, she jumped away from it, with enough force to knock Peter's elbow, spilling the water he was about to drink right into his lap.

Sheila said to both Peter and Sarah, "That was fun! I got you both." Then she came and sat with me to watch what happened next.

Peter's children watched and waited to see if he was going to get mad at Aunt Sarah for spilling his water on him. He was just about to get indignant, when he realized his audience and caught himself. It took a few seconds before he laughed, but then everyone followed suit. He got up calmly and went to the bathroom. He muttered and chuckled slightly to himself.

Everyone looked at her. She said, "Sorry," and shrugged her shoulders. Normal conversation eventually resumed.

I shook my head at Sheila. "Did you have fun?" I asked with an innocent tone.

She smiled and said, "You know I did!" We all laughed again.

The more the angels laughed, the lighter the mood at the table became. Slowly the smiles came back to their faces and the pleasure of being together as a family was felt all around. The adults, who had only picked at their food, started to eat. Every now and again, someone looked my way and all they saw was an empty chair. The angel of that person pointed out the sad face of their charge to someone nearby who then comforted the sad one. Everyone and every angel made a great effort to keep the mood light and loving. It was one of the best dinners I'd ever had with my family.

The remainder of the evening passed in much the same manner. Everyone was there to support one another. Each had their moments, when the reason that they were all together overcame them. We angels made sure that everyone had a shoulder to cry on, strength to draw from and love to share.

After everyone had gone to bed, I went to check on my new family. I wanted to put them to bed for the night, too. When I showed up, the girls were in their rooms, fast asleep. Jeannie was in her bed already. She was writing something, lost in thought.

"What's going on, Pearl?" I asked her angel.

"She misses Jeremi, so she's writing him a poem."

"She writes poetry?" I asked, don't know why that surprised me, I could see her creativity everywhere..

"She wrote a lot when she was younger, this is the first time in years she's even tried."

Another angel entered the room. He looked over Jeannie's shoulder and read what she had written so far. "I like it," he said to her. Then he came over to Pearl and gave her a hug. "Hi, Pearl. What's going on?"

"Jack, I want you to meet Martin," Pearl said, introducing us. "This is Jeremi's father. He's only been here with us for a few days."

"It's nice to meet you, Jack."

"I'm Jeannie's brother. I've been on this side for nearly four years now. I heard she was writing poetry again; I wanted to come see her and check it out. I love to visit her, so I thought this would be a good time. You and Jeremi are her inspiration, I see."

"What do you mean?" I asked.

"What do you mean 'what d'ya mean?'" Jack asked. "You need to read her poem. Go carefully look over her shoulder and read her poem. Just stay in front of her."

"I've already been introduced to that little tidbit. Why is that?" I asked.

"Me, it's my fault," Jack admitted. "When we were children, I used to sneak up on her all the time. Sometimes, I'd wait down the hallway and jump out. Sometimes I'd tiptoe up behind her and tickle her and make her jump a mile. I was relentless. We had fun. She developed the self-defense of facing everything pretty early and I guess it stuck with her." Jack laughed, probably remembering some of those times. When he finished, the three of us turned small, sat on her shoulder and watched her write like we would watch a movie. The paper she wrote on had more things erased than written.

"She's started over about four times now," Pearl said. "Relax, Jeannie, you're doing fine." Jeannie took a deep breath and let out a heavy sigh. Then she wrote the next line and stopped again, put the pen in her mouth and stared off into space.

The line she wrote was "I feel your stress, I feel your strain."

Then Jack said, "Let me help you ease your pain." Which was what she then wrote down. I liked that line. Then Jack looked over at me to explain "We wrote songs together all the time when she still lived at home and I'd come to visit."

"Would she have come up with that one on her own?"

"Something similar, maybe, and she still might change it. We can only make suggestions, she's the one doing the writing." Jack looked back at Jeannie, who wrote another line. "I can help, I've been there, too." She stared back at the ceiling, seemingly at a loss for words.

So I said, "Lean on me, I'll see you through." Which to my amazement, she also wrote down.

"Good one!" Jack said. "Writing songs like this brings back a lot of fun memories for me."

I looked at Jeannie, she still stared at the ceiling, but now she had a slight smile and a very distant look. I think Jack inspired the same memory in her.

We wrote a few more lines, then Pearl reminded Jeannie how late it was and how many things Jeannie had promised to do for other people in the morning. So Jeannie put the pages on the nightstand, turned out the light, nestled her head on her pillow and stretched out her arm like she was going to hold someone's hand. So Jack held her hand. "Hey, Jack, if you are here, thanks for helping me with the poem. And would you say hello to Jeremi's father for me and tell him that I'm really sorry I never got the chance to meet him?"

"You're welcome and he knows," Jack said. He kept hold of her hand until she fell asleep. He kissed her and Pearl good-bye and waved to me. "I'll be back when I can." Then he disappeared.

"Jack and Sheila are part of their connection," Pearl began. "They've had long talks about their respective losses, how they are similar, but different. How hard it was to watch Sheila wither away and how sudden and shocking Jack's mountain climbing accident was. Jeremi and Jeannie both can usually tell when they're being visited. Jack leaves presents behind."

"Presents? How can he leave presents behind?" I needed to be educated about these so-called presents.

"All sorts of presents, but mostly he likes to work with plants. When Jeannie returned from Jack's funeral, the plant that he and his wife had given her was in bloom, even though it was out of season. Another time, he made a clump of flowers grow into a heart shape, during a particularly lonely period, just before her separation. He's done it for everyone in his family. They compare stories and are all sure it's Jack's doing. For the most part, they're right. He took over Guardianship of his son, so he only comes when he can. We'll see him again soon."

Pearl and I went to check on the girls. She was the only one watching over the house this night. Everything was fine.

I thought about George and he immediately appeared. "They're asleep," I informed him.

"Ready to go?" he asked. I nodded and we were back in Heaven, walking down a magnificent road. Now that I was surrounded by even more spectacular beauty, I took a minute to gather my thoughts and reflect on all that I had learned in such a short period of time.

"It's easy to learn a lot in a little while, when you have a completely new perspective." It was Mother.

"Yes, it is," I agreed.

I just launched into telling Mother everything about my experiences. I learned so very much and enjoyed every moment of it. I talked very fast. I related all the details to her, about Glory and Sarah, about Peter, about Jeremi, Jeannie and her girls. How I loved it when the other angels shared stories with me about their charges and how they worked through me to reach my family and my friends. I was so excited about the prospect of helping my family and friends in a way that I never even dreamed possible. This was incredible!

I told Mother about the sunrise that Sheila and I had painted for Glory. We laughed when we talked about all the ways the angels played with babies. I felt so content knowing that I could go back and hold Glory any time I wanted to and she would just know I was there and feel my love. I loved being an angel!

Mother and I walked and discussed the potential to communicate with our living loved-ones. She told me about one of the times she'd used angel light on my brother and me. It was a night we were fighting over something stupid and it had gotten completely out of hand.

"I remember," I said. I knew exactly the incident she was referring to. "There was a scratching at the window, but there nothing was there."

"That was to get your attention," she acknowledged.

"Then there was your rocking chair rocking in the wind. It was all I could see. You were all I could think about. I forgot what we were fighting over. I just watched it rock. I stared and stared at it; it was like you were in it again and I could just imagine what you would say to us. You'd be yelling at us from that rocker, 'If I have to come in there, you'll be sorry! You boys remember you are brothers and put that petty foolishness aside. Lord have mercy!'"

"You may have thought you were imagining it, but that's what I said!" She smiled.

"It stopped the fight."

"I know!" she gloated, and we laughed together.

Suddenly I realized, we'd left Heaven. This walk had taken us back to that old house. We were in the front yard. I stared at it.

"We had some times in that ol' house." Mother said and squeezed my hand tightly.

"Good and bad." I sighed. It was interesting to look at the house now. The rocker was gone from the porch anymore; there was a new family there. They had painted it gray with blue trim. I found it pretty, but peculiar.

I saw the path, leading into the old woods, which started right at the back of the yard and I began to run toward it, feeling like a kid again. There was a young couple close in on the path, who had been lucky enough to steal a moment together. I breezed right past them and the girl's hair tousled a little. They broke their kiss and she looked in my direction. At a loss, she shrugged her shoulders and they started to kiss again. I ran faster and faster and faster and then I jumped into the air and flew. I flew above, in and around the trees. I flew beside the birds and up into the clouds. I looked down at Mother. She'd managed to scrounge up her old rocker and was patiently waiting for me to return. I flew around her a few times. She smiled. I bet she thought I was crazy. I felt free! I never felt so free. I could fly. I could see everything. I could remember everything. I could be anywhere with anyone anytime in Heaven or on Earth. I knew this was only the beginning of a great adventure of learning and growing and sharing and loving. This was incredibly awesome!

After a while, I settled back down and returned to Mother. She shook her head as if I'd pulled some silly stunt like when I was young. "Are you quite finished?" I thought she'd be angry or maybe annoyed. But she was fine. I think she just missed saying stuff like that to me.

"Yes, ma'am," I said, playfully returning her tone. "I missed you so much, Mother."

"I know, son, I know."

I held her hand tight.

We walked through the neighborhood where I grew up. I'd walked these roads many, many times in my youth. It was nice to be here again. It was different, too. I could see everything, people, and all the angels, too, going about their business of teaching and protecting their charges.

I saw other angels, too. There was one young angel at an intersection. He was completely engrossed with the people going through that intersection. "What is he doing?" I asked Mother, perplexed.

"If I were to guess, I'd say that he was killed at that intersection. He was probably doing something stupid or illegal or both. And now it is his responsibility to make sure that nobody else gets killed at that intersection," she explained.

"It is his responsiblity to protect others against what killed him, so that nobody else's family suffers the way his did. Is that right?" I asked, trying to figure out the meaning of this.

"Something like that," Mother confirmed. Then she went on to explain, "God's plan is unique for each of us and second guessing it is a waste of time. Every time I've seen something like this, it is His way of making sure that we all learn from our mistakes and if possible, make sure other people learn our lessons without paying with their lives."

As we passed through the intersection, the young angel acknowledged us with a smile. Then he saw a car trying to run a yellow light, which was about to turn red. We saw the driver's angel trying to get him to slow down. Failing that, the driver's angel motioned to the intersection's angel that his charge was in trouble. So the intersection's angel shined his angel light on the reckless driver approaching, hoping to make everyone else aware of the danger. Each of the other drivers' angels tried to make sure that their charges saw the angel light. One driver's attention was diverted because she was trying to settle an argument in the back seat between her children. The child closest to the window yelled, "Look!" and pointed to the approaching speeding car. Finally all the drivers were aware. The car sped through the red light. The danger passed. All the angels sighed with relief and thanked one another. Their charges continued safely on to their respective destinations.

Mother and I walked on. It was a beautiful, clear night. All the stars shined brightly. We walked along silently for awhile and enjoyed one another's company. "I need to talk to you about tomorrow," she said, in a suddenly serious tone.

"The funeral?" I asked.

"The whole funeral day. The funeral day is an incredibly hard day for the ones who loved you. Funerals amplify family bonds. If they're good bonds, they're strengthened. If they're weak bonds, they're further stressed. It brings to light what the problems are. Sometimes it takes breaking things, so they can be rebuilt. But your family will pull together, like when Sheila died," I agreed. I remembered. "But tomorrow is your funeral day. It's an important day for you, too. You can do so much good for them. It's traditional that the person being let go gives each person left behind a gift. It can be as simple as reminiscing a wonderful memory or staging someone to say something at precisely the right time. It could be helping them unexpectedly find something special you shared with them or presenting them with a new and special gift. It's up to you. You need to spend tonight thinking about it. You need to spend the rest of this night alone. Go wherever you want to go. Go wherever you'll be inspired. Then when you're ready, get to work. George, Sheila, your father and I are only a whisper away. We'll be there when and if you need us. But you go now, son. Go and figure out what it is that you want to give each one of your loved ones and how it is you're going to give it to them." She blew me a kiss and disappeared into the night.

I was alone; without George or Glory, Sheila or Jeremi, Jeannie or anyone else. My thoughts found me flying, I weaved in and out of clouds. I found an eagle soaring, so I soared right beside it. I felt the flap of his wings, I was so close. I thought about Peter and his love of eagles. I thought, I must find a way to give him an eagle tomorrow. I thanked the eagle for his inspiration and flew away, letting thoughts of my loved ones guide me. Sarah, for her it has to be music, it'll be her favorite hymn. I'll find a way tomorrow to play it, so she hears it. My thoughts then turned to Jeremi. I had to give him something he could lean on when he needed inner strength, something to help him find his way. I trusted I'd recognize it when I saw it. I wanted Glory to know that my love for her was undying. The next time I paid attention to my surroundings, I was back in the house.

I was in our bedroom. There was Glory fast asleep in our bed. Sarah was asleep next to her. They both looked so sweet and peaceful.

Naomi and Grandmama sat and talked on the edge of the bed. "Good morning, Martin," they said sweetly.

There was a stack of special cards and letters Glory kept on the desk. I knew the last Valentine's Day card I'd given her was somewhere in there. I stood there, perplexed.

"What's the matter, Martin?" Naomi asked.

"I want to give her my last Valentine's card again," I explained. "But how do I do that?"

"Where is it?"

"Here on the desk, somewhere."

"It's there, third from the top," she said.

"Okay, now I found it. How do I make her find it?" I asked.

We looked around. Then Grandmama suggested, "Pick it up and place it between the desk and the wall, like it fell. Leave a small corner visible, so we can make her see it with angel light."

So I did. Then I sat down in my chair. I watched as Naomi gently woke Glory up. She opened her eyes and looked around like she did every day. Then she looked over at Sarah, who was asleep where I would have been and she let out a heavy sigh, saying, "Oh, Martin."

Naomi, Grandmama and I focused our angel light on the exposed corner of the card. Glory sat on the edge of the bed, her eyes still cloudy from sleep. She rubbed them and when she opened them again, she saw what we wanted her to see. She stared at it a moment, trying to figure out what it was. She got up and picked it up. She realized what it was and it took her breath away.

She sat down at the desk, read it all over again and clutched it to her heart. "Thank you, sweetheart," she said softly. "I'll always love you, too." She blew a kiss in the direction of my chair, which I caught. I got up and kissed her cheek. She got chillbumps. I knew she felt it.

Again she sighed, stood up and said, "Help me get through this day, Lord." She stood the card up on her dresser and went into the bathroom.

"That worked well," I said to Naomi and Grandmama. They agreed. "Well, that's one," I said. "I'd still like to make this easier on Glory today, but I think I'm going to need everyone's help." As they had promised, Mother, Dad, Sheila and George all appeared, right on cue.

"Good show, Martin." George approved of the card as her gift.

"You were watching?" I asked him.

"We all were," he answered. They all smiled. "What would you like to do now?"

"Inspire the older children to make a nice breakfast for the family, so that Glory can relax," I said.

Grandmama stayed to wake up Sarah. The rest of us went to the living room. Children were everywhere. Peter's children and a few extra nieces, nephews, cousins and grandchildren were asleep on the couch and floor in the living room. All the bedrooms were full with visitors, and Peter, his wife, Jeremi and Viv. Sarah shared Glory's room, so that Peter and Melinda could have a room to themselves. The children all looked so sweet when they slept. Everyone's angel was nearby and all of them greeted us as we checked on their charges.

Sheila went to her oldest and did the feather trick with her to get her up. The poor girl ended up flailing and woke up her cousin next to her. A series of "Quit it!" and "Look at what you did!" woke up the other children nearby. About then, Sarah came down the hall shushing the noisemakers, hoping the little children would stay asleep to keep what little peace remained in the house for a while more. Sarah instructed the older girls to follow her into the kitchen. They got busy. Before long, the aroma of fresh coffee, bacon, eggs, grits and toast took over the house.

The angels were busy, too. They made sure things were cooked perfectly, when the girls did all the necessary things to make this a nice breakfast. About the time they had the table set and all the food warming, waiting for everyone to come in, Sarah went over to the older girls and put an arm around each of them. She kissed them each on the top of their heads and told them she loved them. Their angels did the same to each of the girls, too.

Glory came into the kitchen to this wonderful breakfast surprise and proclaimed "Lord have mercy!" The girls both ran to their grandma, who held them tight. "Thank you very much. I know you know how much this means to me." When Glory let them go, she wiped tears from her eyes.

"I guess you'd better wake everybody up," Sarah said.

The girls--who had earned the privilege--woke each one up, with as much force as necessary. After being tickled or kissed, punched or gently nudged, each one of the cousins was awake. The noise that commenced was deafening, but beautiful. The children stretched, yawned, punched each other, tattled, laughed and yelled a little. It was a fairly normal beginning to an extraordinary day for all of us. Glory and

Sarah stood in the kitchen, watched and snickered. Peter and Melinda soon joined the breakfast crew. That was everyone, except Jeremi.

"Henry! Where are you?" I called out.

"In here!" He responded from inside the garage.

Henry called us out to the garage. There was Jeremi asleep, with several empty beer cans in the garbage right beside him. He was slumped up against a box, on the hard concrete floor. Henry, George, and I, stood there watching him. I shook my head, half in disgust and half in pity. I had to spare Glory this. I had to protect her from this.

Henry explained, "He sneaked out last night and bought beer, then he came back and sat in here and drank and cried himself to sleep."

"What are we going to do?" George asked.

I looked around the garage to figure this out. I was at a complete loss. There Jeremi was, laid out. Glory was in the next room. Each one having one of the hardest days of their lives. Here I was, at a loss for anything to do about it.

George asked, "About his present, what did you decide?"

"I decided it had to be a symbol of strength, something he could see, have and touch. I knew that I'd recognize it when I saw it today," I answered.

George, Henry and I looked around the garage with that thought in mind. Our eyes all came to rest on the same thing hanging on a rack over Jeremi's head. It was a symbol of strength, accomplishment and determination. It was representative of something both Jeremi and I loved and shared. He could take it and have it with him. It was the perfect gift for him! I stared at it and stared at it and tried to figure out how I was going to give it to him and how I could make him understand why I gave it to him. Again, I was at a loss.

"Now that we've found it, how do we give it to him?" We pondered the predicament for a bit.

"Would you mind if I did it?" Henry asked.

"By all means," I replied. I watched a master at work. First, he grabbed the present and stretched one corner of it and hooked it on the corner of the box that Jeremi was sleeping on. Then, very gently and quietly, he moved the support behind the box, just a couple of inches. Next, he started to move one corner of the box backward, barely enough for Jeremi to have to readjust. With his readjustment, the box gave way and Jeremi fell back with the box. The present fell down on top of him.

Henry smiled and said. "Mission accomplished!" I applauded him.

Jeremi woke up sputtering and cursing. trying to figure out what had just fallen on him. He frantically pulled it off and threw it to the side. He sat up and looked around and tried to get his bearings. He stretched and still cursed as he accomplished sitting up. He reached for the last swig of the beer that was in the can nearby.

"Yuck! That was nasty!" He said and wiped his mouth, but swallowed none-the-less.

Henry and George pointed their angel light onto the gift to get Jeremi to notice it. I sat beside him. "Son, you've got to get yourself together, today and every day hereafter. You're in big trouble, son, and I'm worried about you. There's something I want you to have. Look over there. Look over there!" He turned his head toward the present and cocked it as he tried to figure out what it was. His eyes got big as he realized what it was.

"Oh, God!" he said and began to cry. "Dad, it's your sweater. It's your letterman's sweater from college. How did it get here?" He looked around frantically, trying to figure out how it had gotten there. Failing that, he picked it up and put it on and sniffed one of the arms. "Oh man, I can still smell your aftershave." He started to cry again.

I put my arm around him. "Jeremiah, I want you to have this sweater. I want you to put it on anytime you want me close by and to feel my arms around you."

Tears rolled down his cheeks. "It feels like your arms are around me when I have this on. Oh, God! Dad, I miss you so much." He sobbed.

"Jeremiah, get yourself together. Your mama's right inside that door and she's waiting for you."

He looked toward the garage door to the house and could hear the commotion of the family gathering at the breakfast table. He stood up, wiped his face with his sleeve, blew his nose on an old dried-up paper towel from the trash and took a deep breath. Having regained his composure, he went inside. We went with him. Everyone turned to see his entrance. He posed proudly in the doorway.

Peter saw the sweater and looked at his mother immediately to see what her reaction was. Glory let out a slight gasp and Peter scooted his chair back and was about to stand to confront Jeremi about the sweater.

Glory grabbed Peter's hand to stop him. She never took her eyes off Jeremi. He stood there anxious to hear her reaction. She was very sure and supportive. "You look handsome, son. You look just like your father." They both exchanged smiles, and Jeremi sighed with relief. "It's fitting that you have that sweater. Yes, it is. Are you gonna just stand there posing or are you gonna come eat?" Jeremi did exactly that. Peter honored Glory's decision and scooted his chair back in and ate his breakfast.

In a replay of the dinner the night before, people picked at their food, even though I could tell it was delicious. Then they began to talk and then laugh. The lighter the mood got, the more they started to eat and act like themselves again.

The only exceptions were Glory and Jeremi. They were both in their own worlds. I went over to talk to them. "Wake up, you two." They both straightened up in their chairs at the same time, realizing they had been drifting into daydreams. "I wish I could tell you how wonderful it is to be here. I wish I could get that through to you, so you stopped aching for me. It's so wonderful here. I'm with everyone. I see everyone, living and passed. I can do almost anything, like paint sunrises, soar with eagles, give you presents." Glory clutched her heart like she'd done with the card earlier and Jeremi smelled the sweater again. They both sighed. "Come on, both of you, eat, you need your strength. It's going to be a long day." I could tell I'd communicated with them, but they still ate very slowly. At least they were eating something, that made me feel a little better.

Glory left the table without eating much more. She had to finish dressing. One by one, they all got up and cleared their plates. Sarah collared the two oldest boys to do the breakfast dishes. They did, but grumbled about it. Sarah promised to fix their attitudes if she heard anything else. They complied.

I saw Peter head out to the backyard by himself. I guessed he needed a moment's peace away from all the children. He sat at the picnic table at the edge of the patio, leaned back, his elbows on the table and his feet outstretched.

"Hey, Dad. I wish you could hear me. There are so many things I still want to tell you. You're my hero. You're my rock. What am I going to do without you? I'm sorry for those times when I was young and stupid and you were just doing what you had to. I said so many hateful things. I kept meaning to tell you how sorry I was for that, but I never got around to it. I was afraid to bring it up again. Now here I am. I want so badly to tell you how sorry I am. I want you to know how much I admire and love you. I wish so much I could tell for sure that you could hear me."

His speech brought tears to my eyes. "Oh, Peter, we're all sorry for things of the past, but we get through them. You've grown into a man that I am so proud of. I am listening and I'll prove it to you. Just stare at the sky. I'll be right back."

I left to find my friend the eagle, the one that had given me the idea for Peter's gift.

He was on his perch on the edge of a cliff. I looked him in the eyes. He saw me. I picked up a loose feather from the ground beneath him. I asked him for his help. I flew away and he followed me. It took a few minutes but soon I could see the house. I could see Peter staring up at the sky. My eagle close behind me, we circled low and wide, right in Peter's line of sight. I could tell he saw us. He stood up and moved toward us, although the yard prevented him from getting too far. I took my leave of the eagle, but he kept circling for me for several more minutes.

While Peter watched the eagle, I gently put the feather on the table behind him. "This is your present, son. Always feel how close I am to you. Always know that I can hear you."

When he turned around, he was startled to see the feather. He took a quick step back. "Whoa!" He looked back up at the sky and the eagle was gone. He picked up the feather and examined it closely. He said, "Thank you, Dad. somehow I just know it's you." He stood there for a minute collecting his thoughts. Then he folded his arms, concealed the feather and walked back in the house. Apparently intending to keep this experience to himself, he went straight to his room.

I took some time after that to talk to each one of my grandchildren. I rode around on their shoulders and tickled their ears from time to time. I told each of them the story of the day they were born and where I was when it happened and what it was like for me the first time I saw them. They'd each heard the story before, but I had fun telling them again.

Before long, it was time to go to the church. The boys were all handsome and girls were all beautiful. Everyone was dignified. They filed silently out the door and got into the cars, without bickering or tattling. I believe that was a first. We drove off to the church.

I decided to go ahead of them to check out the church. George, Sheila, Mother and Dad came with me.

It was so touching. There were several arrangements up near the altar distributed beautifully around my closed coffin. Our church organist was playing very somber, but beautiful, hymns quietly in the background. Some of my friends had already arrived and were seated.

My job was to give them all a gift.

One couple, dear friends whom Glory and I had had dinner with many times, were seated about halfway down. Our children were all about the same ages. We'd sit for hours and talk and talk. Her name was Margaret and his was Jimmy. Margaret had a very sad, reflective look on her face. Jimmy took Margaret's hand and patted it. I could tell he wanted to say something to comfort her, but the best he could do was to let her know he felt the same way. I sat in the pew in front of them, turned around and started to talk to them both.

I wanted to give them a happy memory.

"Do you remember," I began. "that night when Glory and I came to dinner over at your house? Jimmy, you and I were watching game two of the World Series and our beautiful wives were making the preparations for the next church rummage sale. The kids were playing in their room. Do you remember how they were playing? That was the time they were dressing up your tired ol' basset hound, using the laundry they should've been putting away." A slight, distant smile came over Margaret's face; Jimmy looked down as if he were embarrassed. "Then all of a sudden the ladies burst out laughing and we were at a loss as to why, but there was your dog, with your boy's underwear on his head, with his ears hanging out of the leg holes. Thank goodness those shorts were clean!"

Jimmy chuckled to himself, but he still looked down. It was enough of a noise, though, that it startled Margaret. "What?" she asked.

"Oh nothing. I was just thinking about that night when they came over to watch the World Series --"

"And your dog came out wearing your son's drawers on his head!" She finished for him. He nodded and looked away, for fear he'd break out laughing at the thought. "That's funny, I was thinking about that exact same night."

"We had some good times," Jimmy said.

"Let's focus on that. Praise God for the time we did have him in our lives. I'm sure going to miss him." Margaret moved closer to Jimmy and put her head on his shoulder. He put his arm around her.

I went behind them and put my arm around both of them. "Next time your dog comes out of the room with underwear on his head, you'll know I came back to visit." I kissed them both on the top of the head and said, "Thank you for all the good times. I know you'll both help take care of Glory for me."

Another very dear couple was there and I relived another one of my favorite memories with them. As I finished up, recalling the time all our boys' had finished painting our garage (and themselves), I saw my brother at the entrance of the sanctuary. This was the first time I'd seen him since I passed on. I was incredibly happy to see him, but he was distraught. He was rigid and his face was strained. I flew over to him and embraced him. "I've missed you, Lucas," I whispered in his ear. His body began to shake and his wife Lydia grabbed him and we all helped him to the first available seat. He cried as quietly as he could, out of respect for the church, but it was like trying to cap a volcano.

"This is the first time he's let it out," his angel told me. "This is the first time since he found out about your passing that he's cried. Just being here at the church, seeing everything, hearing you now. He needs to let it out." I held him as tight as I could and continued to tell him how much he meant to me. Lydia silently rocked him, held him and comforted him. I thanked her for loving him and being such a good wife to him all these years.

Almost as suddenly as he had started crying, he stopped. A friend nearby went out and got him a cup of water, which he drank and waved a "Thank you" gesture. Lydia helped him up and they went and took their seats in the family section down front.

11

Many people arrived all at once, Glory and the family among them. Peter and Melinda herded the children to their seats. Jeremi held Glory on one side, Sarah on the other as they walked her down the aisle to the front of the church.

Many people stopped Glory on her way. They gave her hugs or kissed her. She was becoming overwhelmed, so Jeremi, politely, headed off the rest of the well-wishers by making eye contact with them or by giving subtle hand gestures that Glory was oblivious to.

They sat down in the front pew. Sarah sat on one side of Glory, Jeremi on the other. Peter and Melinda sat next to Sarah. Vivian and her husband sat right behind Glory. Vivian touched Glory's shoulder and Glory patted Vivian's hand. It was an unspoken moment of understanding between best friends.

All of their angels sat on their shoulders, with the exception of Naomi who knelt at Glory's feet and held hands with her and Sarah. Glory was well taken care of.

I went up to the pulpit and stood behind it. It was a familiar physical perspective, but a very, very different spiritual one. Some people looked up at the pulpit with a longing. I could tell they wanted a sign that I was with them.

It was Sarah's turn for a gift; she needed to hear her favorite hymn. The organist, Lucille, was about to start another song for her prelude.

She organized and situated herself. This was going to be easy. Glory and Peter had picked out the songs for the service, but for Sarah's sake, there was going to be a change in the program.

If Lucille was true to form, she had a meticulously written list of songs with their titles and their numbers. She followed it carefully for every service she played. All I had to do was to change the number. I knew by heart the number of the hymn I wanted. I had sung it a million times, but it held so much more meaning now. I touched her piece of paper and the number for the next song changed. It even still looked like it was in her handwriting. This angel business was incredibly fun! Sheila joined me behind Lucille. We both watched her as she opened her hymnal to the next number on her list. She looked at the book and realized the title was different than what she had written. She looked through her glasses at it, then she looked over her glasses at it. She looked back at the number and back at the book. She sat there perplexed for a couple of moments, before she made a command decision. She always was very professional. I knew she'd avoid fumbling through the index of the book looking for the original song's number. I could hear her mutter to herself. "I could've swore I looked that up last night. Well, Martin liked this hymn, too. This is for you, my dear brother Harper."

"Good girl," I said and kissed her on the cheek.

"Let's sing it for them, Dad," Sheila said. The angels who love to sing joined us on the altar, together in a heavenly choir. We all joined in singing the spiritual.

"Shall we gather at the river, the beautiful, the beautiful river. Gather with the Saints at the river, that flows by the throne of God." It was so much fun to sing. The angels in the congregation swayed and clapped along with the singing. Many people in the congregation hummed along with the angels' singing. My family and friends could hear the singing in their minds, although I knew their minds interpreted it as a memory of when they had heard it before.

A tear rolled down Sarah's cheek and a slight smile started to form on one side of her mouth. She sang lightly along with us. Just like at the dinner table when the mood lightened when the angels laughed, this mood grew more peaceful when the angels sang. It was just the touch that was needed.

When the song ended, Lucille looked over at Glory and their eyes met. Lucille shrugged her shoulders and Glory let her know it was okay that she'd played that song instead of the one Glory and Peter had planned. Lucille sighed with relief that Glory approved of the improptu program change. With a little apprehension, Lucille turned to the next song that was on her list; fortunately, its title matched. She clasped her hands quickly. "Praise Jesus," she said low under her breath. Then she began to play a mellow and slow version of "The Old Rugged Cross."

The service was about to start. I took my seat where I always had, behind the pulpit. My dear friend and associate pastor, Brother Hamilton, sat right beside me. He prayed quietly, under his breath. "Father, please give me the strength to carry the family through this service. May we do all in our power to glorify you, while we here gather to honor Martin's memory, one of your newest angels. In Jesus' name, amen."

"Amen," I said with him.

He took a deep breath and went to the pulpit. He began strong. He came out of the gate preaching. "Friends! We are gathered here today to pay tribute to our dearly departed husband, father, grandfather, brother, friend and pastor, Martin Harper. Friends, I tell you, this is a glad day! This is a day to Praise God for allowing us to have such a wonderful man in our midst for as long as he allowed us Brother Harper!"

A light chorus of "amens" and "praise Jesus" resounded.

"We should be grateful for our Brother Harper has passed through the gates of Heaven! Oh, yes! Let's be glad for Brother Harper, for he is in a better place. He has angel wings and is with his lovely daughter Sheila once again! They are rejoicing in Heaven surrounded by love."

There was a "hallelujah" or two, but the congregation was slow catching up to his level of energy and calls for celebration.

"Friends, Brother Harper was a good man. He had a wonderful family. He had a beautiful wife."

Peter, Jeremi and Sarah said, "Amen!"

"That's right, could I have an Amen? Brother Harper had a beautiful wife!"

And everyone said, "Amen."

"He had two strong sons! He had two beautiful daughters. He was as blessed as a man could be with a loving family. Can I get an Amen?!"

Everyone said a slightly more enthusiastic, "Amen."

"He led this church through lean times and good times. He was there, for you Brother Lester, when your house burned down, working right beside you, helping you rebuild, right?" Brother Lester nodded in agreement.

"And he was there, for you Sister Foster, holding your hand all night long at the hospital after Walter's accident?" Lucille nodded, too.

"And for you, Brother," he pointed at the next unsuspecting soul in the congregation, "And for you, Sister. And we were there for him and Sister Harper throughout their daughter's illness and untimely death?" All the church said, "Yes, Lord!"

Glory put her hands up in the air and joined in the answer.

"He was as blessed as a man could be, with true friends."

And the congregation said, "Amen."

"Each and everyone of us, have some special moment, some memory, that only you and Brother Harper share. Yes?" He waited for a moment, until he got a response from the congregation. "That moment, those moments, those times, those memories, that is the way to keep Brother Harper with us always. Let us pause in prayer, then lift our voice in song, as Sister Foster leads us in playing a song that Brother Harper led us in many times, celebrating the tie we share with him forever-'Blest Be The Tie That Binds.'"

We'd sung that song so many times as a congregation that nobody needed a hymnal. Lucille could even have played it from memory.

When the song ended, Peter walked up to the pulpit, put his handkerchief back in his pocket on the way. He looked around at everybody there and then he took a long, deep breath. He started out reserved and quiet. "I want to thank you all for coming today and for the support you have given us over the past several days. My mother also expresses her gratitude for all your kindness." Glory turned in her seat and nodded back at everyone, then looked back at Peter. "I know that my father would want us to be joyous right now, especially because we are all together, but that's hard to do." He paused for a moment and swallowed hard. "I want to be happy for him, for he is in the Promised Land." The "Amens" and "praise God's" kept coming and as they did Peter got stronger and stronger. "He has gone on, yet he is still here with with us." He patted his left jacket pocket which is where I know he'd put the feather I had given him. "I know he's here, right now, with us and showering his love all over us right now. He's probably sitting in his chair right back here"--he pointed me out--"and saying 'Now go on. Quit your crying. I taught you better than that!' And he did. He taught us better. He taught us so much. He taught us how to love one another. He taught us how to love the Lord and put him first and sit back and watch Jesus and his angels take care of us! He taught us how to be strong in adversity. He taught us how to accept help when the strength had left us. He raised us to be proud of who we were and what we were a part of, our family, our church, our neighborhood, our world. He would want us to remember that--always!" He stopped abruptly. He began again quietly. "Today we come to honor my father, our father, my mother's husband, our pastor and the best example I've ever seen of what a real man is." He stopped, looked down at the coffin and said, "I promise, Dad--" but he stopped short and turned around and looked at me in my chair instead, "I promise, Dad, I will try to be the best father I can. I will do it by living your example and remembering all you taught me, so that I can teach it to my children. We all miss you, Dad, and love you so much." He took his handkerchief back out of his pocket, wiped his face with it as he went back to his seat.

"I'm so proud of you, son," I said right back.

Brother Hamilton went back up to the pulpit. "Thank you, Peter," he began. "Please remember, whenever your heart gets heavy with the burden of your life, that whatever troubles you face, whatever loss you have suffered, in the words of another of Brother Harper's favorite hymns, 'Heaven bears up all of Earth's sorrows.'" He nodded over to Lucille, who began to play the intro. "Let's join together now, praising God, the father Almighty and His only son Jesus Christ our Lord, in celebration of the wonderful life of our beloved Brother in Christ." The organ turned up the volume and the congregation sang out loud with a strong and stirring rendition of "How Great Thou Art." The angels sang right beside their charges. I know all of Heaven could hear.

When the song ended, Brother Hamilton said, "Graveside services will be following directly. Then we are all invited to a reception at Sister Vivian Peterson's house to visit with the family." He raised both hands out high in front of him and began preaching his benediction. "God's peace be with you all until we meet again. In the holy name of our Lord and Savior, Jesus Christ. Amen and Amen!"

And that was that. My funeral was over. It was a beautiful service. I wanted it to keep going. I guess I really just wanted all the love in this room to remain as strong as it was this very moment. It felt so wonderful. It was humbling to be the focus of so much love. I did have a wonderful life on earth. I was blessed. I was truly blessed.

One by one my friends filed past the casket. Most of them touched it, very delicately and lovingly and said how much they missed me. As each one filed by, I kissed them, hugged them, patted them on the back or showed some other form of affection that we would have shown to each other during my life on Earth. After they filed by the coffin, they greeted Glory, Peter, Jeremi and Sarah with hugs, support and friendship. Most of them said, "If there's anything, anything, I can do, please let me know." Glory was gracious, but this was all very wearing on her. She was very tired. Finally the last one made their way by and left.

Then it was Glory, Peter, Jeremi, Sarah, Viv, the good reverend, and all the angels gathered around the casket. One by one they took each other's hand and stood there in silence. We angels stood in a protective ring around them. I was right with Glory. Everyone, even the angels were completely silent.

Suddenly, Glory broke down and cried on the casket. Both Peter and Jeremi, who were on either side of her, put their arms around her. Sarah and Viv reached over the men to touch her. All the angels did the same.

"Give her strength, Lord. Please!" I begged.

With a sudden splendor, the sun broke through the clouds and through the windows very brightly. It lit up the golden cross that was on the back wall of the altar. Peter felt a sudden warmth and looked up to see the cross as it radiated the light. Then Sarah saw it, then Jeremi, then Viv.

"Mama," Peter whispered.

She looked up and saw the beautifully sunlit cross. She stopped crying and gasped.

A strong soothing voice, heard with the ears of the angels and with the hearts of those living said, "Let my Father's perfect peace be upon you. Find comfort in your faith and know that I am with you, always."

"Thank you," I whispered humbly, trembling.

"Peace be on you as well, Martin. Your prayers are heard and answered. These angels have been sent to look over your family, as you have requested all of your life and as you have requested now. They will be safe. They will be strong. Take comfort in your faith and know that I am always with you, too."

Tears began to roll down my cheeks. I was overwhelmed. I could barely speak, but I managed to whisper, "Thank you, Jesus."

The beautiful glow on the cross started to slowly fade away. Glory and everyone there, who had been awestruck by its beauty, began to gather themselves back together. Silently and as close as they could be to one another, they left the church and loaded into the waiting cars with the rest of the family for the ride to the cemetery.

The procession was several blocks long. Most of the angels flew a protective circle around the cars. I rode near Glory. She was quiet. She was calm. She was a comfort to me. I put my arm around her and she sighed peacefully. I whispered in her ear. "The Lord promised me that these angels would look after you. They've done a great job so far. I have every confidence they'll do a great job from now on. I love you. I wish I could ease the pain of your missing me."

"What were her choices, Martin?" Mother joined us.

"What do you mean?" I asked.

"You have to realize that her pain is her choice. The only way for her to avoid this pain right now, would be for her to have loved you with less than her full heart. But she did love you with her full heart - you know she did. If people choose to love in life, when they lose those whom they love, they will have pain. The only other choice is to avoid love, but that is to choose to live in pain. Let her mourn. It's her tribute to you and to your love. She wants to do it. She needs to do it. Soon, her peace will overcome her pain." Mother's voice was so soothing for both me and Glory.

We rode silently the rest of the way to the cemetery.

I thought about what Mother had said. I had to allow them their time to grieve. It was necessary, though incredibly hard to watch. Glory, Sarah, Peter and Jeremi had changed. They accepted the peace that had been bestowed upon them by Jesus. The tears stopped flowing and they stood firm and together, silently, reverently and peacefully.

Finally Brother Hamilton spoke the words I'd spoken over so many in my lifetime: "In grief of your death, but in gratitude for your life and in the pleasure of sharing it with you, we commit your body to be buried. Ashes to ashes, dust to dust, rest now at the end of your days on Earth. Rest now, in the hearts and minds of all you love and who loved you."

A few people, mostly my grandchildren, placed flowers on the casket and walked slowly to their cars. Hugs, support and love was exchanged between everyone there. It was touching to watch those whose lives I'd been a part of, give love and comfort to one another.

The cars left for the reception at Vivian's, with angel protection all around them.

I stayed behind and sat down on the cool grass. George stayed with me. "What are you thinking about?"

I looked at him, peculiarly. "You know what I'm thinking. You always have up to now."

"Your mind is so flooded with all sorts of thoughts and it's difficult for me to tell which one is prevailing."

"That's the truth." I did have so many things on my mind. It was hard to sort it all out.

"Funerals are hard days, for both living and angel," he assured me.

I nodded, then asked, "Are you having a hard day?"

"Yes, but yours is probably harder." He put his hand on my shoulder. "Your mind is full of questions. Ask them."

"I have so many questions, it's hard to choose one to begin with. I want them all answered."

"Start with the most important."

"It's about what happened at the church," I said.

"He answered your prayer, Martin. He gave her strength and peace. He appeared to them in a way that they could easily accept and yet they knew it was Him. They will always feel the peace of that moment anytime they remember it. I've seen your prayers answered before, what's so different now?"

"Yes, but I . . ."

"Talked to God?" George finished my sentence. I looked at him, my brow furrowed with a million more questions. "Of course you did." He laughed at me. "You're a new angel! What did you expect? You're in Heaven. Wherever you go, you're in Heaven. You're still thinking like a person, Martin, waiting for some desperate moment to call upon Him. Talk to God anytime you want. Actually, I'm surprised you it took you this long." He chuckled and shook his head. "You'll get the hang of this - sooner than you think."

"I thought He. . . I mean, He's just. . ." My loss for words made me feel so basic.

"He's just what? He's just there whenever you need him. He's just there like He always promised to be. He appeared to you in life, several times. I know because I was there. What's so different?"

"I saw Him. I literally saw God," I said quietly.

"Yes, you did." He was silent for a moment to let me comprehend what I had just said. Then he smiled like a wise grandfather about to bestow the "moral of the story" to a young child. "Do you know what the most beautiful thing about being an angel is, Martin?" I shook my head. "When you were living, you had to walk by faith. Now, as an angel, you get to walk by sight."

The joy of that simple statement was the most profound I'd ever felt. We sat there, I stared into the sky, contemplating all that I had experienced and learned in the last few hours. Sheila was right: It does just keep getting better and better. We sat there just long enough for me to feel rejuvenated. I had places to go!

The festivities were at Viv's, so that's where George and I went. The reception was in full swing. Lovely food, kids playing together and my friends and family talked and told stories. Most everywhere the mood was lively. There were some pockets of people comforting whoever was crying, but they were the exception to the rule here today.

Peter and Jeremi told the story of the cross at the church to anyone who wanted to hear. As soon as they were finished with one group, someone else brought somebody else and said, "Tell them what you told me!" They gladly did.

Glory sat in Viv's most comfortable chair and everyone made sure she was taken care of. Whoever was nearby refilled her plate or glass. They made sure she was comfortable and never alone. Viv was never more than a few feet away, unless she was getting what Glory needed. Naomi held Glory and rocked her from time to time as Naomi felt Glory's mood turn to sorrow. Naomi was quick to get another angel's attention, so that their charge came to visit with Glory. It was abundantly clear that Glory was well taken care of, on all levels.

Slowly people started to drift out. By early evening, it was down to just the family. They were all exhausted. Peter carried his sleeping baby boy out to the car. Jeremi walked out, helping Glory. Everyone followed in a procession, kissed Vivian and thanked her for all she had done. Sarah and a couple of the older girls stayed to help Vivian clean up.

When they got home, Glory took off her coat and her shoes and sat down on the couch. Before the rest of the family even got all the way into the house, she was asleep. They all tiptoed quietly around her and settled into quiet activities.

Peter put his son to bed. He and Melinda started to pack up for the trip back home the next day. Jeremi snuck out to the garage and reappeared after about ten minutes, wiping his mouth and smoking a cigarette. Sarah dragged herself home about an hour later and went to change her clothes but fell asleep on the bed instead.

Jeremi called Jeannie, but just long enough to make arrangements for her to pick them up at the airport the next day. He promised to tell her all about everything when he saw her tomorrow. Then he sat down to watch TV and was asleep before too long, himself.

Finally this day was over.

12

All the angels who could get away for a bit went back up to Heaven and into the garden. We all rested on each other and talked about what a day it had been. Some angels in the group reminisced about their funeral days and how taxing it had been on them. They told me about the presents they had left behind and the wonderful experiences they had had. I attended most of their funerals and now I could imagine those events from their perspective. I could see their angels working and I remembered the presents that they had given me. Some of their presents were similar to what I'd given my friends and family. Some of them were uniquely individual to both the giver and receiver. Only God could mastermind something so magnificent.

I began to feel my strength return. It was surprising to me how drained I felt by the end of this day. All the other angels helped hold me up and were there with me, when I needed them. Being surrounded by that much love and support was unlike anything I had felt on earth, even during our best times. The angel party lasted all night, until one by one the Guardians were called back to their waking or troubled charges.

When the last angel left, George asked me, "What do you want to do today, Martin?"

"Learn," I responded. I'd been rejuvenated. I was eager and ready.

George crossed his arms and studied me for a moment. "Hmmm. A course in Guardian Angel, 101, coming right up."

We were off!

As we flew, he explained, "I want you to get good at knowing how and when to appear to people. We can do a lot of good work here while you're training."

"Okay," I said eagerly. That sounded like a lot of fun.

"You want to learn, so let's go to school," George joked.

Suddenly, we were at some big high school, students everywhere. There was a lot of undeveloped land around it, so it must have been a new suburb of a fairly large city. There was a girl sitting alone, under a tree reading a book. She looked comfortable being alone, like she had done it frequently. There were three boys nearby who talked about her saying truly horrific things. They planned on "inviting her to a party" that only they were going to have fun at. They were definitely already high on something, especially the ringleader. He was angelless with him. The other two had angels who desperately tried to get them to leave, but to without success. The girl's angel, aware of the danger, tried to get her charge to go inside, also to without success.

"Hard-headed teenagers!" I thought.

We heard the leader say, "Look, there she is, all alone. Let's go."

"What are we going to do?" I asked George.

"We're going to only appear to those boys over there. We're merely going to go over and sit with the girl until those boys lose interest in her," George explained.

That sounded easy enough, but there was something lacking in the plan I thought, so I asked, "Are two grown men going to look a little strange sitting by her?"

"Good point," George said. "Imagine yourself eighteen again and wearing, oh, let's say, jeans and a T-shirt." So we both did that. "Now focus on the boys." I did that. Then we walked around the corner and right up to the girl. She turned around quickly, like she had heard us approach. I looked at her.

"Focus on the boys!" George commanded. So I did.

They approached from the other direction and were still some twenty feet away. We stared them down. The girl looked up, then turned away slightly. She showed absolute zero interest in and barely any recognition of the boys.

The leader cussed at his cohorts about their plans being blown. The boys' angels looked relieved, as did the girl's angel. All of them thanked us for our intervention. The boys walked away. Soon after that, the morning bell rang and the girl got up and went into the school.

The boys, who still had angels with them, went into school, too. The angel-less boy stayed out and cussed them out for their choice to leave him. He wandered out into the parking lot and back toward his car and left the school by speeding out of the parking lot. The speed at which he left the lot attracted the attention of a nearby patrol car, which promptly pulled him over.

"Good work, Martin," George said. "How d'ya like that?"

"That was great. But did she see us?" I asked.

"No, but I believe she heard us. You have to maintain focus when you become visible or somebody may see something more than you intended. To a great extent that's where ghost stories come from."

That made sense. I think I'd started a couple of those ghost stories in my day, myself. "What if those boys would've tried to take us on? What would we have done then?"

"I would have caused a diversion and we would have disappeared. The boys would have been left scratching their heads, trying to find us and probably fighting each other. The girl would still have been safe."

"Should her angel have appeared to them? Would that have helped?"

"Maybe, but she probably thought the prospect of those boys seeing two girls might have been more enticing. It's hard to say. We all protect our charges the best way we know how and it's as individual as we are and as they are. We simply gave a helping angel hand. Someday one will do the same for you and you will be very grateful. Wait, you'll see."

13

"What's next, Martin?" he asked.

"Naomi will send word if Glory needs me, right?"

"She'll send word," George reassured me.

"Where are Peter and Jeremi? What time is it there? They're due back home pretty soon. I want to see what happens when Jeremi and Jeannie get back together. I want to be there for their reunion."

"Very well. Let's go."

We went to Jeannie's apartment. She scurried around like she was getting ready for a big date. The girls watched her every move.

"But we want to go with you!" Carole begged.

"I told you, baby. You have to stay here. I want to spend some time alone with Emi. He's got a lot he says he wants to tell me and, well, he'll come over later and you girls can see him then," Jeannie explained.

Pearl, Edwina and Marie laughed together. Marie said, "That makes twelve." They laughed harder.

"Twelve what?" I asked.

"Times that Carole has asked to go with her to get him. They're all excited about Jeremi coming back into town. She's a persistent one," Marie said about Carole.

"But Mommeeee!" was interupted by the doorbell.

"Saved by the bell," both Pearl said out loud and Jeannie muttered to herself simultaneously, which made all of us laugh louder. Jeannie answered the door. It was their babysitter, a young teenage girl, and her angel.

"Hi! I'm almost ready. Carole, would you please show Ashleigh what I've pulled out for you for dinner?" Then she turned to the babysitter. "Keep them out here, please. Let me get finished dressing, then I'll get out of here." The babysitter acknowledged and followed a stomping Carole out to the kitchen.

Marie buzzed by Carole's ear and said firmly, "Straighten up!" Carole stopped her stomping.

Jeannie disappeared behind her bedroom door. When Lynne tried to follow her, the babysitter picked her up and played with her.

A few minutes later Jeannie emerged from the bedroom. She looked very sharp, definitely ready to go out for the evening. "It would appear that they're going somewhere else after she picks them up from the airport," I said, but it was more of a question for Pearl.

"Yes, she and Jeremi have plans to go out," Pearl confirmed.

Jeannie kissed both the girls, gave the babysitter some final instructions and flew out the door before Carole could ask a thirteenth time to go with her. Pearl followed closely behind. We bid the girls' angels good-bye and we were off as well.

Instead of going with Jeannie in the car ride to the airport, we joined Jeremi, Peter, and family in the air. Jeremi stared out the window, lost in his own thoughts. He had on my letterman's sweater. He looked anxious. Henry was nearby, so we joined him.

"How's he doing?" I asked.

"He's glad to be headed home," Henry said.

"We just came from Jeannie's place; she's ready to have him back," George said.

"She's a worrier," Henry said. "This whole time, Pearl said, all she's done is worry about him. He's had things to keep his mind occupied, but he did miss her, that's for sure. He misses you more, though, Martin. You're who's on his mind right now."

"Then let's get his mind on Jeannie," I said. "I want him to quit moping around. Tell us a story about the two of them and make sure Jeremi can hear you."

"Okay," Henry agreed. "Let's see." He thought for a moment. "A few weeks ago, Jeremi and Jeannie took the girls out to go bowling. Do you remember that, Jeremi? When you went to the bowling alley with the girls?" Jeremi was still deep inside his own thoughts. "Jeremi!" Henry clapped his hands near his face and Jeremi jumped. Jeremi looked around for a second to see if he could figure out what had just happened. Failing that, he shook his head, muttered lightly to himself and stared out the window again. "Okay, now that you're with us, Jeremi, let's tell the story of you and Jeannie taking the girls bowling. It was the first time you met the girls." A distant look and a slight smile crept onto Jeremi's face. "It was the middle of the day, so the bowling alley was fairly empty. There were only a couple of die-hard bowlers a few lanes away. You rented these funky-looking shoes and found a colorful bowling ball for Carole. Yours was slick black and had the name 'Al' engraved on it, so you called it 'Big Al' all night." Jeremi smiled wider, on one side of his mouth. "While Jeannie picked out her bowling ball, Lynne helped you enter the names in the machine. Since the girls were with you, you had them put the bumpers up. Carole went first, with her running self and threw the ball. Actually she did pretty good, as long as she ran straight. If she ran up at any angle at all, the ball zigzagged all the way down the lane. She bowled a fifty-six and a seventy-one, really good for a five-year-old. Jeannie did all right, too. But you and 'Big Al' and Lynne had quite a day. You put Lynne on your hip and bowled. You bowled a one-ninety-eight and a two-twenty-five, some of your best games ever." Jeremi's smile grew wider with each detail. "But then you realized you that you were using bumpers and if you bragged about it to anyone, you'd be clowned!"

Jeremi shook his head, looked out the window and mumbled, "Uh, uh, uh."

Peter sitting next to him, asked, "What?"

Jeremi looked over at Peter and leaned back and tried to dismiss his question, "Oh nothing, I was just thinking of something."

"What?"

"Oh, this time I went bowling with Jeannie and her girls."

"Oh, I see," Peter said sarcastically.

"You see what?" Jeremi asked defensively.

"Oh, nothing," Peter teased, knowing how he could drive his brother nuts with innuendo.

"That's right, nothing!" Jeremi said firmly and looked out the window again. Peter laughed. Jeremi bit his lower lip to stop a laugh from breaking out. Eventually, he gave in and chuckled a little.

"Just like when they were little," I said.

A few minutes later the plane landed.

Jeremi got off first. He could see Jeannie behind some other people, when he was about half way down the gateway. She tried to get a good vantage point, so she could see. When she got a glimpse of him, she went to the closest place she could. Peter and his family were behind him. Peter made them intentionally hang back, so they could watch Jeremi with Jeannie.

As soon as Jeremi reached Jeannie at the end of the corridor, they embraced. She had both her arms around his neck. He had both his arms around her waist. They both squeezed very tight and he picked her up off the ground slightly. They fit well together. It reminded me of the Yin Yang. One side was black and one side was white, separately they were a strange shape, but put together, they formed a perfect shape. It was hard to tell where one started and the other stopped. I liked this. This was going to be all right.

The embrace lasted a bit longer than the man behind them was willing to wait. An "Uh-hum," from him brought them both back into the moment. Jeannie looked down and blushed. Jeremi looked around for Peter and the family. When he saw them, he motioned for them to hurry up. Then he got out of the way and let the people behind him pass.

"That was sweet," I told George and Henry.

"Peter thought so, too," George pointed out.

Peter and Melinda greeted Jeannie. Jeremi introduced Peter's kids to Jeannie as they all walked to the baggage claim. They got their bags and Jeannie drove them home.

Once Jeremi had his things unloaded and put in his room, he and Jeannie left. They went to the pub to eat dinner, sing and talk.

George, Henry, Pearl and I watched them from across the room. It was fun to watch Jeremi tell her about the dream. He described it in full detail, with great enthusiasm. His arms flew around. He talked fast. Jeannie was entranced and got chill bumps when he told her what Glory said about the sunrise and that I mentioned decorating it in his dream. Then he remembered he was wearing my sweater. He told her about how it just "fell" on him when he was alone. He told her a few of the elaborate details of the rest of that night, however, he kept much of it in. When he told her about the funeral and the brilliantly lit cross, they both started to tear up.

When he finished, she told him of some of her similar experiences with Jack's death. How she thought he'd painted rainbows for his wife and made flowers bloom out of season, for her. How she thought he'd put on a personal lightning storm for the family because they always used to love to watch lightning storms roll in.

Jeremi started to fall back into sadness when Henry went over and whispered in his ear for him to ask about the girls. Jeremi did and Jeannie regaled him with wonderfully cute stories of the everyday life of her little girls. He told Jeannie how much he had missed them and her. He smiled.

The pub had started the Karaoke for the night. Jeannie and Jeremi had both put in several song tickets. They were eating their salads when he got called up to sing for the first time. He sang a beautiful love song, about a "One in a Million" love affair. Jeremi, being the showman he is, made every woman there think he sang it directly to her.

Jeannie enjoyed watching him sing. She also enjoyed watching the other people stop what they were doing as soon as he sang his first note. He commanded a presence on stage that was remarkable. I loved watching him, too. Pearl told me that Jeannie loved their evenings together, up until his first song. After that, they were never alone again, until they left the pub. His singing was so memorable that many people in the pub came to tell him how wonderfully he sang. He was always very gracious to his fans. Some came up and asked him to sing duets with them. Unless Jeremi had seen them sing before and knew what they sounded like, he usually declined. Then there were some young women who pulled chairs to their table to talk to him. They pretended that Jeannie was invisible. It was these women that ruined the rest of the night for Jeannie. Jeremi should've asked them to leave, but instead he made some blatantly romantic gesture for Jeannie's sake to get the point across to them who he was with. As soon as one left, another showed up. Some bought him drinks and requested he do a special song for them. Jeremi drank up this attention, quite literally. This was all still very new to Jeannie. All this attention made her really uncomfortable.

When both Jeremi and Jeannie sang songs, they enjoyed themselves. So that compensated for some of the other stressors of the evening. Last call had been made on songs, so they decided to leave. They went back to Jeannie's place. The girls were already tucked into their beds when Jeannie and Jeremi got there. The babysitter was watching TV. Her angel was reading a book beside her. Jeannie walked the babysitter home.

Jeremi checked on the girls. He sat down on Carole's bed and rubbed her back to see if she woke up easily. Marie whispered in her ear excitedly, "Jeremi's here!" Carole rolled over quickly and saw him. She hugged him tight around his neck. He hugged her tight.

"Mommy said you might be sad the next time I saw you. Are you sad?" Carole asked.

"A little," Jeremi said. "But if I got another big hug from you it'd really help." Carole squeezed tighter. "I just wanted to get a hug. You get back to sleep now. I'll see you in the morning."

"But --" Carole started.

"Shhh," Jeremi said. "You'll wake up your sister. Your mama will be back soon and she'd shoot me if she knew I woke you up. So keep this our secret. Okay?"

Carole snuggled back under the covers as Jeremi tucked her in. He kissed her on the forehead. He went to Lynne's bed and kissed his fingers and touched her cheek.

Jeannie returned in time to catch Jeremi sneaking out of the girl's room. "Did you wake them up?" she asked with her hands on her hips, in a failed attempt to look disgusted. Actually, I think she thought it was sweet.

"Me?" he looked at the ceiling to avoid eye contact.

Jeannie tried to pass him in the narrow hallway to go check on the girls, but he grabbed her as she went by and kissed her passionately.

"I've been waiting all night for that," he said, when they decided to come up for air. They kissed again quickly, then broke apart. Jeannie went in to check on the girls. Jeremi peeked in. Carole closed her eyes really hard in an effort to look asleep. Jeannie glanced toward the door. She gave him another disgusted look, to which he shrugged his shoulders. She shook her head and smiled slightly. She kissed Carole on the cheek, then she kissed Lynne. "Sweet dreams, baby girls!" she whispered and quietly shut their door.

As soon as Carole heard the door close, she smiled. I bet she thought that she had fooled her mother.

Jeannie followed Jeremi into the bedroom and their door closed.

I watched the other angels for their lead. Were they going to follow them or give them privacy? "What now?" I asked.

"We go," George said. "They will be all right. Marie has the house tonight, so we can go. She will summon us if she needs us."

"This is a special night, Martin," Pearl said. "This is the night your charge will be conceived."

I could feel my eyes get big. "Already?"

They all nodded in the affirmative.

"I've got to tell Glory!" I said.

"Okay, let's go," George said.

Glory sat at the kitchen table. Sarah and Vivian were there with her. Their angels stood behind them, rubbed their shoulders. Naomi and Grandmama greeted us. Vivian's angel, Goldie, smiled brightly.

"May I?" I asked Naomi. She happily relinquished her position and I took her place rubbing Glory's shoulders. Glory readjusted in her seat. I think she sensed a change. "Naomi, Grandmama, Goldie, I want you to meet Pearl. This is Jeannie's Guardian Angel. Jeannie is the mother of our future grandson."

They all smiled and extended her a warm welcome.

"Tell us about Jeannie," Naomi requested.

"Jeannie, oh, my!" Pearl exclaimed. "She's a sweet one, but stubborn like all the rest of her family. She has a really strong sense of humor. Her favorite part of life is being a mother. She's completely devoted to two very sweet baby girls and soon, her baby boy. She works to support her family. She's a computer expert and does very well at it. She has a few really good friends and a lot who, she will find, are only fair-weather friends. She gets along easily with people, until they hurt her feelings. She needs to work on her forgiveness, but that's another story."

"What happened to the girls' father?" Naomi asked.

"He chose a career over his family. He left them for it. When she reached her limit of loneliness in the marriage, she challenged him on it. It was a long, very hard time for her. She gave him many chances and she endured the loneliness for the sake of the girls having a father. They always came first for her. The girls got her through the lonely time and the separation. She and their father are still friendly."

"That's good," Naomi responded. "It's so nice to meet you. Baby girl here," she said, referring to Glory, "is worried to death about Jeremi. She was just saying how much she wished she could've spent some more time with him when he was here."

Pearl went on to further describe Jeannie to them, but I decided to tune into Glory's conversation.

"And I think he slept out there the night before the funeral," Sarah confided to the group. "There were bottles of beer hidden under the other trash in the can that I found this morning."

"Oh Lord. Something's gonna have to happen," Glory said, referring to Jeremi's irresponsible state.

"The rate he's going, it's gonna have to happen *to* him, if you know what I mean," Sarah said, slightly disgusted. "He did say he was seeing someone up there. A lady, with two kids, I think." Glory's look changed from worried to intrigued. She wanted more details. "They met at the pub, she sings a little." Glory sighed.

"What does Peter think of her?" Vivian asked.

"He knows who she is. That's about all. It's a new relationship, a month or two tops," Sarah continued.

"Oh," Glory said, a little disappointed.

"Well, something's gotta happen. He needs to change from what he's doing now, that's for sure," Sarah said. Then she got up from the table and cleared her dishes. She kissed both Glory and Vivian goodnight. Sarah and Grandmama left.

"I should go, too," Vivian said. "It's been a long day. I have a lot of work to catch up on at home." Glory knew the only reason Vivian had gotten behind on her work was because Viv had spent every waking moment of the past few days here. "I'll call you in the morning," Vivian said and cleared her dishes. She hugged Glory, grabbed her purse and let herself out.

Glory stayed seated at the table. She put her hands together and bowed her head, resting it on her hands. "Lord, please have mercy on Jeremi. Please open his eyes to his drinking problem and let him overcome it. Lord, please wake him up." She paused. "Amen."

"You see," George said, "God is answering prayers. That was a vague prayer, to be sure. But when you're at a loss as to how to get something accomplished, just give it up to the Lord. God answers your prayers in ways you never imagined or thought possible. Believe me, very few on earth will see Jeremi's new situation as the answer to that prayer right away. But someday, when everyone looks back on this situation, they will see it. It will be crystal clear. God is the only one with crystal-clear foresight. He does let us angels in on it from time to time."

George was so wise. I was so lucky to have him as my Guardian Angel.

Glory got up and went to bed. I stayed with her. Henry, George and Pearl took Naomi back to Jeannie's house.

Glory got ready for bed, tried to read a book briefly, but had too much on her mind to concentrate. She put the book down, turned out the light and stared up at the ceiling for a while. I told her about all the things that were happening to me, like I used to. When I was alive and excited about something, I'd just talk and talk. She seemed like she was listening now as she had then. For a little while, I felt like I was alive again and she really could hear me. It was a nice moment. After she fell asleep, I rested there with her, watched her, stroked her face and held her hand all night long. I got lost in her beauty.

When morning neared, Naomi returned.

"What happened?" I asked.

"We went to Jeannie's," Naomi explained. "They were all sleeping. Pearl showed me around and told me all about Jeannie, Lynne and Carole. I'll prepare baby girl here about the child. It'll be just fine. Did you have a good night?"

"Pretty good," I said. "She slept peacefully. I enjoyed watching her."

"I know you being nearby made a difference. She's been tossing and turning, sleeping restlessly since you passed. She will sleep well again soon," Naomi reassured me. "Thanks for the night off. I enjoyed getting to know Pearl and her family."

"Thanks for the night here," I said. "I enjoyed being home."

"George told me to tell you to meet him back in the garden when you're ready."

I kissed Glory good-bye for the moment. She stirred slightly. Then I went to Sarah's room and kissed her, then to Sheila's children's rooms and kissed them. Finally, I went to meet George in the garden.

14

George informed me that the baby had indeed been conceived. So I was officially on duty as a Guardian Angel. It was an easy job in the early stages of the pregnancy. So basically we spent a lot of time floating between Glory, Jeremi, and Jeannie, and whoever else was on my heart at any particular time.

Glory was involved in the legalities of closing out my life on earth. Life insurance was paid. She lived in the parsonage and would have to move. The church gave her a generous timeline to get moved. Since it was a reality she knew she faced, she began to make arrangements. It was hard on her, being in that house without me to help her. There was a memory of both Sheila and me around every corner. The change would be hard, but it would be the best thing for her in her new life. I was there every second I could be, to help her make these decisions and to give her strength any way I could.

Lots of other people were on my heart these days, too. I went visiting a lot. A thought of someone blasted into my head, so I'd go to see him or her. They were always thinking about me, too, and often crying. I had a lot of fun during these times, letting them know how close I really was. Sarah always left lights on. If she was depressed, all I had to do was turn one off and she'd snap right out of it. Pretty soon, she caught on to the game. She'd say, "Sorry, Dad," like she used to when I was alive and I turned the lights out on her. On the nights when she missed me the most, I think she left the lights on, on purpose, to see if any seemingly turned out by themselves.

Jeannie was fun during this time, too. Pearl got her to start taking vitamins again. She did it by repeating how "run down" Jeannie felt, making her actually feel more tired than she was. She repeated to Jeannie that she needed to take better care of herself. She'd put angel light on commercials saying the same thing. Finally, Jeannie got the message and dug around her cabinet for vitamins. She came across her leftover pre-natal vitamins from when she was pregnant with Lynne. She picked them up, examined them and chuckled, putting them back on the shelf. Failing to find any other vitamins, she decided to take those. The first time she did though, she said, "Well, I gotta use these up anyways, they were so expensive!" Pearl laughed up a storm. She was successful at getting Jeannie to take vitamins again, pre-natal ones at that. What a slick operator!

Jeannie went to the pub to see Jeremi a couple of times early on in her pregnancy. The first time, Pearl hid her purse to keep Jeannie from buying any drinks. That only worked once. All it did subsequently was make Jeannie more aware of where her purse was, so Pearl had to keep coming up with new ploys to keep her from drinking.

We decided it was time she found out that she was pregnant, since she unknowingly put the baby at risk by still drinking. We decided that the next time she was on Exile, there would be enough time to do what needed to be done.

The stage was set. Her ex-husband had the girls at her apartment. Jeannie went to the pub to get Jeremi and go out to dinner. Pearl whispered in her ear all day about her side hurting. So much so, that Jeannie had begun to favor her lower right side. While Jeremi drove to the restaurant, Pearl's coaching intensified. Pearl made Jeannie think that she was feeling very hot, that her side hurt worse and that she was sick to her stomach. During this time, Jeannie was very quiet. Jeremi sang the songs on the tape deck and was oblivious to Jeannie's changing condition. By the time they got to the restaurant, Jeannie was pale and sweating and sure that she was feeling a very sharp pain in her lower right side.

After he stopped the car, Jeremi noticed her condition. "Are you all right?" he asked, very concerned and slightly shocked at the change in her appearance in such a short time.

"Yeah, I'm fine," she replied, lying to look brave, determined to keep going. Pearl warned us that she was really stubborn about getting sick. "Let's go in," she said, then winced in pain.

Jeremi came around the car to open the door for her. He took her hand to help her out, but as soon as she stood up, Pearl said, "It hurts really bad right here." Pearl touched her, just inside her right hipbone. Jeannie doubled over completely.

"That's it, I'm taking you to a hospital, right now," Jeremi said and helped her back into the car. Jeremi was so concerned that he drove frantically. So Henry, George and I took over the safety stuff. Jeremi reached over and took Jeannie's hand in a sweet gesture of support.

"I'm sorry," Jeannie said.

"For what? There's nothing to be sorry for," Jeremi reassured her. They were quiet the rest of the way to the emergency room.

Once inside, Jeannie was admitted right away for fear she had appendicitis. Once flat on her back, Pearl lightened up on the pain in her side. She had to ease up for fear they'd operate on the poor girl.

The doctor came in and examined her. He discussed all the tests they wanted to do immediately, such as a complete blood count and a urine analysis. Jeannie submitted begrudgingly. According to Pearl, she absolutely hated doctors and she hated tests.

Jeremi and Jeannie waited for the test results to come back in. They could talk all night, if they wanted to, but in this setting it was hard to keep the conversation going. He held her hand. I could tell that he was genuinely frightened for her. Henry whispered to him "You like taking care of her." And as if what Henry had said were his own thoughts, Jeremi nodded yes to himself.

The doctor came back in. "Well, Jeannie," he started, "your white count is normal, so infection is ruled out. We've also ruled out appendicitis."

They both sighed with relief.

"We still have to figure out what's causing the pain."

"They need to put 'Suspected Angel Intervention' on the form!" Pearl said proudly. We cracked up.

"So, we would like to send you down to ultrasound and see if we can determine what's causing this pain," the doctor finished.

Jeannie agreed. "Can my, my... friend come, too?"

"If he wants to. But you'll have to obey the technician about when you can be present and when to leave," the doctor said to Jeremi. They both nodded in agreement with the terms. We followed Jeremi as he followed Jeannie, as they wheeled her down to ultrasound.

The room was pretty dark, only peripheral light in the room. They all helped Jeannie on the table. The instruments provided a little bit more light when they were turned on. The technician took Jeannie's chart and read the doctor's instructions. It read "possible ectopic pregnancy." She realized that Jeannie and Jeremi watched her every move, so she put on a poker face and smiled. "Let's get started, shall we? Just lay back and relax, Jenny."

"Jeannie," Jeremi corrected her.

She referred back to the chart. "So it is. So sorry."

She focused the equipment on Jeannie's lower right quadrant, where the pain had been. She was meticulous and slow to cover every inch of that area, and she was determined to figure out what caused the pain. So she moved the instrument closer to the center of Jeannie's belly. A little white dot flashed up on the screen. She focused in closer. It looked like a little bee, with its wings beating furiously. She kept the equipment on it, moving a little to the left, then to the right, up above it and down below it.

"That's good," she said softly.

"What's good?" Jeannie and Jeremi asked together.

"It's right where it's supposed to be," she reassured Jeannie, who looked at the screen closer. Jeannie laid back down, closed her eyes tight and took a long, deep breath. Jeremi was still at a loss as to what it was, but Jeannie had had ultrasounds before--she could tell what she was seeing was her baby's heartbeat.

Jeremi got really concerned, especially since he was now the only one still in the dark as to what was going on.

"Jeannie?" He patted her hand to get her attention. "Baby, what's wrong?"

"Did the doctor tell you what he was sending you down here to test for?" the technician asked Jeannie.

"To find the source of the pain," Jeannie answered.

"On my notes, it asks me to rule out a tubal pregnancy. I'm so sorry that you found out this way. Are you going to be all right?" she asked, a little embarrassed.

"Jeannie," Jeremi insisted, "test for what? Find out what?"

"Move over here closer where you can see the screen," Jeannie told Jeremi. "See that little white fluttering thing on the screen?" He nodded yes, but still looked confused. "That's the baby's heart beating." He stared at the screen in disbelief, then his leg gave out, but he caught himself.

"Careful over there," the technician said.

Once he caught his balance, he stared hard at the screen and then he stared hard back at Jeannie.

"Evidently I'm pregnant," Jeannie said to Jeremi quite emotionless, very much in shock.

"But I --" Jeremi started, but I made a loud bang in the hallway outside the room to interupt him. The technician left the room to check on the noise.

Jeannie looked at Jeremi. I'm sure a million thoughts ran through that frightened head of hers. Jeremi looked back at her and said, "This is a trip!" He sat down nearby, still holding her hand. A million thoughts running through his head, too, which had to started with the fact that he truly believed he was unable to have children. He stepped up to the plate and was there for Jeannie, he was very supportive.

"Whatever that was, it's somebody else's problem now," the technician said on the way back in. She stayed at the foot of the bed. "Well, we're done here. Your baby is right where it belongs, whatever your pain is, it's something else. Let's send you back up to the doctor. I'll let him know I spilled the beans."

"How long?" asked Jeannie.

"Oh, probably just a couple of weeks along."

Jeremi looked up, startled. He knew for a fact that Jeannie had been faithful to him during that time frame. He tried to stand up, but was a little weak in the knees.

"Do you want a wheelchair, too?" the technician joked.

"Huh?" He missed the joke.

"Are you going to be all right?" she asked him again.

Shaking off his shock, he responded, "Oh yeah, I'm fine. Just a little . . ." he struggled for words, "just a little . . . something, uh, something..."

"Most new dads are like that," she attempted to keep the humor going.

The words shocked him. He looked hard at her and tried to figure out if she indeed thought he was the father. The orderly came and wheeled Jeannie back up to the emergency room. Jeremi followed close behind physically, but a million miles away in his thoughts.

Back in the room, they were both very quiet, very much shocked by this news. Pearl let all of Jeannie's pain subside and even gave her "You feel great!" messages. They looked at each other.

Finally, he started, "But I was wearing--"

"I know, and I was using--"

"So how could--"

"God only knows," she finished.

"Sounds like an old married couple finishing each other's sentences," Henry chuckled and all the angels cracked up again.

The doctor came back in the room. They both looked at him accusingly.

"I understand you had some unexpected news down in ultrasound." They both nodded. "I'm sorry, I should have written better instructions to the tech." There was a silence, then he continued. "Well, the good news is that we ruled out an ectopic pregnancy as the source of your pain."

"The pain's gone," Jeannie said suddenly aware.

"It's gone?" The doctor looked over his glasses at her.

"Yeah. It's gone."

He went over to her and prodded and poked her side. She was fine.

"Well," he folded one arm and propped the other on it, then tapped his lip, deep in thought. "You're single?" He asked Jeannie. She nodded. "Then I'm going to need you to leave, sir." Jeremi was taken by surprise, but obedient. "I'll send her out in a minute; she'll meet you in the waiting area." Jeremi and Henry left, leaving Jeannie alone with the doctor. Pearl went in close to comfort Jeannie.

"Well, if the pain is gone, I'll release you, but..." Jeannie started to get up. "I highly recommend that you make an appointment with an

OB-GYN as soon as possible." Jeannie nodded. "I take it this was an unplanned pregnancy?" Jeannie rolled her eyes, big time. "Do you want any information about alternative--"

Jeannie shook her head, offended at the suggestion.

"You're absolutely positive? There are a lot of--"

"I'm sure."

"You tell him, honey!" Pearl cheered in her ear.

"Well then, do you have an OB-GYN or would you like me to recommend one?"

"I have a good one," Jeannie said.

The doctor looked at her thoughtfully and said, "Then you can go. But make that appointment right away. Good luck."

"I will and thank you," Jeannie said. The doctor left, scratching his head.

Jeannie got dressed, hurried out to meet Jeremi in the waiting room. "What did he have to say?" he asked.

"Oh nothing, really. He simply wanted to make sure I understood my choices."

"Choices?" Jeremi was lost for a second. "Oh," he said, understanding her words. "Oh!" he said, finally getting her meaning. "What did you say?"

"I said that I knew what my options were and that was enough said."

"Is that . . . an option?" Jeremi avoided saying the word that, suddenly was the only word on his mind.

"It is a choice for other people in other situations, my perspective is that I'm a mother first."

"Good," Jeremi said, which took Jeannie by surprise.

"I never thought I'd be in this position," she muttered. "I'm raising two kids by myself, what's one more?"

Then they both walked quietly to the car.

Jeannie's exile still had about an hour to go. So, they went back to the pub. Neither one said anything. Both were lost in their own worlds, still in shock.

Instead of their usual table by the stage, they took a booth back behind the bar area where they could have some privacy. They both watched each other and tried to figure out what the other was thinking. The waitress came to the table. "Is there anything I can get you?" she asked politely.

"I'll have my usual," Jeremi said.

"Better make it a double," Jeannie said in jest. The waitress looked at Jeremi for confirmation, but he looked at Jeannie strangely.

"Okay," the waitress said, "and for you?"

"She'll have a soda," Jeremi spoke for her.

This time it was Jeannie's turn to return the strange glance. The waitress then looked to Jeannie for confirmation, but realized that she was getting nowhere. She shook her head and muttered to herself about being invisible.

"Let's lighten the mood," George said and he went off to the jukebox. A young lady was selecting some songs and apparently George was reselecting them for her. He buzzed back, beaming with anticipation. "Let's see how they like these."

The first song started out with the word "Baby! Oh, baby. Baby, baby, oh baby." Then a few other words and the baby chorus again. It caught Jeremi's and Jeannie's attention casually and they shook it off and continued to stare at each other, but lost in their own thoughts. The next song was the same thing. The lyrics included the word baby at least fifty times. The next song was the same thing. When the conversation dragged, the lyrics of the music got through and they reacted every time they heard the word baby. After the third song, they both chuckled slightly, but the more it persisted, the more it helped them laugh about it. George's plan worked. It broke the tension and Jeannie and Jeremi started to talk about the situation they found themselves in.

"Do you think someone's trying to tell us something?" she asked Jeremi.

"Yeah, that we better get used to hearing the word baby," he responded, lightly sarcastic.

"Something like that," George said.

Jeremi got serious and took Jeannie's hand. She listened intently as he described his struggles in his first marriage trying to have a child and the fact that in those twelve years, they'd never succeeded. He had always assumed it was his problem, but never actually got checked to know for sure. He told her that he had always been disappointed with himself for denying me any grandchildren. I never knew he felt like that.

"Maybe your father has something to do with this," Jeannie suggested.

"Maybe," Jeremi answered unenthusiastically. After considering the possibility for a little while, his tone changed. "Come to think of it, he might've had a lot to do with this." He sat back in the booth and looked up. "It's a trip to think of it that way. The timing is pretty interesting."

"Uh huh," Jeannie, and all the angels said in chorus.

"This is a trip. Wait until I tell Mama," Jeremi said, and got lost in his own world, probably figuring out exactly how and when he would tell her.

Jeannie looked at her watch. "It's getting late. Let's go."

"I'll walk you out to your car," Jeremi said and they both got up and walked to the parking lot.

"Are you going to be all right?" Jeremi asked. "They really never figured out what caused your pain in the first place."

"I know, but I feel fine now. It's like that happened so that we would find this out." Jeannie stopped short.

"That's my girl!" I said, speaking for all us angels.

"I'll call you tomorrow. Get some rest," Jeremi said. Jeannie nodded. They kissed and held each other very tight for a long time. Then Jeannie got into her car and drove home. Jeremi went straight back into the pub, got his drink, sat at the bar alone. When he finished it, he left.

We stayed with Jeremi. We were all interested in what he would do now. He stopped at a liquor store, bought a 44-ounce bottle of malt liquor and took it home. Peter and Melinda were in the living room when Jeremi arrived. The children were already in bed.

Surprised to see him home this early or basically at all, Melinda said playfully, "Look at what the cat--"

Jeremi put his hand up, interrupting her and weakly said, "Spare me your sarcasm tonight, please."

When Melinda realized her ribbing was unappreciated, she asked concerned, "What's wrong?"

Jeremi thought for a moment and looked up at the ceiling. "Someone's messing with my head and I think it just might be Dad," Jeremi bit on his lower lip.

Peter went over and put his arm around his brother and guided him to the couch, next to Melinda. "C'mon, man, sit in here. Tell us what's up."

"It's Jeannie," Jeremi started.

Peter and Melinda looked at each other. "What about her, did she quit you?" Peter asked.

Jeremi kept his head down and shook it.

"Did you quit her?" Melinda asked.

Jeremi shook his head again.

"Did something happen to her?" Peter asked.

Jeremi nodded.

"Did she get hurt?" Melinda asked. Jeremi shook his head. Both she and Peter were extremely concerned. What could possibly have him this upset about Jeannie?

"Did she have an accident?" Peter asked.

Jeremi looked up, with a peculiar look on his face, unsure how to answer that question. "Kinda..."

"Okay, enough guessing games. Jeremi, pull yourself together and tell us what's wrong with Jeannie," Peter demanded.

"She's pregnant," he said low under his breath.

"What?" They both gasped in unison.

"She's pregnant," he said and then heaved himself backward on the couch and stared at the ceiling.

Peter and Melinda were completely surprised. "Thank God," Melinda said, relieved. Then after Peter and Jeremi looked at her strangely, she backtracked, "I mean that it's only... I mean that she's just... Oh forget it!"

"Is it yours?" Peter asked.

"I guess," Jeremi answered. "At least I'm as sure of that as I can be."

"How far along?" Melinda asked.

"Couple weeks," Jeremi responded. Peter and Melinda listened intently as he gave them the evening's details, up to and including all the songs that were playing on the juke box.

"What do you plan to do?" Peter asked.

"What would you do? This is such a trip. How could this have happened?" Jeremi leaned into his brother's strong shoulder.

Peter and Melinda glanced at each other quickly, with what had to be the telepathic thought "You know very well how it happened!" running between them. They all sat quietly. After a few moments of awkward silence, Jeremi took his bottle and went to his room, where he drank himself to sleep.

George and I went to check on Jeannie. She'd gotten home and tucked the girls into bed. She'd gotten ready for bed herself. She was under the covers, but had the phone on her stomach and her address book beside her.

"She's started to call several people, but hung up the phone before she finished dialing," Pearl told us. Jeannie stared at her walls, completely terrified. "She's at a complete loss as to what this all means to her. She needs some time to sort it out."

"Can we get someone to call her?"

"Oh that's a great idea! Stay with her, I'll be right back," Pearl said and disappeared.

So we watched as Jeannie started to dial the telephone, but after she pressed only three digits, she hung up again.

Pearl came back. "Anne's angel is working on her. She'll call here momentarily," Pearl explained. We watched Jeannie stare at the phone, trying to figure out who to call. Then the phone rang. She was so surprised, she jumped. The phone flew off her stomach and onto the floor. It took her a second to get it untangled, to get to the floor and pick up the receiver.

I could hear a voice on the phone. "Hello? Hello? Jeannie, are you there?"

"I'm here," Jeannie said, after she finally got back to the receiver. There was a pause, then Jeannie said, "Oh, I just knocked it off the bed. Sorry."

There was another long pause while Anne told Jeannie a story. Jeannie nodded like Anne could see. The occasional "Huh," "What did you say?" peppered the conversation. "How did my night go?" Jeannie asked, obviously repeating the question Anne had just asked her. "That's a good question. It went all the way to the hospital. Something happened tonight. Something completely unexpected." Jeannie sighed. "I found out that I'm . . ." another dramatic pause as she gathered the strength to say it, "pregnant." Then Anne rapidly asked her a slew of questions. All Jeannie said was, "I did!" "We were." "Yes, Jeremi." And several other short responses, that we could only guess what the questions were. We could tell when the big one hit, "What are you going to do?"

"Well." Jeannie sighed. "Do the best I can to raise three kids, I guess. I'm doing okay now, by myself. If I can raise two kids, I can raise three."

"That's right," Pearl said. "That stubborn streak of yours will get you through. She'll do it just to prove she can!"

"I know this is different." Jeannie's tone was defensive. "I'll know soon if I'm in this alone or not. But if I am, I know that somehow we'll be all right. . . Yeah, I know the apartment is small, but we were going to move anyway, eventually. . . Jeremi took it all right, I guess. I mean, he's pretty shook. . . I suppose he went to his brother's. I hope. He said he'd call me tomorrow. . . Yeah, I hope he does, too. . . I know. I know. I know you'll be there for me. I know I can count on you. . . No, stay there! I'm fine right now. Really! I just want to get some sleep. Suddenly, I'm really tired. . . Okay, I'll talk to you tomorrow. Good night." She hung up.

"She needed that," Pearl said.

Jeannie put the phone away, switched off the light and crawled back in bed. She tossed and turned for a while. A couple of times she smacked herself on her forehead, while she scolded herself. "I should've put that stuff in storage. But I gave it all away. 'I'm done having babies.' Yeah, right!"

Poor girl, she had to have as many thoughts running through her head as I had had at the cemetery that day. Pearl had had enough, so she curled up around her and sang her a lullaby to soothe her spirit. George and I sang the songs with her. Edwina was still in the house and she joined in, too. Jeannie settled down, stopped tossing in her bed and finally fell asleep.

"That was a tough one," Pearl said after we successfully lullabied Jeannie to sleep. "I've never felt her so scared. She talks tough, but she's afraid."

"Are you worried?" I asked Pearl.

"I'm at complete peace with this." Pearl smiled at me. "God chose her for a reason. Soon you'll be a believer in her spirit too."

"Are you going to be all right here?" George asked Pearl and Edwina. They reassured us that they would be. "Then we should be going," George told me.

"We'll see you soon," I said and then we left.

15

I wanted to go check on Jeremi, to see if he had gotten to sleep yet. He was asleep, if you could call it that. He beat the bed worse than I'd ever seen anyone do before. A very worried Henry watched over Jeremi. I would've asked Henry how Jeremi was doing, but it was obvious, he was a mess.

"You can almost see the players in his struggle. He's fighting so hard. The good side of him is right there on the surface. It's the side he shows Mama and Jeannie. However, the side of darkness looms right below it, trying to take him over forever. He's fighting to keep it down, but it's powerful and he's afraid. And it's his fear that allows the darkness in. This is a critical time for him. I have to be alert every moment, waking and sleeping. This is such a critical time for him."

"It's fear against faith," George comforted Henry, "and I'll take faith every time, Henry. We'll be fighting this battle right by your side. We will win him back for God and for his family, present and future. We will." George's tone was solemn and absolutely sincere. George put his hand on Henry's shoulder and gave Henry strength. We all put our heads down and prayed quietly for Jeremi. We stayed there all night because both Jeremi and Henry needed us.

I watched a sad, tired angel that night. I know that Henry had been by Jeremi's side every second in the past several years, except for maybe when Jeannie's angels took over from time to time. I felt the awesome responsibility a Guardian Angel must feel when his charge is in danger. I felt the despair he felt, feeling he was close to losing his charge. I prayed that night, I prayed so hard for my son and for his son and for his angel. I prayed his son would have a sober father. I prayed that Jeremi would want to be a part of, and a positive influence in, his son's life. I prayed that God would show me what I needed to do to help this come to pass, whatever it took.

We were visited in the night by all of Peter's family's angels. They stayed with us and prayed with us. Peter's angel, William, promised to keep Peter nearby at precisely the right moments, to help both Jeremi and Jeannie.

Jeremi woke up early. After he had his first obligatory sip of beer, he called Jeannie. "What's up?" he asked. . . . "I'm sorry, were you asleep? I just wanted to talk to you, to see if you were all right. . . . That's good. Go back to sleep. I'll call you later. 'Bye."

He put the phone down. He was the only one up. He turned on the TV and flipped through all the channels about four times before settling on a music video station. He sat there and stared out into space, seemingly oblivious to his surroundings.

To Henry, this seemed a perfect time to coach. "Calling her was good. That was good, but she's scared you'll leave her and she's scared you'll stay and keep drinking. You need to let her know you'll be there for her and the baby and that you'll be sober. This is the best reason in the world for you to straighten up your life and take care of your responsibilities."

I could tell Jeremi heard him because his look changed from a blank expression to one of deep thought. I could see his shoulders literally start to bear the burden and he hung his head, then shook it.

"I know this is hard to believe, but it did happen to you. This is your lifeline, Jeremi. You know it and I know you feel it too. Take hold. God wanted to give you a reason to stop destroying yourself. This is it. Jeremi, there's a family in your future. If you keep drinking, you could mess this up. Please hear me, it's so important," Henry finished.

Jeremi stayed with his head still down, but now he shook it up and down ever so slightly. George went to get him some company. He led the dog in from the other room and when it saw Jeremi, it wagged its tail and licked his face, since Jeremi had his head down so low. Jeremi was happy for the company. He gave the dog the rubs it wanted. It brought him out of his self-pity mode. It made him feel better, for the moment.

Henry said he would let us know if he needed us, so for the moment, George and I left Henry and Jeremi.

It was time to check on Jeannie now, to see how she was faring this fine morning.

Pearl and an angel I'd yet to meet sat on Jeannie's couch, giggling. There was a persistent knock on the door every few seconds, knock, knock, knock.

"What's so funny?" I asked Pearl.

"I asked Robin here to get Anne out there to spend some time with Jeannie this morning. The knocking is Anne's way of getting Jeannie out of bed, somewhat akin to the Chinese water torture. Watch when Jeannie finally gives in."

After a few more series of the knocks, Jeannie came down the hallway, fresh out of bed, one eye still closed and the other barely open. She just opened the door because she obviously recognized the knock. Anne popped right on in and said, "Donuts and espresso delivery service."

Jeannie collapsed on the couch next to Pearl. "Mmmm, you love donuts!" Pearl said, which caused her to open the other eye.

"What kind of donuts?" Jeannie asked, annoyed that she'd been pulled out of bed and her friend was so lively so early in the morning.

"Your favorite, chocolate! I know you've been watching your waist lately, but those days are over! So let's just indulge!"

Jeannie gave her an evil eye. She seemed a little irritated that Anne was already joking about her being pregnant.

"Did you say something about coffee?" Jeannie changed the subject.

"Café mocha, with whipped cream. Um, um, fattening!"

Again Jeannie gave her the evil eye, but Anne was impervious to it. Anne smiled sweetly as she gave Jeannie the coffee, just to needle her.

"Thanks," Jeannie said lightly.

Anne got herself a donut and her coffee. "Cheers!" she said. She touched her coffee cup to Jeannie's.

"Cheers to what?" Jeannie snapped.

"To whatever will be! Qué sera sera," Anne said.

"Cheers," Jeannie said back to her as lightly as she had said thanks.

"Now, dear heart, we need to figure out a few things." Anne hinted.

"Like what?"

"Like, where are you going to put a baby in this little cramped apartment? Like, what to do about baby supplies? I know you gave everything away before you moved here. Like, when are you due? So we can figure out how much time we have to get things ready."

"Well, that's easy. God only knows. God only knows. And on Monday I'll call the doctor and then we'll know!"

"I can tell you put a lot of thought into those answers," Anne said. She enjoyed being about ten steps ahead of Jeannie on the awake and enthusiasm scales. "Well, do you want some more questions or would you like answers?"

"Oh, answers, please." Jeannie started to perk up.

"The answers are: You are going to put the baby in with you for a few months, then we'll just trust that God will provide an answer between now and then, so we'll consider that one solved . . . at least for the short term. We're going to go garage sale-ing and get you what you need. And last, since you're only a couple of weeks along, I'm gonna sticky my neck out here and guess that we still have the better part of nine months to get this all accomplished. I just wish I knew if you were going to have a boy or a girl, that would make it easier to plan."

"It's a boy," both Pearl and Jeannie said, with identical conviction and inflection.

For the first time this morning, Anne was off-balance. "Excuse me?"

"It's a boy," Jeannie repeated.

"And you know this how?" Anne hoped Jeannie would fill in the blanks.

"Just know. I knew the girls were going to be girls, right?" Anne agreed. "Okay, I only suspect very strongly it's a boy, but if it turns out to be a girl, I'll be *very* surprised. So, how's that?" Jeannie caught up to the same speed as Anne. These girls had a rhythm with how they talked to each other. There was a lot of joking, but through it you could see the deep bonds of a truly special friendship.

"You want to know something funny?" Anne asked and Jeannie nodded. "I had a dream last night that you had a boy." Their eyes locked and grew wide with astonishment. There was a long, drawn-out pause in their conversation.

"There's the look," Robin said, as she and Pearl broke up laughing. Robin hummed the theme to an old science fiction movie. She and Pearl laugh even harder. It seemed to me that Robin and Pearl had a bond as close as Jeannie and Anne did.

"Nice touch, Robin," Pearl said. Robin smiled slyly.

George explained to me later why that was. Robin and Pearl had been friends before they were angels. On earth, many years ago, they were young friends who had been separated when Pearl's parents moved away. After they became angels, they stayed in close contact. Their desire to see each other led their charges to each other. When Jeannie and Anne met, they hit it off right away. The second they met, Jeannie and Anne felt like they already knew each other. That's the sensation people get when they feel their angels reunite. The unexplainable familiarity they feel is their angels' familiarity. What seems a natural part of the human's friendship is the simple love between their angel friends.

Anne picked up the conversation again. She cleared her throat and continued, but her voice cracked a little. "It might be dangerous to plan things based on that assumption."

"Why?" Jeannie countered with characteristic stubbornness.

"O-kay," Anne said, conceding the issue.

The girls talked the rest of the morning about the curve that Jeannie had been thrown in her life. Anne let her know unconditionally, that whatever happened she would be there to help all the way down to being in the delivery room with her at the hospital. Anne was a nurse at the hospital, so that part of it would come together easily. Pearl and Robin spent the rest of the morning making plans of their own regarding upcoming events. They reminded me very much of Naomi and Goldie and Glory and Vivian. Jeannie would land on her feet, if she had support like this around. This scene made me think about my friends. So I asked George, "Did you do things like this when I was with my friends?"

"Of course."

"Tell me about it."

George took me back to the garden and we talked for the longest time about all the times I was with my childhood buddies and what he and their angels did for us. He elaborated, in much greater detail than I wanted to remember about the times my friends and I got into trouble. How, before it got too dangerous or foolhardy, someone would amazingly discover what we were doing and lead us back to our mothers, usually by our ears. The plan was always foiled just in time. My friends and I were always sure that someone was working against us. We had it so backward. We should've known how hard they were working for us. We were sure the powers that be hated us because we could never pull off a successful prank. Thank God, they really loved us as much as they did and kept us from successfully pulling off one of those stupid capers.

George and I reminisced all afternoon about the stunts I pulled and how he and my friends' angels always had to intervene. I asked him about some of the ones we actually pulled off and like clockwork, he countered with the object lesson, it was supposed to teach us.

The grand plan was so marvelous. I wish I could have appreciated it more when I was still alive. I could have taught so many people so much. I was so blind, I should've been able to see these inter-workings. Looking back, it is all so clear. I guess I had a hard head.

Henry's call interrupted our talk, which had apparently lasted the entire afternoon and evening. "George and Martin, you need to come. Jeremi is about to call Mama."

George and I exchanged quick glances and smiles. We wanted to be there for this one. We'd left a standing request with both Pearl and Henry to call us when someone was told about the baby. Surprisingly, we landed at Jeannie's apartment. Jeremi and Jeannie were out in the living room. The girls had already been tucked into their beds. Henry, Pearl, Jack and Sheila waited for us there. We all greeted one another.

"They just had a long conversation and decided that they should tell their families. They plan on keeping the baby and that's the only decision that has really been made," Pearl explained to us. "Jack and Sheila are going to run interference for us." I know I looked perplexed so they explained. "If Jeannie calls someone and they give her a hard time, then Jack will go work on that person to insure against any lasting damage done to the relationship. Likewise, Sheila will run interference for Jeremi."

"Things are about to heat up," George said, rubbing his hands together.

Jeremi was up first. "Let me call Mama." Sheila left in a flash. Jeannie handed him the phone. He dialed slowly. At first he got a wrong number. "Boy, I must be nervous," he told Jeannie. Then he took a sip of his beer and he dialed again.

"Mama? How are you?" There was a long pause; I guess Glory told him quite a bit. "How's Sarah?" There was a short pause and Jeremi laughed. "Really?" He laughed some more.

Jeannie listened intently for Glory's reaction, but Jeremi stalled a bit. So she sat back on the couch and stared impatiently up at the ceiling. After a few minutes of small talk, Jeremi looked back at her and sensed her anxiousness.

He grabbed her hand and took a deep breath. "Mama, I have some news."

Knowing Glory, she got extremely serious and asked, "What kind of news?"

"I'm going to have a baby," Jeremi said.

"WHAT?!" came through loud and clear. It even made Jeannie's head turn.

"I mean, Jeannie and I are. I mean Jeannie is. I mean she's pregnant. We just found out last night," Jeremi stammered, scrambling for the right words. "Mama, are you there? Mama?" There was a pause. "Yeah, I'm sure it's mine." He squeezed Jeannie's hand really tight, when he said that. Jeannie's eyes got really big as she realized what the question must've been.

"Yeah, I know, but we never actually found out if it was my problem or hers. . . . I know it's a shock! Believe me, I know it's a shock!" He looked into Jeannie's eyes when he said that, with a little humor and a little sarcasm.

Jeannie pantomimed sarcastically that it was just a "little" shock. She rested back on the couch.

"We'll know soon enough. She goes to the doctor on Monday." Glory must've asked a million questions when he said "hospital." He kept trying to answer her questions, but she fired them off so fast, it was hard for him to keep up. "Yeah, we-- . . . She, uh-- . . . Of course! . . . I did!. . . Really!"

I could just imagine how fast she was talking. She talked very fast when she was nervous or upset. She must've finally settled down.

"We thought she was having an appendicitis attack, but they did some other tests and that's how we found out. They did this ultra-sound thing. Mama, we saw the baby's heart beating. It was a trip!" His whole tone changed when he said that. He stopped explaining. He sounded awestruck. "I'm sure she'd love to meet you, too, Mama." Jeremi looked at Jeannie when he said that.

"Nod your head, dear," Pearl whispered in her ear, to get her attention.

Jeannie complied with Pearl's request. Her eyes were huge. Jack was sitting on the other side of her. "Wake up!" he said and poked her in her ribs. Jeannie snapped out of it. Then her nodding seemed a much more conscious decision.

"She says she would like to meet you, too, Mama," Jeremi said. "There's plenty of time, we'll figure something out. . . . Okay. I love you, too."

He hung up the phone and sat back into the couch beside Jeannie; both of them stared up at the ceiling.

It was fun to be here for this side of the conversation, but I wanted to see Glory's reaction to all of this, so I went home. Glory was at the kitchen table deep in thought. Her tea had spilled on the table in front of her and she was so fixated on Jeremi the tea had escaped her notice. Naomi was there with Glory. Sheila and Grandmama guided Sarah into the kitchen right on cue.

"Who was on the phone?" Sarah asked casually. Poor unsuspecting Sarah was about to be unleashed upon.

Glory shook her head with a pained look on her face. Sarah saw Mama's expression and got very concerned. Sarah grabbed a napkin from the middle of the table and started blotting up Glory's spilled tea.

"Tell me again what your brother told you about the girl he's seeing," Glory requested of Sarah.

"Oh, let's see. She works on computers, lives in a dinky apartment, can sing when she's practiced, has two little girls and," she paused, "that's all I can remember. Why?"

"That was Jeremi," Glory started. "He called to tell me that, ah-- that, um . . ." Sarah stared intently at Glory and waited for the bottom line. "That she's pregnant."

"Lord have mercy!" Sarah sat down hard and it took the breath right out of her.

"He says he is sure it's his."

"But--" Sarah started.

"I know, he said he never for sure got checked. He says he's sure this baby is his."

"This is what you've been praying for," Sheila said to both of them. Sarah and Glory's eyes met on that thought.

"Do you think--" Sarah began.

"Maybe," Glory said, as she answered the question Sarah avoided actually asking. "I need to call Peter. Maybe he can shed some more light on the situation."

So she did. They talked for a while. Then Glory let Sarah talk. Sarah asked all the same questions Glory did and a couple more. After they hung up with Peter, they stared at each other, still in shock.

"What do you think?" Sarah asked her mother.

"This is what you've been praying for," Sheila repeated.

"I'm glad he's living with Peter, so at least, he can keep an eye on Jeremi for us. Jeremi sounded completely different when he talked about seeing the baby's heartbeat, maybe there is hope there. We'll just have to wait and see." Glory sat back in her chair. "Maybe we have some extra help up there, now." She looked up to Heaven.

"You know he does," Sarah said, she took Glory's hand and patted it, reassuringly.

"Relax, Mama, I'm there for him and I'm here for you two, too," I said and kissed them on their foreheads.

Henry summoned us back to Jeannie's apartment. It was her turn to call her family. She sat there and held the phone and tried to decide who to call. Jack cheered her on and promised to help.

Jack explained to me about some of the very recent divorce experiences. Each member of Jeannie's family had reacted so differently to her separation and divorce that she was afraid about how they would react to this news. She decided to put off calling anyone. She figured she'd wait for someone to call her. She would tell them, then rely on the family grapevine to do the rest of the work. After they heard this plan, Jack and Pearl started to plot and scheme about who they were going to get to call her first. During their conversation, Jack laughed out loud. Pearl knew this meant he knew who he was going to get, and we'd just have to wait for the surprise of it. "I'll be right back," he said and disappeared.

"This should be interesting," Pearl said and shrugged her shoulders.

A couple of minutes later the phone rang, while Jeannie held it on her lap. She jumped a mile. "Hello?" she said very timidly, probably questioning her decision already. "It's Carole's teacher," she whispered to Jeremi while covering the receiver. "Wednesday? Ten o'clock? . . . I think I can swing that. . . . You're welcome." She hung up. She sighed heavily.

"You know you're going to jump like that every time the phone rings, if you let that decision stand," Pearl reminded Jeannie. "You need to call who you want--"

The phone rang again. Jack reappeared with a grin from ear to ear. "Too late!"

Jeannie jumped again, but was more confident as she answered the phone this time. "Hello?"

"Oh, hello." There was a pause. "I've been on your mind?" Jeannie repeated to the caller.

We all looked at Jack for insight into the caller's identity, but he just looked straight back at us with a sly grin. Obviously, we were going to have to glean it out of Jeannie's conversation.

"How've I been on your mind?" Jeannie stalled. . . . "Just staring at a picture of the family, until all you could see was my face? Yeah, that is interesting. . . . Uh, what's new?" Ah, the question of the day. She glanced over at Jeremi, who encouraged her with hand signals. "Well, let's see, Carole lost a tooth last week and Lynne got two more." Her voice cracked a little. . . ."No, nothing's wrong," she said defensively. She took a deep breath. "Okay, here it is. I've been seeing someone. . . . Jeremiah, Jeremi for short. . . . He sings. . . . Yeah, a singer," she said even more defensively. "Serious? Yeah, I guess you could call it serious. . . . A couple of months. . . . It's long enough." Apparently tired of avoiding the topic, she finally gave in to the inevitable and blurted out, "Because I'm pregnant." After an apparent silence, Jeannie said, "Are you still there Bunny Rabbit?"

Pearl, who had listened intently for clues to the caller's identity, exclaimed, "Perfect!" Jack smiled in recognition of his good work. "Bonnie is her niece, she's all grown up now, but Jeannie still calls her Bunny Rabbit . . . long story."

We turned our attention back to Jeannie.

"You're the first one in the family I've told.. . . Secret, right! We just found out last night. . . A couple of weeks. . . Sure, if you want; it'll save me long distance charges. . . I'm fine. Really. . . We'll be fine. . . Okay, call back then. . . Take care, love ya. 'Bye."

Jeannie sat quietly after she hung up the phone.

"What?" Jeremi asked anxiously.

"If I had to guess, I'd say that was planned."

"It was planned," Jack gloated.

"Why?" Jeremi asked.

"She's planning on seeing my folks tomorrow for a family birthday party. She said she'd break the news for me. Remind me to unplug my phone tomorrow," Jeannie joked.

"Coward," Jack teased her, as if she could hear him.

"Just kidding," Jeannie said, "kinda," come out under her breath.

"That went well," Jack told Pearl smugly.

"Ya done good, kid." Pearl kissed him on his forehead.

"My work here is done!" He pulled a pretend cape from behind his back and flew off, imitating a super hero that could only be called "Super Angel."

The phone rang again and Jeannie just looked at it. It appeared she was afraid of it or whoever was on the other end of it. Instead of answering it, she unplugged it. Jeremi looked at her, puzzled. "I refuse to talk to anyone else but you right now." Jeremi took that as a wierd signal she wanted to be alone with him, so he came to her and held her. She tried to respond to his affection, but she was fixated on the telephone.

Pearl whispered to her, "Okay, Jeannie, school's in session."

Jeannie and Jeremi spent the rest of the evening together watching a movie on TV, but Jeannie was still completely distracted by the presence of the phone, even though it was unplugged. After the movie, Jeremi decided to leave. Jeannie needed to get to bed, she needed to go to work tomorrow and get the girls off to school.

"When are you going to plug the phone back in, so I can call you?" Jeremi asked.

"Soon," Jeannie assured him.

They kissed goodnight and Jeannie closed the door and leaned back on it. She looked exhausted and extremely stressed. Pearl walked over to her and seemed to help her down the hall, sounding like a mother more than an angel. "Let's get you to bed now, you need your rest." Jeannie looked over at this evening's nemesis. "Relax about the phone, you'll plug it in in the middle of the night, like always. Let's go to bed now." Jeannie went in to brush her teeth. There were several quotes pasted up in the bathroom, same as the rest of her house. Pearl picked one out for her to read before bed. Pearl shined her angel light on the quote that said, "You can only judge a man once you've walked a mile in his shoes." I could tell Jeannie saw it and read it, but its significance to her situation escaped her at this moment, but Pearl had planted the seed.

George and I stayed to be sure that Jeannie was tucked into bed safely. We left as Pearl laid down beside her in the bed. Pearl stroked her hair and reiterated the lessons Jeannie needed to learn through this experience.

I wanted a quiet night myself. It'd been a big day. George said he'd meet me in the morning back at Jeannie's. I went to see Glory. She was also already in bed, but wide awake. The TV was on, but I could tell her thoughts were a million miles away from what was showing.

Naomi greeted me with a smile. "Will you stay?" she asked. I nodded. "Call me if you need me." I promised and she was off.

I sat up in the bed right alongside my Glory, in my spot. She rearranged herself a little, like she would have if I had been alive and I'd just gotten into bed with her. She reached over, as if to hold my hand like she used to do, then looked over and suddenly felt foolish.

"I'm right here. I know you can feel me close to you. See with your heart, Glory, feel how close I am and you'll see me right here with you." She ended up patting the bedspread right where my hand was.

"I miss you, Martin," she said aloud.

"I'm right here with you, Mama." I decided to change the subject. "I know you're thinking about Jeremi. I know you're wondering about Jeannie." Glory turned her eyes to Heaven, shook her head and heaved a sigh. "See, I knew you were. You're probably wondering if Jeannie is a good or bad influence in his life. You're worried about his drinking. I am, too, but Jeremi has an amazing team of angels in his corner. We will make this right. Just keep praying for us."

Glory closed her eyes and clasped her hands and prayed for Jeremi and Jeannie. She prayed that I would be close by when they needed me. I prayed that she would be blessed with peace and that my presence here would comfort her and that she would have a restful night.

Right after she prayed, she turned out the light, slid down in the bed, acted like she was watching TV for a few moments and fell fast asleep. I stayed and watched over her and Sarah for the rest of the night.

17

Morning came. Naomi returned. I went to meet George at Jeannie's. She was getting the girls ready for school and herself ready for work. There was more coaching than normal this morning because Jeannie was very distracted by her situation. The girls' angels helped them find their socks and whispered to help them remember various other details. Lynne and Edwina played out in the living room, so George and I joined in a game of peekaboo with them. Little Lynne laughed so loud, a half-dressed Jeannie came out to the living room to check on her. All Jeannie saw was a smiling baby girl covering her eyes. Jeannie said, "Peekaboo," Lynne looked up, saw that Mommy was playing the game too and giggled even louder. Jeannie leaned against the wall briefly as she smiled warmly at her adorable daughter. After a bit, she went back to the bedroom to finish getting ready.

We got the girls off to daycare and school and got Jeannie to work, almost on time. Still rushing to beat the clock, she finally reached her desk and turned on her computer, put away her purse, changed her shoes and all the rest of the typical morning fodder. Jeannie was edgy this morning, everything made her jump. Judie noticed that Jeannie was jumpier than usual and watched her, trying to figure her out. Jeannie saw Judie study her. Judie even mouthed the words, "What's wrong?" Jeannie shrugged her shoulders in an effort to deflect Judie's attention.

"You look like a Mexican jumping bean," Judie informed her.

"Too much coffee, I guess."

Judie raised an eyebrow and sized her up to gain more information. "Is there something wrong with your coffee?"

"Oh yeah, huh," Jeannie buried her head in her computer terminal without any further explanation.

A frustrated and worried Judie left and went into the kitchen area to pour herself another cup of coffee. She decided to read her horoscope. Pearl had anticipated this move so Judie's horoscope read, "A friend needs you now more than ever. Be ready to listen today." Judie read it and looked out the door in Jeannie's direction, as if she could see through walls. She decided to read Jeannie's. It read, "Life is teaching you lessons. Learning is easy, if you are a willing student." Judie left with her coffee and went back to the desk. As she sat down, she studied Jeannie again.

Jeannie felt the stare, bristled up and saw Judie watching her. "What?"

"Nothing." Judie started to type on her keyboard and smiled.

"What's so funny?" Jeannie demanded.

"Nothing," Judie said innocently. Then she muttered under her breath, "Life needs to teach you to be more pleasant when your friends are trying to figure you out!"

They both went back to work, but they were both very conscious of how much they watched each other.

Jeannie, still extremely jumpy, heard a noise behind her. She turned quickly and spilled coffee all over her lap. Luckily, it was barely lukewarm. It forced her out from behind her desk to make a hasty dash to the ladies room to try to wash it out. She left the room without saying anything to anybody.

Judie gave her a bit of a lead, then followed her. When Judie got into the bathroom, she saw Jeannie washing out the stain and muttering to herself, close to tears.

"Are you all right?" Judie asked.

"Oh, yeah," Jeannie answered. "It was pretty cold coffee."

"Jeannie, I want to know if you're all right, you've been overly tense all morning and now you're about to cry over spilled coffee. Something's going on. Did something happen with Jeremi?"

"You could say that." Jeannie bit her bottom lip.

Judie put her arms around Jeannie and led her to the couch in the bathroom's lounge area. Jeannie broke down.

"Did you guys break up?" Judie asked, but Jeannie shook her head. "Did you guys have a fight?" Again Jeannie shook her head. "Did you guys . . . eat ice cream? Either give me a decent clue or just tell me what's wrong."

A peculiar look came over Jeannie's face and she stopped crying momentarily. "Ice cream?" She paused for a moment, then continued very sarcastically, "Yeah, that's it, we ate ice cream. I ate so much ice cream that my rabbit died." Then Jeannie waited long enough to see if Judie had understood the clue.

"How could ice cream kill a--? Oh, my!" Judie fell back on the couch and looked back at Jeannie. She stared at her friend, in shock for a few moments, then covered her mouth to conceal the fact that she'd started to giggle.

"Are you laughing at me?"

Judie shook her head, then let more laughter escape between the fingers covering her mouth. She finally let go and broke out laughing. "I'm sorry, I'm sorry, I'm sorry." She kept laughing, however.

"Then what's so funny?"

"I'm sorry." She swallowed hard to try to gain control. "I'm sorry. Did you read your horoscope this morning?" Jeannie shook her head and looked at Judie with anticipation. "Life is teaching you lessons." Judie laughed again. "I guess 'black' is a significant color to you now, eh?"

Pearl busted up with that one. The rest of us angels were already laughing. Judie laughed so hard she had to hold her sides. After watching Judie howl for a few moments, Jeannie gave in and began to laugh a little, but it was obvious, she was still pretty upset.

"I'm sorry, this is serious," Judie said. Then accidentally snorted, attempting to keep the laugh in.

"I'm glad I could amuse you."

"I'm glad you could, too," Judie said and kept on trying to regain her composure. After a few more moments, she settled down. "Okay, I'm sorry. I'm sorry, let's talk."

Right then another lady walked into the restroom and both Jeannie and Judie immediately clammed up.

"Let's take a walk," Jeannie said and they both left quickly.

Pearl and Judie's angel took off with the girls, but George lagged behind. When I questioned him, he pointed. From behind a partition in the lounge where they kept a cot, another lady peered around the corner to see if she could get out undetected. She had obviously heard everything the girls had said and this gossip was just too hot to keep in. Her angel talked with us.

"You let her hear everything," the angel scolded George. "You could've blocked her hearing and just let her rest? You know how much she loves to gossip. We keep teaching her the same lesson over and over and over again, but she keeps gossiping."

"I bet we can work this out so they both benefit from this one. Will you work with us on this?" George asked her. She agreed. "Buy us some time and we'll be back."

"Okay," the angel agreed.

We caught up with Judie and Jeannie on their walk. Jeannie was deep into her story about the night at the hospital.

Pearl asked us, "Where were you guys?"

"Talking to Marla's angel in the bathroom. Marla was behind the partition," George answered.

"I know," Pearl said. "Once I saw her there, I was sure she was the one I needed to help me with this. How can I say this nicely? Marla has a lot to say, even when there's only a little to really say. Darlene, her angel, has tried time and again to teach her about talking about other people, but she continues to do it. What did Darlene say?"

"She agreed to help," George said.

"Good. Then we need a plan," Pearl said.

"With what objective, exactly?" I asked.

"School's in session for Jeannie. She's about to be the subject of a whole bunch of gossip and from people who barely know her, but who have a whole bunch of opinions about how she got into this situation and what she should do about it," Pearl explained. "In essence, she has done this to herself. When her friends came to her--pregnant and before they were married--she was very supportive, like her friends are to her now. If it was someone she only knew in passing, without trying to find out any more about them, she was fairly harsh in her judgment of the situation. She's merely receiving back what she's given in the past, all at once. It will be hard for her, but she will hopefully learn a whole lot about how that feels. How hard the lesson will be, depends on her. You know a lesson must be repeated until it is learned."

"So she's going to reap what she's sown in the past. But when she's gathered up this harvest, she'll be a better person for it--much more patient and much less judgmental. At least that's the plan," George concluded for Pearl, who wholeheartedly endorsed what he said.

"So how does Darla and Marlene--" I began.

"Marla and Darlene," Pearl corrected.

"Sorry, Marla and Darlene, fit in?"

Darlene joined us at that moment. "Marla got sent on an errand to the statehouse, so she's stuck standing in line at the Treasurer's office. I've got a few minutes. Another angel there will call me back if there's a problem."

Pearl introduced us. "Martin, this is Darlene, he's the baby's Guardian. Darlene, Martin was just asking us how we could help each other here."

"Good to meet you, Martin," Darlene said. "I think we could do a lot of good for both of these girls."

"So how do we get them together?" I asked.

"Without them knowing they're together."

"We can handle that like they did this morning," Pearl said. "Then Marla can tell Karen. You know Karen will shut Marla right down."

"I can arrange that," Darlene said.

"Who's Karen?" I asked.

"She sits across the room from Marla. They were both recently reprimanded for their lack of professionalism and personal conduct in a similar situation," Darlene answered.

"So the plan is to have Jeannie hear them talking about her?" All the angels confirmed my guess. "Then let's go to work."

"Right," George said.

"Marla will get caught," Darlene commanded.

"By Jeannie?" I asked.

"No, by someone who can really make her think about spreading gossip while she's at work. Someone who makes sure she'll be reprimanded expressly for that," George answered.

"And worse than the last time," Darlene added.

"Her boss?" I asked.

"I think it'd be better if the director caught her," Darlene said. "Her boss caught her before. This time we'll put the heat on the boss through the director, and hopefully Marla'll get that message."

"Will that jeopardize her job?" I asked.

"We'll maintain the proper boundaries," Pearl said. Then she looked at Darlene for confirmation. Darlene agreed quickly.

"But to make it all the more effective, I think Marla needs to see the direct result as well," Darlene said. "We need Karen to tell Jeannie what was said about her and by who, while Marla is listening."

"Okay, so we have a plan. Places everyone," Darlene said, then left.

Judie and Jeannie were almost back to the office. Judie's tone had grown more supportive. Jeannie seemed more relaxed. "It's just every time the phone rang last night I jumped out of my skin. I had to unplug it," Jeannie said, continuing her story.

"Well, if you resist telling your family and wait until they call you, you're at the mercy of the whims of fate. It you might be in really terrible shape some night when they just decide to call. Just call them and get it over with! You sound like you know what you're planning to do. Let them deal with it," Judie counseled.

"You know, she's right," Pearl told Jeannie.

"I know you're right," Jeannie said, "That sounds really very logical on the surface, but remember what happened when I told them about the divorce. I'd really like to avoid that. That was crazy-making!"

"Honey, that's old news," Judie said with a drawl.

"Boy, it is now! Okay, now, please for now, let's keep this our secret." Judie agreed. They went back into the building without saying another word and quietly went to their desks.

Pearl started to work on Jeannie. "Jeannie, you're so tired. You should go lay down on the cot in the bathroom."

Jeannie yawned. She looked over at the coffee cup she had spilled earlier and gave it a look like, "You're kidding, right!"

"You're pregnant; you're tired. Go lie down. Nobody will miss you for a few minutes."

Jeannie looked around to see if she thought anyone was watching--nobody was. She got up and went into the ladies room. She snuck up to the partition, in case some might already be there. All clear. She set her watch alarm for fifteen minutes, lay down and closed her eyes.

Within moments, Marla and Karen came in. Marla was so excited to tell Karen this news, she skipped the usual precautions of looking around to see if anyone else was in the ladies room. "This one is so big, you'll just, just, I gotta tell someone, this is so big," Marla said.

"You said that already. What is it this time?" Karen asked, with a giant lack of enthusiasm.

"Jeannie is pregnant!" Marla blurted out. "Can you beat that?!" Marla snickered.

Jeannie stayed behind the partition. She covered her mouth quickly. Her eyes were huge and they darted back and forth trying to figure out how Marla could've found out. Realizing she was where Marla had to have been, her figuring gave way to anger very quickly.

"She just got divorced. I doubt she's pregnant. Why would you make something like that up?" Karen asked in disgust.

"Honest to God! I heard her tell Judie this morning. I was back there, lying down. I heard it all." She pointed toward the cot. Then she whispered, "I had cramps."

Jeannie made a face like she was grossed out at this information and squirmed away from the center of the cot, like there was something on it.

"Careful," Pearl told Jeannie, "you still need to stay hidden."

"I think that's absolutely the stupidest thing I've ever heard?" Marla tried to get Karen to gossip with her. "If I were her, I'd-"

"Well, I doubt Jeannie will ever ask *you* for advice, so I'd keep whatever you were planning to say to yourself, and since this is what got me into trouble the last time, I'm getting back to work and you better too." Karen left.

"Humpf," Marla snorted.

A toilet flushed and out came the director, who adjusted her skirt. Marla realized that she had been caught in the act. She left hastily, but it was too late.

Jeannie knew full well there was still someone in the ladies room, so she stayed hidden. The director left and Jeannie got up and left, too.

"Naptime's over," Pearl chuckled.

"Phase one, mission accomplished," George exclaimed.

We followed Jeannie back to her desk. She was even jumpier than earlier.

The director was already in a closed-door session with Marla's boss. Marla cringed at her desk. Karen worked across the room, oblivious to Marla's predicament.

Judie saw Jeannie come back in. "Is something wrong?" she whispered. Jeannie nodded and sat down.

Judie motioned to her to go down the hall, but Jeannie was emphatic. "Later... much later!"

Judie shrugged her shoulders and went back to work. Jeannie tried to work, but kept making mistakes. The more she tried, the more frequent the mistakes. She took several deep breaths and kept on at the task at hand. Things eventually got better. She was still very jittery.

Darlene called us over when Marla was called into her boss's office. The director was still in there. There was a little yelling, then it got quiet briefly. Then the director came out. After a few more minutes, Marla came out. Her eyes were downcast and she sheepishly walked back to her desk.

Karen was oblivious to Marla, but I could tell that something still bothered her. Karen got up and went over to talk to Jeannie. As soon as Karen left the room, Darlene got Marla to go to the restroom and wash her face. Karen knocked on the post closest to Jeannie's desk. Jeannie jumped a mile. "Can I talk to you?" Karen asked.

Jeannie nodded. They also went to the ladies room.

"They invented conference rooms, ladies," I said sarcastically, when we got there for the third time this morning.

"They should try that, huh?" Pearl replied. All the angels laughed.

Marla heard people coming in. She quickly turned the water off and hid in the stall that had the door that looked most closed, without actually being shut.

Darlene shook her head in disgust as she watched her charge stand on the toilet. "I knew she'd do that!"

"It's all just part of the plan," George comforted her. Darlene sighed, but agreed.

Karen said, "I know I should do this at break time or after work, but I thought you should know that Marla is spreading gossip about you, that you're pregnant."

Jeannie looked down and was close to tears. "I know."

"Well, I just thought you want to know," Karen said.

"I appreciate that very much," Jeannie said.

"Marla is such a liar. She's gotten in trouble so much, you'd think she'd learn when to quit," Karen vented.

"Well, unlike the rest of Marla's gossip," Jeannie took a deep breath and said softly, "it's true. I am pregnant."

"Whoa, Jeannie, I'm sorry," Karen said sympathetically.

Jeannie looked at her, shocked. "Sorry? Why would you be sorry?"

Poor Karen was shocked by Jeannie's response and started to back pedal. "I mean I thought that you . . . I mean, you just got a. . . I mean, oh the heck with what I mean, I thought you'd be upset."

"I am upset. I'm upset at Marla. I wanted to be the one to tell people, when I was ready. I really wanted to wait for a while."

George decided it was time for Marla to be exposed. George imagined a doctor's hammer and tested Marla's reflexes. Marla's leg went right out from under her and George and Darlene helped her to the ground. Marla fell as quietly as she could, but the fact that something fell was very obvious. After hearing the noise, Karen and Jeannie went to investigate, only to discover Marla sitting on the ground in a very awkward position.

"I'm outta here!" Karen said angrily and immediately left, totally disgusted.

Jeannie glared at Marla, almost like someone from an old science fiction movie. She should have had laser beams come out of her eyeballs to melt the person in front of her. I think if she could have, she would have.

"I know what you've been saying. This is none of your business. When I want someone to know about this baby, I'll tell them!" Jeannie yelled at Marla.

"I bet," Marla snapped back sarcastically.

"What's that supposed to mean?"

"I bet you were going to take care of the baby before you told anyone about it." Jeannie gasped.

"Maybe that's the way you'd handle it, but--"

"If you were smart, that's the way you'd handle it."

"You really think that?"

"Yes, I do."

"I pity you," Jeannie said quietly. "And now I know so much more about you. Stay away from me. Quit talking about me. I mean it!" Jeannie turned and left Marla on the floor, without so much as offering to help her up.

Instead of going back to her desk, Jeannie left the building and walked around the corner very fast to get out of the situation. Once she got out of eyesight of the building, she sat down on the curb and cried.

Pearl stayed right with her. "I know this is hard, darling, but you need to think back. Think back, Jeannie. Do you think you ever made anyone feel like that? Unfortunately, you did. Without thinking about what you said, you hurt their feelings over these exact circumstances. You need to remember that. You need to reflect about that and learn from it so that it never happens again. The next time you run across this situation in someone else's life, you need to have the perspective of acceptance, judgment just wounds people. Think long and hard about that." Then Pearl put her arm around her and held her tight.

Jeannie cried harder for a while, then finally slowed down, then stopped. After another little while, Jeannie got up and walked the rest of the way around the block and went back into the building to her desk.

Judie was waiting for her. She met her at the door and whispered, "Are you all right?" Judie saw Jeannie's tear-stained face.

Jeannie shook her head, then went to her desk and got ready to leave.

"Just go, I'll tell them you felt sick and left. That's the truth, right?" Judie asked and Jeannie agreed.

Jeannie packed up her purse and the rest of her things and left through the back door.

George and I went to talk to Darlene to see if we had helped Marla at all. They were back in with Marla's boss. Marla's head was down and the boss was scolding her again. Karen had apparently complained to him.

"Is her job in jeopardy?" I asked. The way the boss talked was pretty severe.

"No," Darlene said. "Marla does a good job. She always gets off with a warning, although she's never had two in the same day before."

"It's been a busy day," I said.

"Martin, George, I need you now!" Pearl's voice blasted into our conversation.

"And the hits just keep on coming!" George said. "Take care, Darlene. We have to go now."

Darlene waved good-bye and we caught up with Jeannie and Pearl. Jeannie was out of control. She had fresh tears rolling down her cheeks. She was speeding. She muttered angrily to herself. It was a good thing we showed up, poor Pearl was doing the work of three angels trying to calm Jeannie down, keep the car safe and warn the other drivers.

Jeannie drove straight to the pub. Jeremi was there. She walked right past him because her objective was a drink..

The bartender knew her by name and said, "You're in early today, Jeannie."

"Bad day," Jeannie muttered.

"Are you all right?" he asked, genuinely concerned.

"I really need a drink, gimme a beer!" Jeannie ordered. The bartender promptly served her. Jeremi walked up as she paid for the beer.

"Thanks, babe," he said flirtatiously. "You must've bought this for me." He motioned his eyes toward her stomach.

"Give it back; I've had a really bad day!"

"I'm sorry, but we both know why," he said forcefully, but as low as he could to keep the conversation private. "Scott, she'll have a spring water!"

"You drink the spring water, I came in for a beer." As she glared at him, she reached for the beer again, Pearl held on to her little finger and let go of it suddenly as Jeannie's hand was coming around the top of the glass. To everyone but the angels, it looked like Jeannie spilled the beer all over herself. All the angels present cheered for Pearl, who took a quick bow.

Jeannie yelled at Jeremi for spilling the beer on her. He pulled back from her. Jeannie stormed off to the bathroom to dry herself off.

"Do you think the lesson sank in?" Pearl asked us.

George nodded in agreement. "Tantrums usually signify that it needs to be repeated. I agree, same lesson, different players?" he asked.

"Pretty much," Pearl confirmed.

After Jeannie had rinsed herself off, she went into one of the stalls and put her head down and cried some more. Before too long, two young girls came into the bathroom to freshen their makeup. The first one let the other in on the hottest gossip to hit the pub in a while.

"And," she gloated, "at first, they thought it was her appendix, but turns out, she's pregnant!"

Jeannie quietly gasped.

"You've got to be kidding me?" the other asked in disbelief.

"God's honest truth!" They both laughed.

"She seemed so much smarter than that."

"Poor Jeremi," the first girl said, while fixing her lipstick. She blew a kiss toward the mirror and they both left quickly.

Jeannie was so taken aback with that conversation that she stopped crying. She was hurt, offended and extremely angry. Now she wanted to find out who that girl was who was taking pity on "poor Jeremi." Jeannie flew out of the stall, the bathroom and the hallway to end up in the bar area where Jeremi was waiting for her. She saw the two girls walk sexy past him. The first ran her finger across his back as she walked behind him and said, "See ya, Jeremi."

To which he nonchalantly replied, "See ya."

Jeannie sat down beside him. He looked over at her and saw she was really upset. "Do you want the water?"

"You know what?" Jeannie started, "It was stupid of me to come here. I've got to get out of here." She picked up her purse and started to leave.

Jeremi grabbed her arm, "Do you want to go and do some-"

"Yeah, right," Jeannie interrupted him angrily pulling away.

Jeremi watched perplexed as Jeannie stormed out of the bar. Then he and the bartender continued the conversation they started while Jeannie was in the bathroom.

Jeannie looked like she had every intention of driving off as crazily as she had driven to get here. So Pearl pulled the keys out of her purse a few parking places away from her car. "Let's skip the 'DWI' part!" Pearl announced. The keys landed on the ground without a sound.

"How could she get a DWI, Jeremi did all her drinking for her."

"DWI - driving while infuriated," she corrected me.

When Jeannie got to her car, she frantically dug through her purse to find the keys. She finally threw it down and sat on the curb in front of her car in complete frustration.

"Please," Jeannie looked up to Heaven, "please tell me what you want from me! I'm sorry for whatever it is I did, just please, please, give me my car keys back so I can get out of here!" She put her head down and cried some more.

"You say you're sorry for whatever you did. Honey, you've got to be more specific than that," Pearl coached her. "You're moving in the right direction, but reflect on this day, the encounters of the day, the people who upset you." Jeannie started to cry harder. "Did you know your thoughtless comments hurt your schoolmates the same way? How about your in-laws, remember how you talked about them?" Jeannie looked up and sniffed, but she began to calm down.

Jeannie looked up to Heaven again. "God, help me please. I just want to go home. I want to go get my girls and go home. I'm sorry for whatever I did. . ." Pearl cleared her throat. "I'm sorry if I. . . if I--" Jeannie swallowed hard. "I'm sorry if I ever made anyone feel like this. I'm sorry if I ever thought someone else in this situation was stupid. I'm sorry if I ever thought I knew what they should do better than they did. I'm sorry."

"That's my girl!" Pearl said. Then she shined her angel light on Jeannie's keys. Jeannie saw them, retrieved them, got into her car and drove out of the parking lot carefully. She was completely drained.

Poor Jeannie was exhausted by the time she got the girls home from daycare. She went into the kitchen and opened the refrigerator and promptly closed it. "How's pizza sound?" she asked the girls, who jumped up and down excitedly.

Jeannie went over to the phone to order pizza. The answering machine's light was blinking. The whole time she was on the phone ordering the pizza, she stared at the blinking light. When she hung up, she unplugged the phone and the answering machine, too.

"Why did you do that?" Carole asked.

"Because I want it to be just us guys tonight, just us three," Jeannie said and got down on her knees and hugged her girls.

All the angels present joined in on the hug. It seemed to be the medicine Jeannie needed. She went into her bedroom and returned a few minutes later, having changed into sweat pants and shirt. She popped a movie into the VCR, grabbed the girls and said, "Let's get comfy." They all snuggled together on the couch to watch TV.

The girls enjoyed watching the movie, snuggled up close with their mom. Jeannie's thoughts were far away. Her eyes were glazed over. Carole had to nudge her mother about three times when the pizza was delivered before Jeannie was back in the moment and aware their dinner had arrived.

It had been a tough day on her and a tough day on Pearl. It had gone well, but it took a large toll on both charge and angel.

George and I stayed with them for the rest of the evening to support them with our presence. After pizza and the movie, Jeannie put the girls to bed. Then she went back out to the living room. She stared at the phone and turned away to clean up the kitchen.

"Jeannie, stop being afraid!" Pearl said. "If you call the family and face this, it'll be easier than if you wait until it all catches up with you. Stop living in fear of your phone. You need the connection to your friends and family intact. You'll need them now more than you have in a long time. Quit being so proud. You know that you need them. You're strong enough, and help will be there when you need it, unless you alienate them. It will be all right, stop being afraid. Face your fears head on! I'm right here with you."

"This is silly!" Jeannie muttered to herself and turned around and plugged in the phone. She took a deep breath and pressed the play button on the messages. There was only one message from Anne about garage sales this weekend. Jeannie breathed a sigh of relief. She went back to cleaning the kitchen.

As she finished cleaning up, there was a knock on the door. It was Jeremi.

"Can I come in?" he asked timidly.

"Yes. I'm feeling much better now."

Jeremi gave Jeannie a quick hug. "What was wrong?"

"I had a really bad day," Jeannie told him and pulled away. "Everyone at my work knows I'm pregnant and now apparently so does everyone at the pub."

She sat down on the couch.

Jeremi was close behind. "I know," Jeremi said. Jeannie looked at him suspiciously. Jeremi shrugged his shoulders. "It out now. Scott must've told."

"Who told Scott?" Jeannie demanded and leaned back into the couch and stared at the ceiling. She let out a heavy sigh and so did he. Then there was a long moment of silence. They both seemed lost in their own thoughts.

Jeannie broke the silence. "Do you ever feel like you're being 'tested'?"

"Tested?" Jeremi asked, surprised.

"This feels like a test."

"What's being tested?" Jeremi asked.

"Maybe my character, my principles, you know, the things I always said I'd do. Now it's the moment of truth. I know, I'm rambling, but there is something important I need to understand here."

"Yeah, maybe I know what you mean." Jeremi picked it up where she'd left off. "It's like someone's up there watching us, waiting to see what we'll do. I know it's my dad. He's saying 'Son, get yourself together, you've got responsibilities now.'"

He was so close that I wanted to give him a signal that he was right. I made the power blink in the apartment. Jeremi jumped.

"What?" Jeannie asked.

"Did you see that?" Jeremi asked. "The lights flickered. That was Dad; I know it was."

Jeannie looked around the room. Her heart pounded and she breathed a little faster. I think Jeremi had spooked her. "Man, I've got chill bumps."

Neither one said anything for a little while. Eventually Jeannie yawned and Jeremi decided he needed to go and let her get to bed. After all, tomorrow she had to go back to work. They kissed goodnight and Jeremi left. An exhausted Jeannie made her way down the hallway, turned out lights as she passed them and plopped into the bed. She was asleep in a couple minutes.

George and I gave Pearl, Edwina and Marie the night off. "I suppose I'll have to get used to guarding the house sometime, it may as well be tonight."

They thanked us and went off together. George and I spent this night in Jeannie's apartment talking about the things angels need to do for their charges. Occasionally we checked on our sleeping girls.

Somewhere around midnight, Carole got up and went in to sleep with her mother. After another hour, Lynne got up and climbed in on the other side of the bed.

"Where's she going to put the baby?" I joked with George.

"On top!" he answered. We chuckled and kissed the girls and nudged them away from the edges of the bed, closer to the middle.

I wanted to get to know Jeannie better. I wanted to get inside her thoughts and discover why her family finding out about the baby upset her so much. I understood the things that Jack and Pearl had told me, but I had questions, a lot of questions. If I could talk to her, I thought I could help her.

"I want to meet her in a dream, like I did with Jeremi. Can I find a way to keep it from being as traumatic as it was for Jeremi. Can I do that?" I asked George.

"Relax, this one is easy. If she knew who you were, it would be harder. Since you never met, it will simply be a very vivid, memorable dream."

"Should I go back to the beach, like I did with Jeremi? Where's a special place that we can both share?"

"Walk with her around her work, like she does with Judie Plant that seed in her dream, that she's walking with Judie around her work," George suggested.

I took her hand and stroked it gently. I began describing the beautiful neighborhoods where she and Judie walked everyday.

Suddenly, we were there. Jeannie talked, the way she always talked to Judie. I stepped up right beside her, where Judie would have been. She kept talking.

"It's beautiful out here at night, do you agree?" I asked her.

"It sure is," she said and looked over at me. "Do I know you?"

"I know you," I answered, testing to see if I could get away with being very vague.

"How do I know you?"

"Through Jeremi. We're close."

"Oh," Jeannie let it go. We walked a little farther.

"Tell me about Jeremi," I requested.

She smiled. "He's cute. He's the best singer I've ever met. He's easy to talk to. We have a lot in common." Then her smile disappeared. "But he drinks too much and that scares me."

"Why?" I asked, although I already knew the answer.

"Because of the girls and because of the baby. I know I can handle it, right now they are too young to understand about his drinking. When I think about the future, that thought really bothers me."

"Are you ashamed of him, that's why telling your family about the baby is so hard, because he drinks?" I asked. I thought I might have a handle on the situation.

"That has nothing to do with it," Jeannie answered strongly. She took the wind right out of my sails!

"Then why?"

"Each member of my family had a different opinion of what I should have done about my ex-husband once we split. Each one treated me like I was a little girl again and gave me orders on how to run my life, much the way they used to tell me to clean my room. Then each one was offended when I solved my own problems, on my own terms. I made them all mad because I was me. There are so many more facets to this situation. I know each one will have a different opinion again; it'll be the same thing. I'll offend each one again. I know what I need to do. And believe you me, none of them would advise me to do what I know I have to do. I know they'll all be disappointed in me--again."

Jeannie told me exactly what I wanted to know. I think this helped her specifically identify her fears, too.

"What do you wish they'd understand?" I asked her, in hopes she'd continue.

"That I feel like this is my destiny and this baby is meant to be and he will be incredible." Jeannie patted her stomach.

"Why do you say that?"

"Because, from the second I knew he was there, I've felt a determination, a strength coming from him. I've felt like this baby is using me to get here. That there's a much greater purpose for him coming into this world than just to be a part of my life. He's strong and special. I can really feel that."

"You seem sure it's a boy."

"From the second I knew he was there, it was like there was a voice that told me that," Jeannie said, sure of herself.

I chuckled to myself and thought about all the times a little voice had told her that exact thing.

"What do you think this baby's purpose is?"

"It's beyond me. I'll treat him the way I want to be treated and let him figure out his own destiny, but somehow, I just know it's going be important," she answered, then went silent. It seemed she was finished giving me answers. She began to look to me to answer some of her questions. Time to plant the seed.

"When was the last time you went to church, Jeannie?"

"Last Easter," she replied. "Regularly, you mean?" I nodded. "Oh, it's been a long time."

I took her hands and looked into her eyes, as deep as I could see. "When I feel like I'm in a situation that's bigger than I am, I turn to someone bigger than I am. If you want answers, ask God and then be quiet and listen to what comes to you."

She looked back into my eyes and indicated she understood.

"I should go now," I told her. I was back in her bedroom. I continued to stroke her hand. She tossed in her sleep and reached out. "Shhh. Stay asleep. Dream a sweet dream of your baby. Shhh." She settled back down and thankfully, stayed sound asleep. Thankfully, we avoided the jolt like Jeremi did, especially since the girls were right next to her in the bed.

George waited for me. "Did you have a nice talk?"

"Yes, we did."

"What did you learn?"

I quit stroking her hand. George and I went out to the living room to talk. I wanted to look at her family pictures more. There she was, in each one of these old family pictures. Someone was always holding her. I could see why she would be sensitive to standing on her own two feet.

"I learned she's very strong-willed and independent. But her family still thinks of her as a little girl. She can handle her problems independently. But she really has to work hard to prove to them that she can handle her own responsibilities. I think she really wants her family in her life, but on her terms. They really need to respect that she can make her own decisions and right now. I think she needs to set some reasonable boundaries with them. I get that, but it's hard for people to change in relationships, I also get that. This is going to be an adjustment for everyone."

"She'll come around and they'll come around, all in the fullness of time. After all, Jack is there to help all sides and Pearl will keep it from getting out of control. There will be some stress, and strain, there always is. They call 'em 'growing *pains*'. Jeannie needs some space right now. She needs to make her decisions herself and be at peace with those decisions, so she can stand up for them. She needs to attain that kind of inner strength to stand up for her choices and own that they are hers and hers alone."

What a productive night!

If I had been alive, I would never have been able to have such an enlightening conversation with her. I really looked forward to getting to know her and her family better in the coming years.

A few minutes before the girls were due to wake up, Pearl, Edwina, and Marie, returned. We told them about the night and what had been accomplished. Jeannie's alarm clock rang and the snooze button was pushed, pushed, and pushed again. Morning arrived again at Jeannie's house.

When Jeannie got to work, she told Judie about the dream. Judie was intrigued and asked her when the last time was that she had gone to church. Judie was to play the organ next Sunday at a church close to Jeannie's apartment. They made plans to meet there.

That seed had sprouted; I prayed it landed in good soil.

The next few weeks gradually turned into months and Jeremi saw Jeannie frequently, practically every day and most nights. They grew very close. Jeannie had gone back to church, fairly regularly. Occasionally, Jeremi went with her. I considered that progress They were going in a good direction when they were together. His drinking got worse when they were apart, especially when he was alone. He now used beer to chase his brandies when he was at the pub. He used to only drink beer, with the occasional brandy. This escalation was frightening. The more he drank, the less Henry could get through to him. Henry was getting more and more frustrated about his lack of influence over Jeremi.

Unfortunately, any positive influence in his life filtered out when he drank and all sorts of negative influence freely flowed in. The people Jeremi associated with during these times were evidence of this. He sat at the bar and sometimes bemoaned the fact that he'd been thrust unexpectedly into fatherhood. His mates at the bar always put in their two cents' worth, none of which was flattering to Jeannie. According to them, she was either trying to trap him into marriage or find a way to get part of his paycheck for the next eighteen years or just plain stupid. They advised him to run away, to break up or find someone else. The girl who had called him "poor Jeremi" in the bathroom a few weeks before, frequently cozied up to him, if he was alone. Jeremi was always polite, but he knew in his heart that she was trouble and discouraged her. Unfortunately, she persisted.

Meanwhile, Jeannie went to church and acquired some baby supplies at garage sales with Anne. Jeannie's parents came for a quick visit to check out the situation. Their relationship had been strained, but it was healing for them to be together. Her parents left reasonably satisfied, but still quite concerned. Jeannie's girls now understood that Mommy was going to have a baby and were very excited. When Jeremi, or Jeannie's support team, was around her, she was optimistic about the situation. When Jeannie was alone, she worried a lot, mostly about Jeremi. He always seemed to be on her mind. Sometimes she would call the pub to try to find him. It depended on how much he had had to drink whether she got a warm reception or a brush off.

The bar cronies teased Jeremi about his "ball and chain" as soon as he hung up the phone, which simply amplified the pressure Jeremi was already under.

One very unfortunate night, toward the middle of her pregnancy, Jeannie was home alone. Her girls had gone to the house of one of their father's sisters for the night. Anne was out of town on vacation with her family. Jeannie called the pub to see if Jeremi was there. He was and had been there for quite some time and he was drunk. The "poor Jeremi" girl was also there and getting closer and closer to him. He took Jeannie's phone call. She could tell he was drunk, but she asked him if he wanted to go to a movie and out to dinner with her anyway. As he repeated the words, movie and dinner, the girl at the bar loudly ordered "Two more brandies here for Jeremi and me!" Jeannie heard what the girl had said, but covered that fact up with Jeremi. Jeannie planned to come to the pub to pick him up. They hung up.

Jeremi sat down again, after the routine jeers of the "ol' ball and chain" and quickly shot down the brandy the girl had bought him. He thanked her, then turned and talked to the man on the other side of him. That man left shortly thereafter. Jeremi turned to the only other person there to talk to, the girl. When she offered to buy him another drink, Jeremi agreed. These days, he never turned down a free drink.

Jeannie got ready and hurried to the pub. When she got to the door, she saw Jeremi and the girl talking and drinking together. The girl caught a glimpse of Jeannie at the door, but Jeremi was oblivious. The girl put her arm cozily on his upper thigh. As soon as Jeannie saw this, she started to hyperventilate. She refused to go into the pub. Pearl, George and I tried to get her to go in, but her emotions and pride were too strong.

Henry tried to get Jeremi to turn and see Jeannie, but he was too far gone. He pushed the girl's hand off his thigh, but Jeannie had already left before that happened.

She whipped around the corner of the building and tried to catch her breath--tears streamed down her face--from the shock of actually seeing what she had told Anne she feared most--seeing Jeremi with someone else. Pearl did everything in her power to hold her up, but she slid down the side of the building into a sitting position nonetheless.

It took several minutes, but Jeannie regained most of her composure. She made it to a pay phone and called the pub to tell Jeremi she'd changed her mind, without giving him a reason. Then she got into her car and drove away. She was in such a state that I really felt like I had to protect my charge. She sped away from the pub, right past her apartment. After a close call at a stop sign, Jeannie settled down, but she was crying.

"We've got to get her off the road and get some people around her," Pearl said.

"I think she's about to have a flat tire," George said. Jeannie pulled her car up to the stoplight, into the left lane and rolled over some broken glass that George had spread there. As she stopped, Jeannie heard a crunch and then a hissing noise. She rolled down her window and stuck her head out and could see that she had air rapidly escaping out of the left front tire.

"There's a tire repair place up about a block, you need to get there," Pearl said.

Jeannie looked up and saw the tire sign. She muttered some very mean things about the tire and the timing of this problem. She pulled into the parking lot and right up to the garage stall. The fellow who worked there happened to be out having a cigarette when Jeannie pulled up. He heard the hissing coming from the tire and directed her into the repair bay. She stopped the car and got out. He jumped in and pulled the car into the stall and up onto the hoist. Jeannie stood on the outside and looked in, while he pulled a large piece of glass out of the tire with pliers. He informed her that she would need a patch and it would take just a few minutes. She took the news pretty well, considering. She went inside and sat down. Pearl coached her to take deep breaths and calm down. She picked up a magazine and tried to thumb through it, but her mind was obviously elsewhere.

"Is it all right if I talk to her?" I asked.

"By all means," Pearl answered.

There was a restroom in the lobby. I went in there to get ready. I decided to wear a short-sleeved cotton shirt and a pair of jeans. I thought the age I was was appropriate for the situation. So, I made the toilet flush loudly. Then I came out and sat in the waiting room a couple of chairs away from Jeannie.

"He looks familiar Jeannie." Pearl coached.

"You know him from somewhere, but where?" George added.

Jeannie looked at me, nodded hello with a faint smile. I returned the greeting. Jeannie tried to keep up the appearance of reading the magazine, but occasionally looked over at me. As soon as I looked up, she quickly looked back at her magazine.

"He looks familiar, but where do you know him from?" Pearl continued her coaching. About the fourth or fifth time this happened, Jeannie started to snicker and so did I.

"I'm sorry for staring, but you look really familiar," I said to her.

"I know. I mean, you do, too. Do you know how we know each other?"

"Do you come here often?"

I gave her an expectant look and then she got the joke. "Just every flat I get."

"Me too. When was your last flat?"

She chuckled. "I know I know you. Do you work out at the airport?" I shook my head.

"I was there several weeks ago. I thought that's where I might've seen you. Where do you work?"

"I'm a guard," I said.

"What do you guard?"

"People."

"Like a body guard?"

"Something like that."

She shook her head no. "Nobody I know needs a bodyguard."

"Everyone you know needs a bodyguard!" Pearl said. I heard all the angels laugh. Jeannie got a peculiar look on her face as if she'd heard what Pearl said.

"I know where it was from!" she exclaimed. I panicked for a second remembering our encounter in the dream. I looked for George. He motioned that it would be okay. "A couple of Sundays ago, you were at the church on Washington street. You stood up when they asked who was visiting."

"That's right. I did," I said, relieved. "Good memory. I greeted you in the narthex after the service, with your little girl, was it?"

"Girls," Jeannie corrected.

"I met so many people that day. Nice people, all of them,"

"You'll find that there."

The man came in to tell Jeannie her car was ready.

"Nice talking to you," Jeannie said. on her way out. "Maybe I'll see you again soon."

"I'm certain of it," I said. We smiled at each other and Jeannie paid for the repairs and left. She waved as she left the waiting room.

I stayed in the chair until the mechanic left the room and Jeannie had driven away. Then I went back to only being visible to angels. The mechanic came in a few minutes later to check on something. He looked at the chair I had been in and then he looked around the waiting room and outside the door. He shrugged his shoulders and left.

George and I caught up with Jeannie and Pearl. Jeannie's driving was quite a bit calmer now. She drove to the movie theater. Pearl explained to us that when she is really hurting, Jeannie goes to a movie and tries to get lost in it. It's a good way for her to distance herself from her situation. She picks a movie whose situation is as far removed from her own as possible, that she can just forget for a little while. Today, she picked a movie about a military trial; without a love story, without pregnant women. Jeannie calmly watched the movie about the military court martial. We had her settled and she would stay calm for a few hours. "She's fine. You better go help Henry," Pearl told us.

We went back to the pub. Jeremi was still there and the girl was still beside him. I had never seen Jeremi this drunk in my entire life or death. Henry was beside himself. These were the most miserable times for Henry. If he was going to be able to protect Jeremi, it was going to have to be in spite of Jeremi. The bartender tried to get him to leave. He offered to call a cab. Jeremi refused. The girl told him she knew where there was a party and she would take him. He agreed to go with her to this "party." Jeremi got into the car with the girl and they drove away from the pub, without saying goodnight to anyone. George, Henry, and I went along because this was shaping up to be a disaster.

As I suspected, the "party" was nothing more than liquor at her house. Jeremi protested until she pointed out her large selection. One of the many bottles was the brand of brandy that Jeremi drank the most often. It appeared to me that this girl had had this "party" planned for a quite a while.

All of his protesting behind him now, Jeremi asked what movies she had to watch. She pulled out an assortment of films from action to X-rated. Jeremi picked an action movie. She made him a drink and sat down on the couch next to him, very close. Jeremi squirmed a little, but she persisted. Before too long, she made her move. He gave in and soon, they were kissing very intensely.

Henry made the phone ring to distract them. She took it off the hook. George made her car alarm go off. She got up briefly, looked out the window, pointed a remote at it and turned it off. On the way back to the couch, she flipped on the stereo, turned off the TV and the lights and unbuttoned her blouse. I tried to talk sense into Jeremi, but it was a lost cause!

It became terribly clear that she and Jeremi were going to have sex. I was afraid this was going to ruin everything we had been working for. "Well, what do we do now?" I asked George and Henry.

"We need to make sure that he at least uses a condom to keep him from getting exposed to anything she might have. Beyond that, it would take an intervention beyond what is appropriate," Henry said.

"What is this going to do to the plan?" I asked anxiously.

"The future is unwritten," George said.

"She's a spoiler. She's angel-less. She knows his weakness and she's using it to get to him. Exactly why remains to be seen," George explained.

"We've got to stop this!" I insisted.

"Shy of an earthquake, probably not. Besides, the way she's using our interventions against us, she'd like the ride. No, I'm afraid not," Henry said.

"At least they are practicing 'safe sex,'" I said.

"There's nothing safe about this sex," George said and shook his head with disgust.

"I've got to get out here! This is too awful to be any part of," I said. I never wanted to see this side of Jeremi. I looked to George for direction.

"Henry, call us if you need us," George said. Henry nodded. We went back to talk to Pearl and to check on Jeannie.

The movie was almost over. Jeannie had settled down considerably. You could see her thoughts return to her problems as soon as the lights came up. She walked slowly out of the theater. When she got back to her car, she rested her head on her hands on the steering wheel. Eventually, she took a deep breath and drove slowly home. She got there and dragged herself out of the car and into her apartment. Without turning on any lights or even checking her phone messages, she drug herself down the hallway dropping things as she went. She fell back onto the bed, face up, eyes wide open. The occasional tear fell down her cheek. Eventually her eyelids started to droop and she fell asleep. She stayed in that exact position for the rest of the night.

"She is so hurt. I've never seen her like this before," Pearl said. "She's been hurt in her life before, but betrayed like this in love like this... This is brand new territory for her. She's devastated."

"But she only suspects that Jeremi slept with the spoiler," I said. "Do you think she's holding out any hope that it'll be okay?"

"Her hope for a happily ever after is shattered," Pearl answered "I think right now, this whole situation has taken her to one of the lowest points in her life. She's pregnant, alone and the father is cheating. Despite the strong face she tries to show the rest of the world, she is hurt, lonely and scared."

"What can we do?" I asked.

"There's only one message for nights like these," George said and Pearl nodded. I looked at them perplexed, so he went on. "Life is hard, but God is good!" I nodded in agreement.

For the rest of that night, we sang every song we knew, quoted every piece of scripture with that theme, preached sermons with that message, so that idea would seep into Jeannie's subconscious, then conscious mind, so she could start fresh in the morning.

Henry called George and me back in the morning, before Jeannie woke up. We went to see what we could do. Jeremi was beginning to stir. He had fallen asleep on the couch and the spoiler had curled up on the couch with her head on his lap. He opened his eyes quickly, looked around and realized where he was and what he had done. He grabbed his head. It looked like a combination of shame and pain. She was still asleep. He moved very slowly, cautiously and tried to get her head off his lap. Once he did, he got his things together, swigged the last of the brandy on the table and got out of the house.

Once outside, the sun hurt his eyes and his head. He put his sunglasses on. He looked around and tried to figure out where he was. He picked a direction and walked away. He looked at his watch and shook his head. I could tell he was trying to cook up a story to tell Jeannie about where he had been. He rehearsed it silently in his mind, outwardly with his hands. He looked pretty ridiculous. He made it to a street he recognized and stuck out his thumb as cars went by, but nobody picked him up. He kept on walking. Eventually he made it back to the pub, where he got into his car and drove straight over to Jeannie's.

She was still asleep. The look on her face was much more peaceful now than the expression she'd had when she went to sleep. She woke up abruptly to the knock on the door.

She looked out the peephole. She could see a smiling Jeremi. She opened the door, but blocked his entrance. Undeterred, he breezed right past her. "So what happened to you last night?" he asked her.

Flabbergasted, Jeannie's jaw dropped, "What happened to me?"

Jeremi took control of the conversation. "Yeah, I thought we were going to a movie, then you call and cancel at the last minute without giving me a reason. You stranded me there! Did you get a better offer or something?"

"No," Jeannie was really caught off guard. Apparently, Jeremi thought the best defense was a good offense. This was hard to watch. We all shook our heads in disbelief and disgust.

"So what did you do, last night?" he asked her.

"I went to a movie, BY MYSELF!" Jeannie was very emphatic.

"What movie?"

"That new military one, at the mall."

"You went without me? You know I wanted to see that one." Jeremi tried to act indignant.

"So sorry," Jeannie said sarcastically. "I figured you already had plans for the night, you were well on your way when I came into the pub last night."

"Here we go!" Pearl said.

"What are you talking about?" Jeremi tried to act innocent. It was despicable.

"I came to pick you up at the bar and I saw you with *her*. I figured three was a crowd." Jeannie turned her back on him.

"Her?" Jeremi acting ignorant.

"Yes, 'her'! I saw you sitting at the bar next to her. She had her hand on your thigh and she was buying you drinks. You looked quite cozy!" Jeannie accused.

"Oh that. You've got it all wrong. I just know her from the pub. We're just friends." He waited for her reaction.

"If I did that with my male *friends*, you'd go ballistic. She was all over you!" She started to cry.

"I'm sorry, baby. I wish you'd come in and we could have avoided all this," he said.

"Well, most of it, anyway," Pearl chimed in.

Jeannie turned around and looked him in the eyes, tears in hers.

Jeremi put his arms around her. "Stop crying, baby, I'm here. I'm here for you now." She sobbed in his arms for a few moments.

"She's gone," Pearl said.

"Do you mean she believes him?" I asked.

"She wants to believe him more than she wants to believe what she saw and as you said before, she only suspects, so there is a lot of room for doubt in her mind right now," Pearl said.

"Then he had better do something to earn her forgiveness," I said, sounding again more like a father than an angel.

"What forgiveness?" George asked. "Instead of confessing, he tried to make her think it was her fault that she's feeling this way."

Unfortunately, George was right.

However, it appeared that Jeremi's guilty conscious-despite his hangover--got the better of him. He treated Jeannie like a princess that day. He made her breakfast, then he took her to a movie and after that they went out to an early dinner. The girls returned and they all went out to a playground where Jeremi played with the girls.

He decided to stay away from the pub. He quit his job there and got a job in a department store. He avoided the spoiler like the plague. He stayed very close to Jeannie and the girls. It appeared that things were going to be back on track, momentarily.

20

Several weeks later, Glory decided to visit Jeremi, Peter, Melinda, and their kids and take the opportunity to meet the mother of her next grandchild. Peter invited Jeannie and the girls over to a big family dinner. One evening they all talked and got to know each other better. It was only about a month now, before the baby was due. Each Guardian had fun whispering story ideas into their charge's ears for them to tell. Jeannie enjoyed listening to stories about everyone else. Marie whispered to Carole and Carole told a story about her mom, after which, Jeannie, although embarrassed, smiled, but shot Carole a look like: You just wait until we get home.

Glory pulled Carole close to her and got her to talk some more. Glory told Carole she could call her Grandma. Everyone laughed, talked and got along well all evening long.

It was a lovely time, the first union of my two families into my new expanded family.

Glory made it a point to pull Jeannie aside and let her know that regardless how things worked out between her and Jeremi, that she was now family and that she intended to stay close. Peter let Jeannie know that he would be happy to help, if she ever needed it, regardless of her relationship with Jeremi. It Jeannie was relieved and thankful to receive such support from Jeremi's family. She and the girls left a little after that.

Melinda and the children went to bed, leaving Peter, Jeremi and Glory alone to talk.

The three of them looked at each other. None of them seemed to want to start the conversation.

"Cute girls," Glory said, breaking the ice.

Jeremi and Peter nodded in agreement. There was an awkward silence again.

"So what's going on with the two of you?" Glory asked. "Peter says you spend a lot of time with them."

Jeremi looked at Peter, who shrugged his shoulders and tried to look innocent of the charge of "talking about him behind his back." "Yeah, I spend some time with them. It's just a trip that she's pregnant."

"Is she the only person you spend time with?" Glory asked.

Jeremi hesitated, then said, "Recently, yeah." I could tell that this question unsettled him.

"How recently?" Peter asked.

"Recently. You know, recently," Jeremi snapped defensively. "Look, I like her. She's having my baby. She's the only one I'm seeing, and that's enough for me."

"Is that enough for her?" Glory said in a very soft voice and looked down at her hands.

Peter shot Jeremi a disgusted look and motioned his head toward Glory.

"I'm sorry, Mama. I'm sorry I snapped. I'm just finished talking about whether we should get married because..." Jeremi looked around deciding he was probably outnumbered in this argument. "Just because."

"Have you talked about it with her?" Glory asked.

"Only once. The night we found out about the baby. We both decided getting married just because of the baby would be a mistake."

"That was months--" Peter began, but stopped when Glory put her hand up.

Glory nodded, pursed her lips and kept her words in. However, I could tell that her mind was going a million miles an hour.

Peter changed the subject and the conversation lightened quickly. Jeremi got restless so he told them he was going to bed. He kissed

Glory and said, "Peace!" to Peter and quietly went down the hallway to his room. A familiar clink could be heard coming from the direction of his bedroom.

Glory and Peter both heard it, recognizing it for what it was.

"There he goes again," Peter said.

"Is it every night, still?" Glory asked, concerned.

"And every morning."

"Lord have mercy," Glory looked up. "Is Jeannie like that?"

"Once she found out about the baby, she quit drinking anything."

"Well, that's something," Glory said. Peter nodded in agreement. "Do you think he loves her?" Glory asked.

Peter answered. "I think he probably does, but I think his drinking is between them." Glory stayed quiet. "He just does really stupid things when he's drunk."

"Like what?"

"Like going to parties with other women," Peter said.

"Lord, have mercy! Does Jeannie know?"

"Mama, I'm sure she suspects."

"He'd better be careful, Nothing bad is going to happen to my grandbaby!" Glory said sternly.

Peter nodded. "I guess we'll have to wait and see what happens."

They talked for a few more minutes and then Glory went to bed. George, Naomi and I stayed with her. She got down on her knees and prayed quietly and earnestly for about half an hour. We all got on our knees right beside her and prayed right along with her. This was the most intent I'd seen her for several months now. This situation worried her immensely. I knew she felt she shouldered this burden alone.

I wanted to let her know that we were right here with her. "Talk to me," I said to her.

She reacted to my words, with her body. She got into bed and turned out the light. I laid down beside her and again I said, "Talk to me." She sighed heavily and rolled away from me. "Talk to me, Glory, I'm right here."

"I've never had this hard a time getting her to talk to me. What's the problem?" I asked George.

"It could be a multitude of things. She's afraid she'll wake someone by talking out loud. Maybe she's just so preoccupied by the situation that nothing else can break into her thoughts," George explained.

"What can I do to bring her back to me?"

"Déjà vu dreams are helpful at times like these," George said. I gave him my usual perplexed look, so he explained further. "Déjà vu dreams, it's a dream where we guide our charge through the problem they're having. They tell us how they would like it solved. Then we show them the solution they've described and the probable outcome. We work through the problem, until they are at peace about it. It's different from dreams where we're actually talking to them. Here we simply guide them. They really do all the work. Then like all dreams, if she has any memory of it, it will fade from her conscious mind. If their solutions come true one day, they might remember bits and pieces of it. That's why they call it déjà vu, because they've already seen it. It's a good way to get them to work out a problem, so they release their stress about it."

"They just forget it?"

"It's their thought processes, Martin. They already know the solutions and they can rethink them again when they're awake. They're actually working these things all out for themselves, we just give them the venue."

My blank stare kept him explaining.

"Do you ever remember waking up with the solution to a problem that had been bothering you when you went to bed?"

I nodded. "Yes, many, many times."

"Okay, then. We worked it out while you slept. I know you forgot that part, but do you remember having the solution when you woke up?"

"You never cease to amaze me, George."

"This is all part of the grand plan. And grand is an understatement." George looked toward Heaven with appreciation.

"It is indeed."

George and Naomi looked at me and when our eyes met, the three of us joined Glory in her dream.

"What's troubling you?" George asked.

"My son," Glory replied.

"What's troubling you about him?"

"Many things." There was a pause, then she went on. "He'll be having a child, his first, but it was quite unplanned. He drinks heavily and he's getting worse. I'm scared for him. He's messing around with loose women, when another one is having his child. He's going to lose his child if he keeps acting this way. I'm afraid I'll lose my grandchild because of the way he's treating the child's mother."

"Those are heavy burdens."

"Yes, they are."

"Do you see solutions?" George asked her.

"He has to stop drinking!" she said emphatically. "Then with a sober mind, assess his responsibilities and his relationships."

"How would you do that?" George asked.

"Get him some help. I think he needs serious help. If he could see the damage he's doing, he'd stop. He's a good person at heart; I know he is. We raised him to take care of his business. Something stronger than he is has control of him and we have to break its grip. We need to get him some help. Then it should all fall right back into place."

"Do you think he's ready to ask for help?" I asked.

She shook her head. She recognized my voice.

"What do you think needs to happen?"

"Something dramatic. Something so dramatic, that it will wake him up. I only pray that nobody gets hurt because of it. That's my greatest fear, that he will get hurt or hurt somebody when he's drunk."

"So let's say something dramatic has happened and now he's in treatment, he's sober and nobody has been hurt. What happens now?" George asked her.

"He's there when his baby comes into the world and every second thereafter. He brings the baby to see me and we stand up together when we have the baby baptized in its grandfather's church." Glory smiled with those thoughts.

"That would be nice," I said.

"Yes, it would!" Glory said, still smiling.

"Just lie here and imagine those beautiful thoughts. Remember the peace you're feeling at this moment," George said and left.

"Please try and feel how close I am to you and know that I'm that close Jeremi also. I love you - both," I said. Her smile grew broader. I left.

Naomi stayed behind to coach some more.

George and I watched Glory sleep. Her look grew more and more peaceful. "I hope this feeling stays with her even after she goes home tomorrow," I said as we left.

21

We decided to look in on Jeremi. He struggled in his sleep as usual.

"We just did a déjà vu with Glory," I told Henry. "She's right about a lot of things."

"Like what?"

"It's going to be impossible to get him to go willingly."

"Get help for his drinking," George clarified for Henry's sake.

"He has enablers all over the place. Even if one went away, another would willingly take their place," Henry said. We all agreed. We knew he meant the spoiler.

"What that boy needs is an education," George said definitively. "We need to make a concerted effort to get the message in front of him. Everywhere he turns, he needs to see the phone number to AA, a pamphlet about the Hope Center, the consequences of drinking and a light leading him out."

"Makes sense," I said and we all agreed again.

"Beginning tomorrow, the message will bombard him everywhere," Henry said.

"Good, let us help where we can," George said.

"You know what to do," Henry replied.

"I do," George confirmed.

George and I left on our mission. We visited all the other family members, including Jeannie. We planted thoughts with them and their angels about obtaining material regarding The Alcoholic and how to get him help.

In the next few days, whenever Jeremi watched TV, he'd flip through the channels. Every time there was a drunk who looked stupid on a show, the remote would quit working for a few moments. Jeremi would flip the remote harder to get it to change. He would be intent on the screen to see if the channel had changed, therefore, he was forced to watch the whole drunken escapade. Henry had fun making that one work out.

George and I shopped for pamphlets. Once we found several good ones, they appeared in both Peter and Jeannie's mailboxes addressed to "Occupant." Henry made sure Jeremi got the mail that day. Jeremi browsed through the collection and promptly threw them away. Undetered by that, more came in the next day's mail. Melinda got those.

Henry shined angel light on all newspaper sections that dealt with the consequences of drunken behavior, like the listings of the arrests and the gruesome pictures of the accidents. In every instance, Henry was sure to angel light the words, "Alcohol was involved."

It was a massive campaign and everyone with an angel that Jeremi had contact with in some way, shape or form, echoed the message.

Several nights later, Jeremi headed over to Jeannie's house to pick her up for an evening out. Anne had come to get the girls, so they could go out. While Jeannie waited for Jeremi to arrive, she opened the envelope with the brochures that George and I had sent her. She spread them out on the coffee table by the couch and picked one out that apparently appealed to her the most. She started to read it.

Jeremi knocked at the door. Instead of putting the brochure down, she took it with her to the door and continued to read it. She opened the door and kissed Jeremi hello and he gave her a nice hug. Then she turned around to grab her purse, but she kept reading the brochure.

"What's that?" he asked her.

She flashed it at him and resumed reading as she grabbed her purse.

"You've got to be kidding me!" he snapped at her. Jeannie was taken by surprise by this sudden change in tone. "I suppose you think I have a drinking problem, too! Geez, it's everywhere I turn these days!" He got louder and louder. Jeannie watched him, completely in shock.

"Well, if that's what you think, I'm out of here!" He slammed the door, got in his car and sped off.

Jeannie grabbed her purse and went to follow him, but he had driven off too fast. "He went to the pub," Pearl informed her. So Jeannie drove to the pub and as expected, she found Jeremi's car there.

Jeannie went in and sat beside him at the bar. He already had one brandy down and had another one ordered.

"What's wrong with you?" she asked him. "I was just reading my mail and you went ballistic!"

Jeremi softened with his first brandy. "I know, I'm sorry. It's just every time I turn around, someone's throwing a pamphlet in my face."

He eventually calmed down and it looked like things were getting back to normal.

Then George told me, "We've got big problems." Out in the parking lot, headed in to the pub was the spoiler, looking determined.

"What do we do now?" I asked.

"Watch over them," Henry, Pearl and George said together.

Jeannie and Jeremi had their backs to the door. The spoiler spotted them right away and walked around the bar, directly into their line of sight. Jeremi was reaching for his next shot of brandy, when he saw her and his arm jerked and the brandy spilled all over the bar. Jeannie jumped and looked at Jeremi. His eyes were glued on the spoiler. Jeannie followed Jeremi's line of sight and saw what he was looking at. The spoiler walked slowly, sexily, around the back of the bar, never for one second taking her eyes off Jeremi. He tried to avoid eye contact with the spoiler by looking back at Jeannie. She glared at him with the coldest, angriest stare I think I have ever seen. Her hands trembled. Jeremi looked away, toward the bartender, for help. The bartended leaned back, with his arms crossed and watched this all unfold.

"Could I get a rag here?" Jeremi yelled at him.

The bartender threw it at him. They exchanged glares. Jeremi quickly wiped up the spill, then threw the rag right back at him.

"I've got to go," Jeannie said and stormed out the door.

Jeremi was torn between following Jeannie out the door and following the spoiler down the hallway. Jeannie disappeared so quickly Jeremi's only choice was to follow the spoiler.

She was down the hallway, around the corner, wearing a cocky look on her face. She'd been sure he'd follow her. Unfortunately, she was right.

"Hi, baby," she said and put her arms around his neck.

He pulled away, "Karla, get off me!"

"But, sweetheart," she touched his stomach gently with her fingers and drew a couple of circles. He pushed her hand away.

"Get away from me. You were a mistake. I told you before and I'll tell you again, we're through. Get away and stay away from me," he said forcefully.

Karla looked over Jeremi's shoulder and saw Jeannie there, waiting to confront him about this situation. The bartender followed close behind her. The spoiler put her arm over Jeremi's shoulder and put her leg up around his thigh and rubbed it up and down. "But, baby, you were so good, I've never had a lover like you before. When can we make love again? When can we do it again? Huh? Baby?" Her voice was sickeningly sweet. This woman was a piece of work.

"I'd like to know the answer to that, myself," Jeannie said.

Jeremi whipped around and inadvertently knocked Karla to the floor. "Jeannie!" Jeremi exclaimed, very startled. "Jeannie," he said again more softly and went to her. "It was a mistake."

Karla got up from the floor, spitting mad. "Jeremi! So you think you can just screw me and take off! Come back here, I'm still talking to you!" She lunged at Jeremi, but Henry helped her lose her footing. She missed and landed on the ground again. Furious, she took a swing at Jeannie. The bartender saw this coming, stopped her hand mid-swing and pulled her out of the hallway by her wrist. She spit at Jeannie and Jeremi on the way by. Some got on Jeannie's face and Jeremi tried to wipe it off, but she batted his hand away. Jeannie wiped it off herself.

Jeannie glared at Jeremi. "You liar." Her angry voice was low and controlled. "You cheating liar. I knew it. And I let you lie to me, even though in my heart I knew it was all a lie."

"Baby, come on." Jeremi tried to figure a way out of this one.

"Baby, that's was her name for you. You lost the right to EVER call me that again!"

"Look, I'm really sorry," Jeremi said.

"Yeah, I bet you're sorry. You're sorry you got caught!" Jeannie lashed out, trembling with anger and agony.

Jeremi got indignant. "Caught at what? You act like we're married," he snapped back defensively.

The words hit Jeannie like a physical punch. She fell back against the wall. "So you can be in a relationship with someone and cheat and it's okay, up until the minute you say 'I do.' Now I get it," she said quietly, sarcastically and angrily. I think Jeremi realized how much he had just hurt her, so he gently put his hand up to her face to wipe her tears away. She batted his hand away. "Get your hands off me!" she growled at him. Her eyes threw daggers at him. There was a long pause.

"You're still carrying my baby," he screamed at her.

There was nothing but pain in her eyes when she replied, "If you think I'm going to let a drunk like you come near my child, you're crazier than you are drunk. You're dead to me." She paused, then added, "To us."

When he heard Jeannie use the word drunk to describe him, he lost all control. All the angels went into action. Henry surrounded Jeremi, Pearl surrounded Jeannie and I tried to stay between them. The bartender came back down the hallway to break this up and he arrived in time to see Jeremi smack Jeannie's face. He slapped her so hard that she fell down. Pearl cushioned her fall as best she could. Jeannie sat up immediately and grabbed her stomach. She screamed in pain.

Both Jeremi and the bartender rushed to Jeannie's aid. Jeremi pleaded "I'm sorry. Oh God, I'm so sorry. Are you all right? Jeannie, talk to me please. Oh God, please!"

Jeannie groaned.

The bartender told Jeremi, "You need to leave. You need to be gone and I mean now!"

"Jeannie, are you all right! Jeannie!!!" Jeremi yelled back.

"Get away from me," Jeannie growled, glared and groaned.

"Now. I'm about to call the police," the bartender warned.

Jeremi got up. "But I'm sorry, Jeannie. God, tell her I'm sorry!" He pleaded with the bartender. Jeremi looked around, examined his options, then he ran out of the pub.

I tried to help Pearl with Jeannie. Pearl coached, "Breathe, breathe, he-he-hoo, he-he-hoo." Jeannie complied with her. We worked to calm her down and to help her make it through the pain.

Henry just stood there. He looked down and wept. Then he said through his tears, "I've failed. I've completely failed Jeremi, Jeannie, God and myself. It's time I go where I can be of productive service to the universe because I'm finished being of any reasonable good here. God, please forgive me my failure."

I stood up to face him. "Get a grip, man! Jeremi needs you. You're his angel."

George came between Henry and me. "Martin. This is Henry's choice and he's made it. He's lost Jeremi. He needs to go where he will be of more use, spiritually." He turned to Henry, "Go in peace, my friend." Henry turned away from us and simply vanished.

"Well, who's gonna protect Jeremi now?" I demanded of George.

"Nobody," he answered sadly.

"Pearl, how's Jeannie? How's the baby?" I assessed the situation as fast as I could. I knew the baby was my charge, but Jeremi was my son. I was never so torn in my life or death.

"She's going to be all right," Pearl said. "She's more upset than anything right now. The baby is fine. She was knocked down, that's all."

"Call me if you need me. I'm going after Jeremi." I looked at George to discern if we were in this battle together.

"Let's go," he said to me.

22

We caught up with Jeremi, crying and driving - headed nowhere in particular. He kept drinking from a bottle of brandy that he already had in the car.

I told George. "We've got to get him off the road."

"What he needs is to get caught," George responded. "I'm going to go help a police officer find him." He left.

Within a minute, lights flashed in Jeremi's rearview mirror. Jeremi muttered some expletives. He tried to stash the brandy bottle as he pulled into a nearby parking lot. He dug in his pocket for a breath mint and popped it in. He wiped his face and tried to put on a smile to fool the officer, who came up to the side of the car. George was right behind him. The officer's angel waited for him in the patrol car.

"Good evening," the officer said politely.

"Good evening, officer," Jeremi said. "Is there a problem?"

"Do you know why I pulled you over tonight, sir?"

Jeremi shook his head.

"You took that last turn back there awfully wide."

"I did? I'm sorry." Jeremi said as sweet as he could muster.

"Have you been drinking tonight, sir?"

"I had a brandy back at the pub, but only one," Jeremi admitted.

"I'm going to need your license and registration, then I'm going to need you to step out of the car, sir."

Jeremi took his wallet out and gave him his driver's license. He reached down under the seat and spilled the brandy bottle as he opened the glove box to get out the registration. George helped a little brandy get on the registration, to insure the officer smelled it. It worked.

"Do you know it's against the law to have an open container of alcohol in your vehicle?" the officer asked him. Jeremi nodded. "Please get out of the car, sir." Jeremi got out of the car. "Please turn around." Jeremi turned around. "I'm placing you under arrest, on the charge of driving while intoxicated and violating the open container ordinance. You have the right to remain silent . . ." The officer read him the rest of his Miranda rights and led him to the police car.

"Well, now what?" I asked George.

"I'm making this up as I go."

"Well, we got him out from behind the wheel drunk, angry and hurt. That much is good," I consoled myself. "But getting him arrested, this is pretty drastic."

"Even Glory asked for something dramatic to wake him up. This is pretty dramatic. Hopefully, the court will order some type of alcohol treatment or education. But whether they do or not, at least we got him off the streets where he was in mortal danger."

We sat in the backseat of the police car with Jeremi on his long drive downtown. I had to find out if Jeannie was all right. "Will you be all right for a bit? My heart is telling me that I've got to go check on Jeannie and the baby," I told George.

"I'll stay with him," George reassured me.

"Call me if you need anything."

"Go!" George commanded.

Jeannie was back at her apartment alone, except for Pearl. I told Pearl what happened to Jeremi and she told me the bartender drove Jeannie home, then returned to the pub.

Jeannie paced the living room for awhile and then cried. After a while, she collapsed on the couch. Almost immediately after she sat down, there was a knock on the door. With quite a bit of effort, thanks to her prominent stomach and sore behind, she got herself up. She muttered quietly on the way to the door about her bad timing. Then she looked out the peephole and saw Peter. She opened the door and let him in.

"Are you all right?" He rushed right in and gave her a hug.

Jeannie said. "I'm fine." She looked at her stomach, "We're fine." He gave her a look of disbelief. "Really," she insisted.

"I know better," Peter said and pulled her close and held her tight. Then she let finally let down her defenses she started to cry. "That's right, get out all the garbage. Cry it out. I know this is very hard, especially for you."

The more Peter consoled her, the harder Jeannie cried. Eventually she pulled away and wiped her eyes. "I'm all right." She went to get herself a glass of water.

She and Peter sat on the couch to talk things out. Peter reiterated that he planned to be there for his nephew or niece and he would help in any way she needed him to. They talked for over an hour. Jeannie told him how she felt about Jeremi and how badly he had hurt her. Peter listened. Sometimes he'd explain some detail about Jeremi that he hoped would give her insight into his character, and sometimes that helped. Peter got ready to leave after he was fully satisfied Jeannie had settled down and was going to be all right. Then the phone rang.

"What now?" Jeannie said, exasperated. She answered the phone and snapped "Hello."

She listened for a bit, her eyes getting big. She motioned for Peter to come over to the phone. She covered the mouthpiece and whispered, "Jeremi's in jail and since there was nobody's home at your house, he called me to come bail him out."

Peter rolled his eyes, shaking his head, "He's got his nerve."

"This is why you're here, Peter. You need to get him out of jail and into a treatment center. Tell her you'll go get him." William coached.

"How did you know about this?" I asked William.

"George summoned me and told me to get Peter here. He had me turn the ringer off Peter's phone right before I left," Peter's angel explained.

"He's good," I said. William agreed.

Jeannie repeated what Jeremi said to her, for Peter's benefit.

"Tell him you'll take care of it," Peter whispered to her. Jeannie looked at him in disbelief. He encouraged her to say it.

"I'll take care of it," Jeannie said to Jeremi, then hung up the phone abruptly.

"This is perfect," Peter said excitedly.

"How?" Jeannie asked.

"He's right where we want him."

"You got that right."

"No, no. Check this out: I'll bail him out in a little bit, but first I'll make arrangements for him to check into the Hope Center to detox," Peter explained. "Where's your phone book?"

"How are you going to get him to go there?"

"Well, I'll reason with him to see if he sees the predicament he's in. If keeps being hard headed about it, he'll walk his little ass back to jail!" Peter grabbed the phone book from Jeannie. He held the receiver with his shoulder as he looked up the number. "This might be exactly the break we've all been praying for."

Peter made the arrangements, hugged Jeannie and told her that he'd call her tomorrow and let her know what was up. He left.

Pearl assured me that Jeannie and the baby were all right, so I left to go back to George and Jeremi.

Jeremi was in a drunk tank. I explained the plan to George.

"I think I'm getting through to him," George said. "That is, when he's quiet. If he's agitating his cellmates, forget it."

Jeremi vented his anger from time to time by complaining about one of the other's personal habits, but luckily they all pretty much ignored him. Jeremi muttered to himself about needing a drink.

When Jeremi was pitching a fits, George was silent. When Jeremi finally got quiet, George coached, "Jeremi, you know you're big in trouble. You need someone to throw you a life-line. It may seem to you like nobody is there for you, but there's plenty of people and angels who are on your side. We all want to see you get well. You need to get off this poison. You need to sober up and stay sober! You have a son coming. I know you want him to grow up knowing the real you." A tear formed in Jeremi's eye. George's voice softened. Jeremi's closed his eyes and drifted off to a shallow sleep.

"I'll be right back," George said and he went into Jeremi's dream. Jeremi reached out and looked like he was holding on to something. George reappeared.

"What did you do?" I asked.

"I threw him a life-line. It said Hope on it. When Peter gets here, I want that image to be fresh in his mind."

There was still plenty of time to pass before Peter could arrive. So, while Jeremi slept, I needed to understand what happened with Henry. As usual, George knew what was on my mind.

"Are you ready to talk about Henry?"

"Why, yes I am. However did you know?" I replied glibly. He ignored my tone. So I went on, "How could he quit like that? How could he just walk away? When we're closer now than ever to a breakthrough."

"What you need to understand, Martin," George began, "is that there is a terrible battle going on. Evil is constantly trying to overtake the good in the world. There are battles going on everywhere, all the time. Angels need to feel useful. The battle must be continually fought or we will lose good people to the void. Henry felt useless. He's tried to get through to Jeremi and he's tried for many things over many years. Sometimes people lose their angels. Some people can do something so offensive to their angel that their angel in good conscious have to leave. This has been building up for so long, today Jeremi hit the woman who is carrying his baby. That was his breaking point. And unless he turns his life around, he'll probably never get another angel."

"So what's going to happen to him now, angel-wise? Who'll be there to look over him?"

"Nobody, and nobody will again unless he gets back on the right track and earns back the privilege of being guarded by an angel. There are a lot of angel-less people out there, Martin."

"There's gotta be another answer!"

"It's up to Jeremi now..." George tried to comfort me.

The guard opened the door and called. "Jeremiah Harper."

Jeremi was still asleep. As the guard called him a second time, both George and I yelled in Jeremi's ear. He sat up confused and groggy.

"You Jeremiah Harper?"

"Uh huh." He wavered a little getting up, but George steadied one arm and I the other.

"You've been bailed out, buddy; let's go." The guard let Jeremi out and closed the cell door behind him.

Jeremi looked around, saw a clock. It was two in the morning. "It's about time she got here," he sputtered.

The guard heard what he said and asked, "She?"

Peter was there waiting for him. When Jeremi saw Peter he stopped in his tracks. "I thought Jeannie'd be here."

"She handled it. I'm here," Peter emphasized Jeannie's exact words. "Sit down, we need to talk." He motioned for Jeremi to sit next to him and the guard took his seat at the desk. Jeremi sat down.

"What?" Jeremi said impatiently. "Let's get out of here."

"We've got to talk before I take you anywhere," Peter said. Jeremi gave him his attention. "You know I love you." He nodded and got Jeremi to nod back. "But--"

"I knew there had to be a 'but.' Cut to the chase, man," Jeremi snapped.

"Okay." Peter took a moment and rethought what he needed to say. "This is the deal: I've made a reservation for you at the Hope Center. If I bail you out, that's where I'm taking you."

"If?!" Jeremi repeated in disbelief, with a hint of panic.

"That's right, 'if.' If you refuse to do this, then you get to keep your happy behind in jail! If you choose jail, you'll detox here because by the time you see the judge, it'll be tomorrow morning. I doubt that anyone's gonna serve you a beer breakfast in your bunk!" Peter's tone was very firm.

"Then he's looking at least 60 days," the guard said.

"What did you say?" Jeremi asked the guard.

"I said, '60 days.'" Jeremi and Peter looked at him, waiting for him to explain. "The judge he's seeing is on a personal quest to rid the world of alcoholics. A drunk driver killed her sister. She'll sentence you to at least sixty days for the level of booze you had in your blood. Throw an open container on top of that, you're looking at least four, maybe six months. Your only hope is to detox voluntarily." The guard leaned back in his chair and put his arms behind his head and rocked.

"I guess that's the only choice I have." Jeremi snapped at Peter. "This sucks."

"Then is that where we're going?" Peter asked.

"I guess I'm stuck," Jeremi conceded, angrily.

The guard gave Jeremi and Peter both papers to sign. He told Jeremi where to wait to have his belongings returned to him; both Peter and Jeremi went there. They stood in line for a moment, then Peter abruptly returned to the officer's desk.

"Where is this officer?" Peter asked of another guard standing nearby. "I'd like to thank him for his help with my brother." Peter pointed at the piece of paper which was just signed, to help this new guard discern who he was talking about.

The other guard looked at the paper and said, "Oh, he's gone. He left a couple of hours ago."

Peter stood there, perplexed. He looked around and tried to regain his bearings, making sure he was in the right place. He looked back at the paper, the guard's name was clearly written on it. Jeremi waved at Peter to let him know he was ready. Peter left, scratching his head and looking over his shoulder, still trying to sort it all out.

I looked at George, who had on a huge cheesy grin. "Tell me you recognize an angel when you see one."

"Of course!" I said, but he knew he got me good that time.

"I love it when a plan comes together!" George laughed.

We joined a confused Peter and a reluctant Jeremi as they walked silently out to Peter's car.

23

The drive to the Hope Center was just as silent and still. Jeremi hung his head. When they arrived in the parking lot and brought the car to a stop, Jeremi was still in the same position.

"It'll be all right, bro," Peter comforted him.

Jeremi grumbled. Peter got out, went around and opened Jeremi's door for him.

"All right, all right," Jeremi snapped at Peter.

"C'mon, bro, they're waiting for you," Peter said. Jeremi looked up, surprised at that statement.

They walked slowly into the facility. Peter tried to put his hand on his brother's shoulder, but Jeremi shrugged it off. Peter stopped at the front desk to ask directions. The lady pointed and they followed a corridor in the direction she indicated. They went through a doorway and sat down in a waiting area.

"This is messed up!" Jeremi complained to Peter. "Get me outta here. I can quit drinking by myself. Give me a chance."

"Do you want to take your chances with the judge the guard talked about?"

"I bet you put him up to saying that."

They walked the rest of the way in silence. Once Jeremi had had enough quiet, he went on the offensive again.

"This is all Jeannie's fault. If she just come into the pub, sat down and listened to my explanation, none of this would've happened," Jeremi vented.

Peter looked at him in complete disbelief. "You mean if she'd've just believed your lies one more time... Blaming other people for your mistakes, will keep you right where you are man, stuck. You were the one behind the wheel. It was only a matter of time before you were stopped and you know it."

"I'm out of here," Jeremi said and stood up.

"Mr. Harper," a nurse called, right as Jeremi stood up. Jeremi froze in his tracks.

"It's your choice, my brother. Let booze screw up your life more than it has already--or get rid of the demon that has control of you. What do you think your future son or daughter would want you to do?" Peter spoke very softly. "What would Dad want you to do?"

Jeremi stared Peter down. George, William and I prayed hard that those thoughts would make a difference and Jeremi would turn around.

"Mr. Harper," the nurse called again.

Jeremi turned and went to sit at the admitting desk. When Jeremi's back was turned, Peter raised his eyes and clasped his hands together and mouthed the words, "Thank you."

They went through the typical admission questions, statistical information: height, weight, age, etc. Peter filled out another form quietly behind him, a form on his impressions of Jeremi's problem. Jeremi was asked to fill out the same form. His answers differed significantly from Peter's. However, I suppose that was pretty common for this situation.

Peter was informed about the rules regarding contact, they will be denied contact for three to five days, depending on his progress. They also gave him a list of necessities; like clothes, pajama's, etc. that he would need to bring to the unit for him.

He told Jeremi, "See ya, bro. I'll be praying for you."

Jeremi grumbled some more as they led him into the unit.

"He'll be just fine," the nurse assured Peter as he watched Jeremi go.

"I sure hope so," Peter said.

A nurse led Jeremi to a room and gave him a gown, pajama bottoms and slippers and asked him to change. He went behind a curtain and came out in the pajamas. She took his clothes and put them in a bag and put it by the door. Jeremi swore under his breath. The nurse told him to lie down on the bed and she took his vital signs. He was a rude, uncooperative patient. George and I watched and shuddered as each new request was made. It got to be funny after a while, to every one but Jeremi. Jeremi asked for a cigarette and the nurse promptly slapped a nicotine patch on his arm.

"You rest, I'll be back in and check on you in a little bit," she said and took the bag of his clothes and left.

Jeremi laid down, but he was stiff as a board because he was so tense. He kept grumbling. "Rest, ha! You stick yourself in this bed and try to rest. This sucks." He replayed the night's events in his head and tried to figure out who to blame for his predicament. "All I wanted to do was have a nice night out, but she had to get all up in my face about drinking and Karla. If we were married, that'd be different. Hitting her was wrong, I know and that cop, where did he come from? I was set up. I get harassed everywhere I go. Then this crap, he's my brother, he should've bailed me out and let me handle my own business. I could quit if I wanted. Problem - ha. This place is the problem!"

"Hey man, shut up!" an agitated voice came from the bed by the window. "Some of us are actually trying to sleep here!"

"Leave the new guy alone." A much more pleasant voice came from the bed right beside him. "Hey, new guy, if you're gonna blame everyone else in the world but yourself for your situation, would you be a little quieter, please?"

"Blame everyone el--" Jeremi was incensed. "Like you would know!"

"You'd be surprised," the pleasant man continued.

"What's that supposed to mean?" Jeremi demanded.

"Paranoia is normal, friend, just relax. We've all been where you are. We know what you're going through. You'll figure that out soon enough," the pleasant one explained.

"Oh yeah, do you want to come over here and say those things?" Jeremi tried to sound tough, which cracked the other two up. Through their laughter, Jeremi protested bitterly, "Yeah, well, did you guys just get dumped here by people who supposedly care about you?"

"You'd be surprised," the pleasant man repeated.

"Yeah, well, maybe you idiots wanted to be here, but I've got better things to do. Come morning, I'm out of here."

"You'd be surprised," they said in unison and laughed again.

"That's enough!" Jeremi whipped down his sheets and jumped out of bed, like he was going to take someone on. Neither of the other men moved a muscle.

"C'mon, friend, you've probably already done enough things you regret for one night. My guess is that you have a list about a mile long already," the pleasant man said.

"Whatever they told you, they're making a big deal outta nothing," Jeremi insisted.

"Of course," the one who was agitated said under his breath.

"And by the way, nobody told us anything," the pleasant one continued. "Like I said, we've all been where you are. Now would you please lay back down? We've got group in the morning."

"You might have 'group' in the morning, but I'll be gone by then." Jeremi dug himself a deeper hole.

"Like as not, friend, you'll be *gone* in the morning. But we need our sleep, so can you keep it down? Please?" the pleasant man concluded.

Jeremi got back in bed, still tense, but stayed silent.

The nurse came back every hour and checked on all the people in the room. Jeremi watched her like a hawk the first couple of times she did. In between nurse visits, George and I tried to talk to Jeremi to get him to calm down.

We also got to know the pleasant-voiced gentleman's angel, Claude, who was in the room with Jeremi. The man's name was Don. Don had been here over a week and would be going home in a couple of days. He was making very good progress. The other man in the room, whose name was Tony, was angelless. He'd been here about two days. Claude said that he was doing all right, but all had hoped he'd do better. There were angels that came and checked on him, but none that stayed very long. They were his children's angels. Tony had been sent here by court order. Don had been brought here by his wife and grown son.

Apparently, the unit tried to stagger the roommates, so that the new ones were put into rooms with ones that were working the program already, as extra support for what they were going through. Claude told us that when Don first came in, the experienced one in the room was an incredible help to him, especially the first few days, so he feels a great need to pass that on. Luckily, Jeremi will be the recipient of that payback.

Jeremi drifted off to sleep, finally. He still fought his sleep battles. The nurse made her third round to check on them. Jeremi's hand started to twitch noticeably, then vibrate constantly. Then his other hand did, too. "It's the beginning of the DTs," Claude told us. The nurse was on hourly rounds and she'd just been here. So, Claude pushed the nurse call button on Jeremi's bed.

"They're gonna notice--" I began to protest.

"Relax," Claude stopped me short. "Too much will be going on, too many ways that could've been pushed and nobody'll care."

Jeremi shook all over and he cried out in his sleep. Claude joined George and I in a prayer for this phase of withdrawal to pass quickly and without injury to Jeremi or anyone else. We prayed hard, while we kept him from falling out of bed and smacking guardrails with his head, hands and feet. Jeremi made enough noise that Don woke up and rushed to Jeremi's aid, first pressing his nurse call-button. Almost immediately, two nurses rushed in. One stayed and started shouting instructions to Don. Anything she said to do, we tried to help Don do. The second nurse came back with a syringe and once they had both stabilized one of Jeremi's arms, she administered the injection. Almost at once his tremors decreased, until eventually he lay there still, save for the occasional twitch. One of the nurses stayed with him for several minutes and monitored his vital signs. Don got back in bed and watched Jeremi from there and eventually fell back to sleep. Claude, George and I heaved a collective sigh of relief and sat down next to Jeremi on the bed.

"I hope the worst is over," I said to George.

"Hardly," Claude said. "He's still got a long road ahead."

George and I heaved that same sigh again. We continued to pray for him the rest of the night. Pearl came to check on us and promised to pray for us. William did the same. Word had gotten to Glory that he was here and Naomi checked in on us, too, and left with our prayers on her heart as well. The battle had begun, but we had prayer warriors on our side.

Morning came and Jeremi was still asleep, although it was more peaceful right after the shot, but at least the flailing had stopped. He moaned mostly. The occasional word came out, but it never made any sense. "Do you think we should go into his dream?" I asked George.

"He's too far out of it to. Maybe later."

The nurse came to wake Don and Tony for their morning routine. They took turns getting themselves ready in the bathroom. She checked on Jeremi and took his vital signs again. She patted him on the hand, as if he could hear her and said, "You hold on, honey; we'll pull you through this."

The angel with her looked back and gave us a wink. "Keep praying," she encouraged us.

The other men went to their therapy sessions and Jeremi was left alone, save the hourly nurse visit. The nurse's angel, Constance, was a great help, explaining the situation to us. She told us how exhausting the withdrawal was for his body, DTs and all. Couple that with very little sleep the night before and nobody expects him to wake much before dinnertime.

It was three o'clock when he finally began to stir. He woke up groaning and moving very slowly. He looked around at his surroundings and seemed to remember where he was and groaned even louder. I went to see if Constance could bring her charge back into the room. She did.

"I had a feeling you'd be stirring about now," the nurse said to Jeremi. Constance winked at us again. "How are you feeling?"

"Like crap," Jeremi groaned.

"That's pretty typical," the nurse continued. "You did some serious dancin' last night. We had to give you the potion to settle you back down. You might be a little sore today." Jeremi groaned again. "I'll go get you something for the pain." Jeremi's expectant eyes met hers. "Just aspirin, that's all you need." He groaned again.

She left briefly and came back with a cup of water and two pain relievers. She helped him sit up and he took the pills. "Drink it all," she instructed him. Which he did, but very slowly.

"Are you hungry?" she asked while she took his vital signs, but Jeremi shook his head. "Are you strong enough to get out of bed?" She helped Jeremi sit up. "Let's start small. How's about you go wash your face and do whatever else you might need to do by now." Jeremi slowly dragged himself to the bathroom and closed the door. "I'm right here if you need anything," she said and knocked on the door lightly.

When Jeremi emerged, she asked, "Feel better?" Jeremi nodded. "Well then, let's catch up with your group session." The nurse held the door, but Jeremi sat back down on the bed and stared at her with a look of disbelief. He and his hard head went back to bed. She stood there at the open door, still being very pleasant about it.

George and I decided to take control. Jeremi sat very close to the edge of the bed, with his arms crossed. It would be easy to put him off balance. So I suggested to him that he cross his legs. As he picked the one leg up off the floor to cross the other, George kicked him in the behind. He fell off the bed and landed on the floor. I was there to break his fall. The only thing that really got hurt was his pride.

The nurse laughed lightly. Constance, George, and I, did laugh out loud. The nurse came over and helped him up, which he tried to fend off. So we kept him down until he decided to accept her help. Once she got him up, she hooked her arm in his and walked him out the door.

Down the hall, in a large open room, "group" was underway. Jeremi and the nurse quietly came in through the back door. He tried to bolt once, but the nurse held tight. There was plenty of room on a couch near the center of the room, so the nurse directed Jeremi there. He sat down, his arms crossed and very tense. She went over and talked to the group leader. I listened, but she just told him his name, the fact that he was there for alcohol detox and that he had just awakened for the first time since experiencing the DTs. He acknowledged and she left.

There were nearly twenty people in the room watching a video. Some in street clothes, like Don, some in pajamas like Jeremi. Claude came over to see us. He explained that one could tell how long someone had been there or how well they were doing by their clothes. The new ones and the troublemakers were in the pajamas. Getting to put their street clothes back on was a privilege they had to earn.

The video they watched was about relationships and how devastating an addiction is to the "other person." It made the point, very graphically, that "I'm only hurting myself" is a tremendous lie. Jeremi chose to watch the ceiling instead of the video. He looked around the room and scoped it out. With the exception of the group leader, who acknowledged him, he looked away quickly if anyone else tried to make eye contact with him.

When the video ended, the leader introduced Jeremi as the newest member of their group and explained the rules of the group to him: Basically, they only participated if they wanted to. The group discussed the video and its parallels to their own lives. They told sad stories about how their relationships with everyone from their parents, to their spouses, to their kids, to their bosses, to their neighbors had been affected adversely. Jeremi sat there quietly with his arms crossed. It seemed like he actually listened every now and again. Don and Tony occasionally contributed to the conversation.

"It's okay if he's quiet during his first group session. He's very tired and he's feeling sick in body and spirit right about now. Take heart, his participation will pick up soon," Claude explained to us.

After the session ended, there was a dinner gathering in the back half of the room. Several of the group members' families came in. The hospital served up a buffet-style dinner of sandwich meats, breads, fruit and cheeses and punch, lots of punch and water. Almost everyone in the group converged at the back of the room to meet their visitors. Don stayed behind. Jeremi just sat there.

"Hey, you're looking better," he greeted Jeremi.

Jeremi gave him a blank stare.

"Last night, in the room. I'm your roommate," Don explained.

Jeremi continued to stare at him blankly.

"That's okay, friend. You were actually pretty out of it when you came in. Let me introduce myself to you now. My name is Don, we're roommates." He extended his hand. Jeremi kept his arms folded, but wiggled a few fingers to acknowledge Don. "Well, I'm going to go eat. I'll be seeing you around. If you want to talk just let me know." Don joined the others in the back. Jeremi turned his back on Don as he walked away. Don took it in stride.

"Let's let him see how silly he looks," Claude suggested. "Get him to look at me." George and I got to work.

Since Jeremi's back was turned to him, Claude made himself visible, only to Jeremi, however. Claude sat in the chair at the end of the couch. George and I cast our angel light onto Claude. George tapped Jeremi on the shoulder. Jeremi, being the stubborn soul he is, refused to turn around. So I called, "Hey, Jeannie!" in a voice only Jeremi could hear.

Whether it was the name I called or the sound of my voice, it worked and he did turn around. Then Claude caught his eye. Claude had decked himself out in identical pajamas to Jeremi and sat in the exact same position as Jeremi and had the same expression on his face. Jeremi sneered at Claude. Claude sneered at Jeremi. Jeremi crossed his legs away from Claude and stared away in a different direction, so did Claude. Occasionally, Jeremi would look back over his shoulder to see if Claude was still watching him. Every time he did, Claude did whatever Jeremi did. They both jerked back away from each other. Finally Jeremi had taken all he could stand, got up quickly and joined the others in the back of the room, to get away from his mirror. When he got to the back of the room, where the rest of the people were, he looked back in the last place he had seen Claude, who was gone. Jeremi looked all around trying to figure out where Claude could have gotten to.

To anyone else watching him, his behavior was completely bizarre. "You okay, friend?" Don tapped on his shoulder.

"Get away!" Jeremi whipped around, but he stopped himself when he realized it was Don behind him. "Sorry, I thought you were someone else."

"Who?"

"That wierd guy in the ugly pajamas," Jeremi said, then he looked down at himself and apparently realized he had the same ones on. Don gave him a very concerned look. "I just want to go back to the room."

"Have you eaten anything?"

"What I want is a drink."

"There's water and punch over there."

"You know what I mean."

"I do know, and that's why there's still water and punch over there," he repeated with the exact same inflections.

Jeremi gave him a dirty look. "I'm going back to the room," he announced and started to leave.

"Hold on, friend."

"What for?" Jeremi snapped.

"For your escort. People in pajamas have to have escorts in the hallways. I'll get you one." Don left. Jeremi threw his arms up in disbelief and frustration. He took this time to look around again, even under things, to find Claude.

Don returned with the group's leader. "This gentleman wants to go back to his room."

"Shall we?" the leader asked and swept his arms in a graceful manner in the direction Jeremi needed to go. He had an angel. He rode small on his shoulder. Jeremi and the leader left.

"Are you tired?" the leader asked Jeremi.

"I'm tired, pissed off and really want a drink."

"That's pretty common," the leader said. "Especially on your first day."

"This place is a trip."

"It's meant to be anything but that," the leader joked with him.

"I'm sure."

"My name is Bill," the leader said pleasantly.

"Jeremi Harper." They came up on the room. "Can we just keep on walking? I feel like crap. I'd rather walk than sleep right now."

"Let's keep on then." They walked on in silence around the corner and down the hall. Bill pointed out a solarium where nobody else was. "Do you want to sit?"

Jeremi nodded.

They both sat down, Bill in an oversized chair, and sat back and relaxed. Jeremi sat in the middle of the couch, close to the edge and held his head in his hands.

"Does your head hurt?" Bill asked.

Jeremi nodded. Then shook his head. He glanced at Bill. "I just feel really sick and strange."

"You're in a transitional stage, somewhere between figuring out if you can admit you have a drinking problem, doing something about it and denying responsibility for everything that has happened to you lately," Bill said gently.

"Denying what! They stuck me here." Jeremi said defensively.

"Okay. I was just like you on my first day - mostly just pissed off." Bill spoke very softly. Jeremi looked up, slightly shocked. "That's right, I'm an alcoholic. I've been sober for eight great years now," Bill said reassuringly.

"I figured all you psycho-babble types were book learners."

"Once I got sober, I went back and finished school. I got my counseling certificate and I started to help the people who wanted out. I could relate to where they had been and I knew how they were feeling. This is the best job in the world for me, it helps me remember where I came from," Bill confided. "Tell me your story, Jeremi. Where did you come from and how did you come to join us here at 'Hope'?"

"It's just a big misunderstanding, really. I'm here because this cop convinced my brother that it would help my case."

"DUI?" Bill asked. Jeremi looked down, but nodded in the affirmative. "What did you blow?" Bill asked.

"Point one four," Jeremi mumbled.

"It was point one seven," George whispered to me.

"I believe it." Bill's angel came to join us and we introduced ourselves and he introduced himself to us. "My name is Bill, too, Bill Senior. Bill's my son."

"Jeremi is my son, too," I told him.

"Are you his angel?" Bill Sr. asked me.

"Momentarily," I answered.

"I see," Bill Sr. said.

Bill Jr. let Jeremi vent. He told Bill Jr. all about the events that led up to his being brought here last evening. He left out some critical events of the evening however, like knocking Jeannie down and the fact that he'd had an open container in the car. The yarn that Bill Jr. heard was definitely told through Jeremi's brandy-colored glasses.

"I hope Bill Jr. can tell the difference between the truth and this manure. Jeremi's shoveling. If Bill's even getting half the story, I'd be amazed."

"He can tell," Bill Sr. answered. "Watch Billy's fingers." Bill Jr.'s hands were folded in his lap, so I went over and looked over his shoulder. Sure enough, Bill Jr. counted as Jeremi told his story. Almost every time Jeremi said something that either was a half-truth or was an outright lie, Bill Jr. scored another one. He caught almost all of them. I waas impressed.

"Billy simply lets them talk themselves into realizing their problem. Right now, he's gauging how far he has to go based on how many lies or denial of responsibilities he can see," Bill Sr. explained.

"How do you think he's doing?" I asked Bill Sr. eagerly, hoping for a positive read.

Bill Sr. shook his head and said, "Billy's got his work cut out for him this time." I looked down, but Bill Sr. put his hand on my shoulder and continued, "Martin, this is going to be hard, you need to know that, but I can feel the prayers around Jeremi; that alone will carry him a long way. He'll find that he can draw strength from those prayers and without even knowing how he's doing it. I take it you and George'll be here, plus he's got my Billy working on him. I think he's going to make it, regardless how long that road is."

"Thanks," I said. I needed a little pep talk.

"So that's it. He left and dumped me here," Jeremi concluded. He watched Bill Jr. intently. I think he was trying to figure out if Bill Jr. believed him or not. Bill Jr. nodded as if in agreement with Jeremi. So Jeremi relaxed a little.

"So, it's because she was reading a pamphlet, that now you're here," Bill Jr. said.

"Exactly!" Jeremi said emphatically and apparently amazed he'd fooled Bill Jr. so easily. I looked over at Bill Sr. in disbelief. Bill Sr. smiled slyly and pointed back to the action.

"Or you could say, it's because Karla showed up, now you're here. That works too, right?" Bill Jr. continued.

"You got it," Jeremi agreed, wholeheartedly.

"And because that cop caught you driving drunk with an open container, that now here." Bill Jr. smiled ever so slightly. "And if your brother could have just trusted you to handle your own business, you'd be in your own bed right now," Bill concluded.

"You do understand!" Jeremi was practically cheering.

"Yeah, I understand. I understand perfectly." Bill Jr.'s tone changed and he stood up in front of Jeremi and stared him down. "I understand that you refuse to take responsibility for storming out of your girlfriend's apartment in a rage because she was trying to get information on how to help you." Jeremi's jaw dropped. "I understand that you refuse to take responsibility for a confrontation between yourself and two women you had been romancing at the same time." Jeremi's eyes got really big. "I understand that you refuse to take responsibility for driving after you had been drinking." Jeremi stood up. "Sit down!" Bill commanded and Jeremi complied, but his face filled with rage. "I understand that you refuse to take responsibility for anything. Well, Jeremi, let me tell you, it's your choice. Right now is where the rubber meets the road. Either you can choose to start taking responsibility for the choices you make in life and get sober or you can leave and continue on the path to self-destruction, which believe me buddy, for you is just around the corner. The door's right there." Bill took a dramatic pause, but never lost eye contact with Jeremi. He softened, "It's your choice, Jeremi, life or death. For your sake, I hope you choose life. You only get to stay if you *really* choose life are serious about getting sober. If you intend to waste my time by being someone who'll jerk me around, there's the door. Go enjoy jail and all the rest of the problems that are about to crash around your feet as soon as you leave this building. I have too many people who are serious about getting well." Bill walked calmly out of the room. Before the door closed, he said, "I hope I see you tomorrow."

Frankly, I was as dumbfounded as Jeremi. "Why did he do that?" I asked George. Bill Sr. had left with Bill Jr. "He's all alone here; he'll bolt like a frightened horse."

George sat down next to Jeremi, who still stared straight out into space, completely taken by surprise by Bill Jr.'s turnaround. George coached him. "It has to be your choice, Jeremi. You've just been told that you have to make the choice to stay. Your destiny is in your hands. Let's change it forever, for the better. Take hold of that life-line." Jeremi's fingers looked like they might've tried to grab at something. "Hold that life-line tight." Jeremi clenched his fist. "That's right. Hold tight."

"All angels within the sound of my voice, pray with us," George called out. "God, help us now! Let your hand be on him now as he makes this decision. Grace us with your healing presence."

The room began to radiate a wonderful light. Jeremi saw it, too; he sat on the edge of the couch and he lifted his face to Heaven. The Lord stood right in front of Jeremi and touched him on the forehead. Jeremi looked right through Him. I could tell he only saw the light.

After the Lord touched him, Jeremi dropped to his knees, still with his face lifted up. "They're all right, I am lost. I'm so confused. Help me, Jesus!" Jeremi cried.

The Lord spoke directly to Jeremi's heart. The Lord stroked his head and chill bumps appeared all over Jeremi. "Jeremi, you know the way. Follow the light of love and you will never be lost. I will carry you when you are too weak to do it alone. You will feel my love for you when you are lonely. You will be healed if only you ask."

Then the Lord looked at George and me. "Be strong, my angels." He left and the light eventually faded.

Jeremi fell off his knees and readjusted himself, sitting on the floor. He leaned against the couch and stared into space. His look was deep and troubled. He rubbed his arms where his chill bumps had been. Jeremi sat there for about half an hour, with the same soul-searching look on his face, then he got up and went back to his room.

He knelt by the side of his bed and prayed aloud. "Jesus, I need your help. I want to get sober. Please Lord, please help me. In your name, I pray. Amen." Jeremi got up off his knees and climbed into his bed and soon fell asleep. For the first time since I'd died, he slept peacefully. He'd finally fought off all those demons. His heartfelt prayer chased them all away.

George told me to tell the other angels our good news; he'd stay with Jeremi and summon me, if need be. I left to thank Glory, Naomi, Sarah, Grandmama, Pearl, Jeannie, Edwina, Marie, Peter and William and all the rest of the angels and people who prayed for us.

I spent the night with Glory afterward. I told her everything that was going on. When morning came, I went back to the hospital. Pearl was there with George. She'd told him the story of Jeannie's day yesterday. She repeated it for my benefit.

"Her friend Anne decided to whisk her off to the border town casino for the night. It was about a two-hour drive. They talked a lot on the way and Jeannie cried a lot. When they got there, they played roulette for a little bit. Jeannie's ,mind was elsewhere, too much downtime between spins, too much time to think about her situation. So they decided to take in a show, with a young comedian who made them both laugh. That was really good for them. When Jeannie was ready to leave, she pretty much had a smile on her face, but on the way out of the casino she stopped short and told Anne she wanted to try something. She took a silver dollar she'd won at the roulette table and put it in the last machine before the door. As she put the money in, she said, 'I need a crib for the baby' --she was having trouble budgeting a crib in between now and the end of the month. The lights on the machine started flashing. Jeannie realized she'd won something, but was having a dickens of a time trying to figure out what. She won a hundred dollars. The crib she wanted cost ninety-two dollars.

"Since there was plenty in her reserves, we gave her the needed boost. It was Robin's idea, but we made it happen. She and Anne are going out to buy the crib today."

"So you and Anne are keeping her mind off her problems here with Jeremi?" I asked.

"We're trying," Pearl said.

"What are her reserves?"

"Heaven keeps track of your giving, your generosity," Pearl explained. "If you give a lot, Heaven allows you to receive a lot. The converse also being true, when you take, you are taken from. The reserves or the debt, is what we call it. When we want to do something extra-special for our charges, we need to check the reserves. If it is enough to win the lottery, that'd be great, but if your charge is generous, then there are extra rewards in Heaven and on Earth. Jeannie gave away all her baby furniture to needy people after she got her divorce. Much of what she has now for the baby has been given to her, now that she's in need. She never expected all the help she's received and is amazed at the generosity extended to her, but since she gave it away first, it's been returned to her. It's simply how it works."

I really did know that, but to learn that there was an actual system in place that dealt was fascinating.

Jeremi started to stir.

"I'll let you gentlemen get back to your work now. I'll be praying for you," she said.

"We'll be praying for you, Jeannie and the children likewise," George said.

Pearl left.

Jeremi sat up in the bed and rubbed his eyes. He looked around to get his bearings. He rubbed his arms like he'd done the night before, remembering, I think, what had given him his chill bumps last night. He got out of bed and went to the window to look out. He took a deep breath.

He stood there for a few minutes, then the nurse and Constance came in to wake everyone for the day. "You're looking better today," the nurse told Jeremi quietly.

"Yeah," Jeremi said.

"Are you hungry yet?"

Jeremi thought for about half a second, then he said, "Yeah."

"I'm glad to hear that. Breakfast will be in a few minutes."

"Good," Jeremi said.

The nurse smiled, I think surprised to hear such a pleasant tone out of the man she'd had to wrestle up off the floor yesterday. "You'd be smart to get into the bathroom and freshen up before I wake up your roommates."

Jeremi went right in, with a noticeable little spring in his step. The nurse shook her head in disbelief at the changes.

Constance told us how happy she was for his transformation. The nurse woke up Don and Tony and then left. When Jeremi came out of the bathroom, Don was waiting to go in. "Good morning, friend," Don said.

"Yes, it is. Don? Right?" Jeremi said. "I'm Jeremiah, call me Jeremi." Jeremi extended his hand.

Don nodded and took the opportunity to shake the hand that had been refused him the night before. "This is Tony." Don pointed over to the bed.

"Hey, man." Tony waved from the bed.

"Hey," Jeremi replied.

Don went into the bathroom and Jeremi sat on the edge of his bed. "So what are we supposed to be doing?" Jeremi asked Tony.

"We'll go to breakfast, then group, then lunch, then group, then counseling, then dinner, then group. Then tomorrow, we do it all over again," Tony said in a dry, monotone voice.

"Okay," Jeremi said hesitantly detecting Tony's negative tone.

"Next," Don said cheerfully on his way out of the bathroom. Tony took his turn. Don put some things away in the dresser by the bed and asked Jeremi, "Are you ready for breakfast?" Don went to the door and held it for him.

"Do you want to wait for Tony?"

"He knows his way," Don assured him. Jeremi shrugged his shoulders and left with Don. They went down the hallway into the cafeteria. Both Don and Jeremi loaded up their trays with breakfast food, fruits, cereals, toast and juices. Jeremi started out ravenously, but quickly maxed out.

"What's up with this?" he asked Don, "I was so hungry. But if I eat another bite, I think I'll get sick."

"Happens," Don said chewing his toast. "You're really used to drinking your meals." Jeremi looked down, like that statement embarrassed him. "It's okay--that's how we all were."

Jeremi looked back at Don, surprised. "Nobody understood me ever before in my life..." Jeremi just stared at him.

"Man, we all understand. We've all been there and some are still there. That's why you're here. If it's any consolation, I only ate about half of what you just did at my first meal. But now look at me." Don stuffed the rest of his toast in his mouth and gulped some juice. Then he sat back and patted his stomach. Once he swallowed, he continued, "I've been here nine days now and I think I've gained at least fifteen pounds."

"Is that going to be Jeremi in a few days?" I asked Claude.

"God willing and some hard work."

"That's hard to imagine." I said.

"It's probably hard for Jeremi to imagine that, too."

After breakfast, Don told his story to Jeremi. "About two weeks ago, I decided to take lunch at a bar across from my work, instead of the building's cafeteria. I was having a really bad morning . . . you know, the boss wanted me to work." Jeremi cracked a slight smile. "You know how they can be demanding like that." Jeremi nodded. "Well, I ordered up a burger and a beer. The beer came first, naturally, and it was gone in nothing flat. So I ordered another. Well, it was gone by the time I got the burger, so I ordered another with my meal. Then I decided, what the Hell, let them wait. So I got one more for the road, you know." Jeremi nodded again. "Well, I finally went back to work, about half an hour late. The boss left a note on my desk. He put the time on it, just to let me know that he knew I had taken a long lunch. Well, that just chapped my . . . well, you know. I mean, how dare he want me to come back in on time?" Jeremi cracked another little smile, every time Don's tone got more and more outrageous.

"So I sat there and decided to read this manual, you know, look like I was busy. But it was the most boring thing I'd ever read and the next thing I know, my boss is waking me up by tapping me on the shoulder. He said 'Can I see you in my office, please?'" Jeremi grimaced. "Well, it was my fifth write-up in three months. He fired me, then and there. I grabbed my stuff and went home. I hated telling my wife. I told her what a jerk my boss was, etcetera, etcetera, but she told me she could smell the beer on my breath still. I told her that was because I stopped on the way home, that it had nothing to do with the job. But she knew I was lying. Anyway, I filed for unemployment; it was denied. I decided I'd rather drink than worry about looking for work. So, I sat on the couch and drank beer all day long, starting first thing in the morning and all through until evening.

"My son--he's thirty-five--came for a 'surprise' visit. She'd called him and the next thing I know, I'm a resident here at the Hope Center. It was hard on me being here, especially at first, but it was twice as hard for her to stand up to me like that. That took guts. That took real love. It was the best thing she could've done for me. I'm just sorry I made it so hard for her."

Jeremi listened intently to every word. A bell interrupted their conversation. Don looked at the clock on the wall. "Well, friend, it's time for us to go to group." Jeremi followed Don and put up the dishes. They walked down to the same room they had been in the night before.

"I hope that weird guy's in some other group," Jeremi said to Don.

"There's only one 'group.' What weird guy?" Don asked.

Jeremi tried to talk using his hands, but nothing was coming out. "Never mind," he finally said. When Jeremi entered, he scoped out everyone in the room carefully, but failed to find the "weird guy." Claude was doubled over laughing at Jeremi's expressions. George and I also enjoyed the show..

Don and Jeremi sat on the couch. Some people were already in the room, Tony among them. Some still filtered in from breakfast. By the time everyone got there, there were about eighteen people. Bills Sr. and Jr. came in the room and spied Jeremi right off. Bill Jr. smiled at Jeremi. Jeremi made eye contact with him, and for now, that was enough.

"Well, let's get started today, shall we?" Bill Jr. began. "Let's start with saying the first three steps. Number one."

Many members of the group chanted, "We admit we are powerless over alcohol or drugs, that our lives had become unmanageable." Jeremi took a breath, but stayed quiet.

"Number two," Bill said.

Again they said in unison, "We have come to believe that a Power greater than ourselves could restore us to sanity."

Jeremi rubbed his arm like he had last night and looked up to the sky.

"Number three," Bill said.

"We've made a decision to turn our will and our life over to the care of God as we understand God."

Jeremi nodded slightly and looked down at his hands folded in his lap.

"Okay, good start." Bill was full of enthusiasm. "Last night, we discussed one of the great lies of an addiction. 'That we are only hurting ourselves.' Many of you saw your families last night right after that. Is there anything anyone would like to share?"

A few people looked around the group sheepishly. I think they wanted to share, but were hesitant to go first.

"I do," Don said after there'd been several seconds of awkward silence. "When she got here, I gave Deanna a huge hug and apologized to her for everything. I've apologized before, of course, but it was the first time since I really thought about what life was like for her living with all my lies, temper and bad attitude. I truly hope some day I can make it up to her."

"I know what you mean." A woman across the room spoke up. "When I finally put myself in my daughter's shoes. I could feel how she must've felt because she was embarrassed to have her friends over because I'd always be drunk or drinking. It really hurt."

I watched Jeremi as the discussion went on. His look was distant, but his head turned in the direction of each of the new speakers, so I think he listened to what was said, but his thoughts were somewhere else. I wondered if he thought about people his drinking affected. He might have been thinking about Jeannie or Glory, Peter or Sarah, his first wife, or maybe me. Wherever he was, he was definitely in a better place than a couple of days ago.

The conversation went on for about half an hour. People related how they finally realized they'd really hurt other people, especially those closest to them. Then it diverged into related topics for the rest of the session. Jeremi never did speak up. Claude and Bill Sr. encouraged us about the progress he had already made.

After the session was over, Bill found Jeremi and two other new pajama-clad arrivals and handed them the necessary books and a book bag. There was a big notebook and some smaller books.

"Before our next session, I want you to read the daily inspiration." He took a small book out of Jeremi's bag, found the day's date on a page and showed it to the three. "We'll get you caught up on your assignments later. There will be plenty for you to do and throughout your recovery. These books are yours to keep." Bill patted Jeremi on the back as he left.

The three looked at each other briefly and the man on Jeremi's left mouthed the word "Assignments?" with a slightly panicked look. Jeremi chuckled a little, took his new belongings and sat down on the couch. He started to look through them. He held the daily inspirations book on his lap. Then he briefly rifled through the rest of the bag. He opened the daily inspirational book to today's date:

"When we first come to Recovery, the most common form of self-pity begins: 'Poor me! I should be able to drink just like everybody else! Why me?' Such bemoaning is a surefire ticket right back to the mess we were in before we came. When we stick around Recovery for a while, we discover that being alone in this struggle is a thing of the past--we become involved with people from all walks of life, who are in exactly the same boat. Ask yourself: Am I learning all I can about how others have dealt with their problems so I can apply these lessons to my own life?"

It looked like Jeremi read and reread that passage. Then one by one he looked around the room at the people who had spoken in the last group session. He seemed lost, deep in thought, when Bill called them all back together again.

"So who wants to read today's passage?" Bill asked the group when they reconvened.

A lady across the room did.

"And. . ." Bill encouraged more conversation.

The same lady who had read the passage offered, "When I came here, I felt so isolated, like I was crazy, and that nobody in the world could possibly understand what I was going through. I thought, for some bizarre reason, that I was special, somehow, in my misery. Once I opened up to the process, I realized in a less than a day that this is a disease, with specific symptoms and that runs a specific course, just like the chickenpox. The details in everyone's life may be a little different, but we are all suffering in the same way. It really does help to go through this with people who understand."

There was a little bit of a murmur in the group, mostly of agreement and support for the speaker.

Then Jeremi spoke up, "I've only been here a couple of days,." The murmuring stopped in respect for the speaker. "But I was doing what this quote said, especially the first night I was here, blaming everyone in the world but myself for landing here. But something happened to me the second night I was here, it's hard to describe, but I realized that I wanted to get sober. I came in here and listened to you guys talk and really listened, you know? It's helping me because I can relate to what you're saying and to what you did. I can see myself in those exact circumstances and I-I-I'm learning a lot."

There was more murmuring after Jeremi finished and a couple of "Good for you's."

Claude winked at us and said, "See, I told you." George and I smiled, very proud of Jeremi for this first big leap of faith.

Another voice contributed to the conversation. "I was doing the same thing as. . .what was your name, friend?" he asked.

"Jeremi," he answered.

"I was doing the same thing as Jeremi here did, at first. But when I listened to the other people in the group, especially the ones who'd been here for a few more days than I had, I did finally get it. They made a difference for me. I think they were the difference between life and death-really-I know that sounds dramatic, but it's true. If I were alone in my hospital room, like I imagined places like this to be, I would've just withered away. We need to talk. We need to get it out. We need each other."

This group session continued with lots of people expressing deep gratitude for the fact that they were together in this struggle. Some broke down and cried. Others hugged those who had testified, specifically made a difference to them. Many praised Bill for his candor about his recovery and his subsequent decision to be a counselor. It was a very emotional group session.

When lunchtime came, it seemed that everyone was wiped out, emotionally and physically. They dragged themselves down to the lunchroom for soup and sandwiches. Jeremi ate with Don, Bill, and Eric, the fellow who'd spoken up right after he did. Eric's angel's name was Floyd. After all the introductions, they sat down to eat.

"So what's your story, Jeremi?" Eric asked candidly as he took a bite of his sandwich.

Jeremi looked a little panicked to be put on the spot like that. He shrugged his shoulders, "What do you want to know?"

"Start with how long have you been here?" Eric suggested.

"A couple of days."

"Who brought you here?"

"My brother. My brother, Peter."

"What happened?"

"It was either agree to come here or he go to jail for 60 days or better," Jeremi answered.

"Why were you arrested?"

"DUI."

"First time?" Eric kept going.

"Yup."

"You married?"

"Used to be." Jeremi was playing it very close to the vest.

"Do you have someone now?"

"Maybe, I hope so.."

"Why maybe?"

"Because I messed up. We had a bad fight, a really bad fight."

"Fool around?" Eric asked through his full mouth. Jeremi nodded. "Yikes, that's a tough one. Is anyone pregnant?" Jeremi nodded again. "Which one?"

"Jeannie, the one I care about."

"So you'd go back to her, if she took you back?" Don asked.

"I guess."

"You just said you cared about her," Eric reminded him.

"I do and I care about the baby she's carrying, it's all just a trip." Jeremi paused and the questions ceased for the moment. "She's also got these two adorable little girls. I miss them, too." Jeremi's look grew sad and distant. Then he shook it off. "Whatever, I doubt if she'll ever speak to me again after all that's happened."

"Steps eight and nine will really help you sort that out, Jeremi," Don said.

"You need to get yourself better first, then worry about your relationships. because without sobriety, your relationships will fall apart anyway," Bill cautioned him.

"But there's things I want to tell her," Jeremi said.

"Then you know what you do?" Jeremi shook his head. "Write her a letter," Bill suggested. "An open and honest letter, get everything out you want to say. Get it out of your head and on to paper. Work on it for a few days, then after a few days are over, you'll be in a much better state of mind to make these decisions. You're barely dried-out. You need some time to sort it all out. Take it slow, so you stop hurting yourself and others."

"I'll try. I will really try."

All this talk about Jeannie made me want to go check on her. George promised to stay close to Jeremi and call if he needed me. Claude said he would also back him up. So I left to find Jeannie. I caught up with her and Anne at the mall. They were out crib-shopping, like Pearl had said. Jeannie's eyes were red. I could tell she'd been crying quite a bit. Anne's face was pretty somber too. She cared about her friend very much.

Pearl and Robin welcomed me aboard. "They just bought the crib. They put it in the car already. She actually has a couple of dollars left," Pearl told me.

"How's she holding up?"

"I've heard the words, 'Why me?' a lot today," Pearl said. "She's trying to figure out how things got so far out of her control."

"I have just the ticket. See that curio's shop over there? Direct them in. I'll be waiting," I instructed Pearl and Robin.

I went into the shop and looked around. There was a specific message that I wanted to give Jeannie and I needed to find a way to give it to her. I went to a wall covered with delicately decorated, beautiful bookmarks. There was only one I wanted her to see, the one I just made for her.

As the girls got closer to the shop, I shined my angel light on it. As soon as Jeannie and Anne came in the store, Pearl and Robin shined their angel light on it, too. Both girls came over to the wall. It attracted them like a magnet. Anne scoured the other bookmarks along the wall, without picking a favorite, but Jeannie went straight for my bookmark and read it right away.

Jeannie sighed heavily. "I got my answer."

"Huh?" Anne still scoured the bookmarks and was only giving Jeannie a small portion of her attention.

"Why did we come in here?" Jeannie asked Anne.

"Because you wanted to."

"I know. But I've never been in this shop before. Suddenly, it was like it was the only shop in the mall. It was all I could see." Pearl pointed to herself proudly. "Then we come straight over to this wall." Anne turned to look at Jeannie, knowing there was more to this story. "And out of all these bookmarks on the wall, I really only saw one. So I picked it up." Anne opened her eyes wide in anticipation of the point. "And this is what I read." She showed the bookmark to Anne. Robin and Pearl smiled, as they read it for the first time.

"Trust in the Lord with all thine heart, and release your need to understand. Proverbs."

"You just gave me chills," Anne said.

"Me, too," Jeannie replied. "I guess someone's trying to tell me something."

"So listen already." Anne attempted a Yiddish accent.

Pearl said, "Now stop asking 'Why me?' and start trusting that God is in control."

The look on Jeannie's face changed. She had a faint, peaceful smile. Ever so slight, but it was there. Anne chuckled at her a couple of times in the checkout line.

"So, is that all you're going to get?" Anne asked her.

"Was there something else in this store?" Jeannie joked.

Pearl, Robin and I laughed at that for the rest of the day.

I went with them back to the apartment. It took quite a while and it was quite entertaining to watch them put the crib together. All the women, living and angel, participated in the construction. It was classic. Pearl, Robin, Marie and Edwina helped provide some necessary comic relief during the construction effort. The ladies were fair as carpenters, but it got very interesting at times, especially when Lynne and Carole 'helped.' They eventually got the job done. When it was completed, Jeannie put some crib sheets on it and a bumper pad that had been given to her. The girls each offered a stuffed animal to put in the crib for the baby. Jeannie took the bookmark and hung it on the wall, right at eye-level in the hallway. Now every time she went down the hallway, she could see it, if she started to slide back down the path of doubt.

Jeannie and the baby were doing fine. It was time to return to Jeremi and George. I went back to the Hope Center. When I got there, they had barely finished dinner. It was time for the evening group session.

"Is he eating any better?" I asked when I arrived.

"A little," Claude answered. "It takes a couple of days."

Bill started the group session. "Today we talked a lot about the steps we're going to take to make ourselves better. Tonight we'll be talking about the promises that we're going to be making to ourselves. The first is that 'We are going to know a new freedom and a new happiness.' I think most of you can already taste that new freedom. You are going to control your life from now on. The days of your addiction controlling you are over."

There were a few murmurs in the group.

"Secondly, 'The past is the past and must be accepted as is. Denying the events of the past will only to deepen the wounds suffered in it.' The past will always be there and changing it is impossible. It needs to be seen as merely the path that you were on that led you here. For that, we should be grateful for it. What we choose to do from this moment on will be much more defining to your future than anything you did in your past up to this point."

Again the group quietly murmured, some talked to the ones closest to them.

"Three and four are 'We will comprehend the word serenity' and 'We will know peace.' These promises we will make to ourselves and we will keep them for ourselves. Our lives will be richer, more free, more serene and peaceful. Our lives will turn away from the pain of the addiction to the happiness that comes with sobriety."

The group's murmurs turned into enthusiasm. "Okay, let's talk about this. The first promise is that we are going to know a new freedom and a new happiness. Does anyone have anything to add to this?" Bill asked.

Eric spoke up first. "I do feel freer than I've ever felt before. If you knew where I was just a week ago--my only thoughts were about booze. When was I going to get my next drink? I still think that, but I'm free from letting that control me. I can change my thoughts, and therefore change my life's experience. I call it my new freedom. I can think and concentrate on whatever I want and when, due to force of habit, the thought, 'Where is that next drink coming from' does cross my mind, I'm happy when I realize that that I have a choice and that choice is to live."

"That's very good," Bill said. "Anyone else?" Nobody spoke up, so he continued. "The past is the past and must be accepted as is. Denying the events of the past will only to deepen the wounds suffered in it.' If we regret the path that got us here, we'll be doomed to repeat the lessons of it. We are who we are because we have done what we have done.

"I can embrace that I'm an alcoholic. I am a recovering alcoholic, and because of that, I am here helping you and countless like you. I shudder to think of my life continuing on the way it was going. I am happy that it took the abrupt left turn where it did and now I'm here and my life experiences help me do the job I now love doing. Whatever path you all set out on will be likewise altered. In my case, that was a very positive change. You must also make that choice, release your regrets, the past is the past, but come to the present and take your life on from this day forward, the only way we can, one day at a time."

A woman sobbed uncontrollably in the corner. Her angel tried to comfort her. Another angel appeared, she also wept and wiped the woman's tears away. The weeping angel simply repeated over and over again, "I'm sorry. I'm so sorry." A couple other members of the group, who were close to the woman, put their hands on her to comfort her.

When the woman's sobbing ceased, the weeping angel left. Then the woman spoke out angrily. "How can you say that? I have regrets. I have so many regrets, too many to count! It's because I was so busy drinking, that I missed the warning signs. If It's because I was so drunk, that I was such a lousy mother. I should've been there when she needed me, but I..." she sobbed. The group gathered in around her, when she looked up, she glared at Bill, "Of course, I have regrets, it hurts so much."

"What's happening?" I asked Claude.

"Her daughter committed suicide. The angel who appeared and disappeared, that was her daughter."

I tried to figure this out from the way it was playing out, but I was at a loss.

George took over the explanation from there. "The daughter wiped away the tears that were shed because of her selfishness. We all make it to the other side, Martin. Now that's she's an angel, because she committed suicide, she must wipe away every tear that was ever shed for her. In that way, she has a front row seat and witnesses every bit of agony caused by her selfish selfish action. Suicide is worse when you're on this side."

"Like the angel at the intersection," I said.

"Somewhat," George said. "This one is much harder because the suffering caused was intentional. She can never become a free angel until the last bit of suffering caused by her suicide has passed. In between tears that fall, they work to prevent other suicides. You've heard the stories. The record played on the radio, at exactly the right moment. The DJ saying he changed his mind at the last second, even so far as announcing another record, but playing the one that prevented the suicide instead. Things like that. They work desperately to prevent other people from causing the suffering they caused their families to suffer."

"That's heartbreaking," I said.

Both George and Claude agreed.

The woman was now venting at Bill. "How can you say we must release our regrets?"

Bill spoke very softly and reassuringly to her. "One of the hardest parts of the past to accept it as it is. Release all your 'what-iffing', changing it is impossible. Where we are is where we are. Your situation is particularly tragic, I know that. But trying to figure out which day you should've lived differently will change nothing. Even if you could've figured out the day, the time and place, where's the guarantee the outcome would have been any different? You've got to stop beating yourself up for your loss. You need to grieve and through your grieving, heal. We're all here to help you, if you'll let us."

She began to cry again and her weeping angel daughter appeared again. She disappeared again when the tears stopped.

A few more people shared tragic stories of the horrible happenings while they were drunk. Bill's messages were always the same. "*Respect* instead of regret the past. You must realize that you are who you are because of everything that's happened to you thus far. If there are things that are particularly bothersome, instead of regretting them, try to find a way to make amends for them."

Their assignment for the next morning session was to write down three things that they felt they should make amends for. Jeremi took that assignment very seriously. He only put down the names of the three people with whom he wanted to make amends: Jeannie, Glory and Peter.

That night back in the room, there was a great air of excitement from Don. His wife was going to pick him up the next afternoon. He could go home. The rest of his treatment could be as an outpatient because he'd done so well. The talk in the room was quite excited for most of the night. Even so, Tony came in and went straight to sleep. So Don and Jeremi whispered and kept the conversation going. Don was making plans on what to do with his life as soon as he was back with his wife.

"I'm going to make her a dinner fit for a queen," Don explained. "I love to cook, especially barbecue, so we'll be having the best steaks in town tomorrow night. Then I'll take her out, wherever she wants to go. I'll be so happy to be with her, I'll be thrilled to even go see one of those date movies. I'll just be watching her anyways. It's gonna be so great!"

Jeremi got a distant look in his eye when Don talked about the plans he had.

"Jeremi?" Don asked.

"What?"

"If you could do anything with Jeannie, what would you do?"

"I'd like to know that, too," I said.

"Well, if she'll take me back, the first thing I want to do is make sure she's all right. I'd hold her, just hold her, for as long as she'd let me. Then I'd tell her how sorry I was for all that happened. Then I'd just want to sit somewhere and talk about the baby and our future. I've picked out a name, if it's a boy," Jeremi told Don.

"What's the name?" Don asked.

"Well, I wanted to honor Dad and Sheila with the baby's name. So, I wrote down both names and rearranged the letters until I had something I liked."

"What was your father's name?"

"Martin," Jeremi answered. "So, I took letters from Sheila and Martin and came up with Marshal. With one 'l.'"

"That's nice," Don said. "It honors both people and yet it's his own name. I like that. Did Jeannie have any names picked out?"

"We never talked about it."

"Well, good luck; I hope she likes it. You guys will get back together. I just feel it."

"I hope so."

"You will."

The room quieted down after that. Jeremi drifted off to sleep first, then eventually Don did, too.

"So what are you going to do after the baby is born?" Claude asked George.

That question struck me as bizarre.

"Well, I presume I'll be given another charge and try to do as well with him as I have with Martin here." George smiled at me like a proud father.

"I thought you'd still be with us, for a while at least," I said to George.

"You'll be ready by the time the baby comes, then it'll be my time to go," George said confidently. Suddenly, I felt scared. What would it be like without George at my side?

"Relax, Martin; you'll be fine." Claude reassured me, too.

George, Claude, and I, kept watch all night long. We talked about the futures we felt we had and that Jeremi and Don were going to have.

As we talked, my mind drifted to the recent past. We were close to accomplishing the task at hand, getting Jeremi sober, but the players involved were sometimes surprising.always, like the spoiler, the cop, the crazy guy in pajamas The ones I would have chosen to get the job done would've been much different, if I were to script it. I was having trouble sorting that out.

True to form, George came into my thoughts and said simply, "It takes lemons to make lemonade."

I shook my head and tried to clear my thoughts, in an effort to comprehend what he said. "Lemons?"

"What's in lemonade, Martin?"

"Lemons."

"And?"

I thought for a moment. "Well, there's also sugar and water."

"So how did Jeremi get here?"

"Well, Peter brought him here--"

"Sugar," George said.

"Because he was arrested--"

"Lemon."

"Because he was driving drunk--"

"Lemon."

"Because he and Jeannie had a fight over the spoiler," I finally finished.

"Jeannie is the sugar. Karla is both," George explained.

"What?" I asked, trying to comprehend how something could be both sugar and a lemon at the same time.

"For Jeannie she was a lemon, in that it shook the foundations of their relationship. But for Jeremi she was sugar, because their involvement shook the foundations of their relationship." I did my usual head tilt. So he added. "It was because their relationship was pushed like this, that we had all this drama. It's because we had all this drama, that Jeremi ended up here - this quickly."

"Okay, I get it, the ol' things happen for a reason." I pondered that for a moment, but I still wanted to know one thing. "So what's the water?" I asked.

"Time. Time is what it takes to bring it together. Some people's lemonade is sweet, lots of sugar, few lemons. Others, well, there're more lemons than sugar. Still others have some combination in between and the flavor changes, depending on the time it is in their lives."

"'All things work together for good for those that love the Lord,'" I said, quoting a favorite scripture.

George nodded at me. "The masterplan will always remain a mystery to us, Martin. We're only messengers - in the very literal sense, that is what 'angel' means. So sometimes we get just as many surprises as our charges. It helps us to learn and grow, too. We have more powers and get glimpses into things that are to come, but God holds all the lemons and all the sugar and doles them out at his discretion, but ultimately, they all make lemonade."

I had to agree. I now had a completely different perspective (and label) for the people and situations that had been involved in this struggle. Lemonade! How wonderful!

When morning came, Don got up early and packed his things. He tiptoed around the room. He certainly was excited to be going home. When the nurse came in to wake them up, Don was sitting on the edge of the bed with his suitcase beside him. He smiled like he was keeping a secret.

"I'm going to miss you, Don," the nurse said.

"I'm going to miss you too, Claude," Constance echoed.

"Me, too," Don and Claude said in unison.

The nurse woke Jeremi and Tony. Then as she left, winked at Don. He, in turn, blew her a kiss.

"Did you sleep well?" Don asked Jeremi.

"Pretty good."

"What about you, Tony?" Don asked.

"Yeah, yeah," Tony said rudely as he went into the bathroom.

"I hardly slept," Don said. "I am so ready to get out of here." Jeremi smiled at him. "So when do you get to leave?"

"After afternoon group, just before visiting hours." Don answered.

Tony came out of the bathroom and left for breakfast. Jeremi went in and freshened up. The nurse came in while Jeremi was in the bathroom and put his clean and folded clothes on his bed, as well as another bag of clothes, which I presumed Peter had brought in. She stood there with Don as Jeremi came out of the bathroom; then both she and Don smiled at Jeremi.

Jeremi was clueless as to why they were smiling and checked himself out. "What? Do I have something on my behind?" He looked over his shoulder. Don and the nurse laughed.

Then Jeremi looked over at the bed. "My clothes!" He went over and picked up the shirt and smelled it. "Clean, even. Cool." He looked at the nurse. "You mean I can change into these and out of these nasty PJs?"

"Well, you have to wait until I leave the room first," she said as she nodded. Jeremi put his hand on his hip, tapped his foot impatiently and looked at her, like it was time for her to leave now. "Okay! Okay. I'm going! Congratulations for making street clothes. You're doing great." She left.

"Thank you," Jeremi said graciously after her. He picked up the shirt and smelled it again. "You never know what you got until it's gone. This is my new favorite shirt!"

"Well, you made it part of the way. Now you'll have to make it the rest of the way without me. But you can do it. Just trust in God and believe in yourself and remember your dreams."

Jeremi stopped dressing and made eye contact with Don for a couple of seconds, then he said sincerely, "I will."

"Well, you better. If I have to come back here and whup your behind, I'm gonna be dammed disappointed!"

Jeremi gave him an "Are you serious?" look, and smiled through it all. They both laughed some more. So did we all. It was nice to see this friendship develop.

Jeremi started to rifle through the other bag; it held some more clothes--right on the top was my old letterman's sweater. "I'm glad Peter packed that for him," I said to George.

"You're sure it was Peter?" George asked me.

"Did you do that?" I asked him. He never did answer me. So I watched Jeremi as he pulled it out of the bag and smelled it, too. He clutched it tight to his breast.

"Are you okay, Jeremi?" Don asked, concerned that his demeanor had changed so quickly.

"This was Dad's," Jeremi said to Don. "Do you have any idea how special this sweater is to me?"

"Please tell me why that sweater is so special."

Jeremi put it on over his clothes. "This makes me feel like my dad is here with me, y'know."

"I know." Don consoled him and patted him on the back.

They went off to breakfast.

"George, do you think anyone is coming to see Jeremi tonight at visitation?" I asked as we walked down the hall.

"Well, I'm sure we can arrange it."

I nodded. "Do you want me to go, or you?"

"You go. I'll stay here and take care of Jeremi."

I wanted to check on everybody. Then I'd decide who I'd encourage to visit him. I checked on Glory first; she and Sarah were eating breakfast and talking, Naomi and Grandmama close by. I checked on Jeannie, who was hard at work, typing on her computer--Pearl playfully reminded me to stay in front of her--her friend Judie was working, as well. I went to check on Peter; he and Melinda were talking.

William was there. "Hello, Martin," he greeted me. "How's it going with Jeremi?"

"He just graduated to his street clothes."

"Fantastic!"

"Tonight is visitation. Does Peter know? Is he going?"

"Yes, he knows it's tonight. He's apprehensive about going, though."

"Why not?"

"He's afraid Jeremi might still be angry with him for leaving him there. He'd really rather avoid reliving that night. Peter's problem is that he's oblivious to Jeremi's progress. So the last experience he had of Jeremi is one of anger. To hope for something different, well -"

"I understand that. What do we have to do to change that?"

"I'd guess that if he picked up some of that literature over there, we could make it read pretty good." He pointed to the pile of alcoholism literature that had come in the mail recently.

"It needs to address this specific issue."

"It will."

William and I both shined our angel light on the stack of pamphlets on the counter. Peter finished his conversation with Melinda abruptly because he'd become distracted. He went over to the stack and thumbed through it until he saw a pamphlet headed WHILE THEY'RE RECOVERING -- THE FAMILY'S PERSPECTIVE. Peter picked it up and went straight to the section entitled CURING APPREHENSION THROUGH INVOLVEMENT, which said: "Unless the family is allowed to keep in contact during the first few days of the recovery, the old relationships and situations keep playing in their heads. The actual progress of the individual in therapy is unknown, so their last impression of the alcoholic is the one they usually hold to. This is unfair to the alcoholic in recovery. Whether their progress is quick or slow, their perspective changes with every passing day. The family is an integral part of the healing process and they should be encouraged to be a part of the recovery at every opportunity."

Peter put the pamphlet down and stared at the floor for a bit. Then he announced to Melinda, "I'm going to visit Jeremi tonight."

Melinda looked up from the newspaper she was reading at the table and said, "I thought you were still thinking about it."

"I was, and now I've made my decision."

"What helped you decide?"

"This," Peter said and showed her the pamphlet.

"Where'd that come from?" She got up and took it from him and examined it.

"It was here in the pile," Peter said.

"Hmmm," Melinda said and spread out the pile and thumbed through it probably to see what else she might have missed.

"She's read most of them," William said to me. "I guess I threw her for a loop. Oh well."

Melinda shrugged her shoulders and took the pamphlet from Peter to read it. When she finished she told him, "Good luck. Give him our love."

"I will," Peter said. They were both quiet for a moment. "I better call and find out what time specifically."

"Seven to nine," Melinda told him.

Peter smiled and kissed her. Then he went up to his bedroom. She continued to look at the pamphlet, turned it over, flipped through the pages, then she finally shrugged her shoulders. "I must've missed this one." She put it back on the counter top in the stack from whence it came.

"Good work," I told William.

He grinned. "Well, we'll see you tonight then."

"See you then," I said and left.

When I got back to the hospital, they were in group. They discussed making amends to people, without being specific about who these people were to them, the recoverees were encouraged to share ideas on what to say or how to make up for some of the bad times that had come before. Love was the presiding theme. If the person was still in their lives or they wanted them back in their lives, the message was just to love them.

Jeremi contributed from time to time, and listened, but he was also writing in his book so intensely I thought it must be something incredibly sensitive and personal. When I saw what it was, I was surprised: doodles! He was drawing pictures. However, these pictures were around the names Jeannie, Marshal, Lynne, Carole and Jeremi. It was cute. He made it like a puzzle. When Jeannie and Marshal shared an "A." Lynne and Marshal shared the "L." Lynne and Carole shared the "E" and Carole and Jeremi shared the "R." Then it came back full circle and Jeannie and Jeremi shared the "J."

"That's interesting," George said.

"It certainly is," I said. "All those names fit together like that. Was that part of the plan too?"

George smiled and said, "We need to make sure the baby's name gets to be Marshal."

"With one 'l.'" I said smugly. George snickered.

Group ended and lunch came and went.

As soon as the afternoon group session began, Bill started it by going over to Don and presenting him with a coffee cup with the serenity prayer printed on the side. "Now remember two things, Don. First, repeat this prayer every day until it becomes second nature and every day after that just because. And," Bill paused and tried to conceal his smile when he said, "this is a coffee cup." The joke was just the comic relief the group needed as several of the women were close to tears.

Bill gave Don a hug and said, "I'll see you in the outpatient groups."

"Now let's tell Don what we wish him," Bill said to the group. "I'll start," he cleared his throat. "Don, I wish you sobriety. I wish you a personal relationship with God. May He always protect you."

Claude, who stood right beside Don, said, "That's right."

"And I wish you love, in life, with your beautiful wife, your son and all your friends, many of whom are in this room. Finally, I wish you peace," Bill finished.

One by one, those who wanted to speak up, spoke and offered Don words of encouragement and love. Jeremi basically echoed the sentiments of Bill, but added, "And I wish you good weather for your barbecue tonight." Don chuckled as he brushed another tear back.

Don was then excused from the group, as his wife had arrived to pick him up. He waved good-bye from the door and said, "I'll never forget any of you." Claude left with him. He echoed the same sentiments to us. We returned the same to him.

28

Group broke up shortly thereafter and everyone was dismissed to their rooms or to their private counseling sessions. Jeremi sat with a new group of people at dinner. Most talked with excitement about visitation tonight. "So who's coming to see you, Jeremi?" the woman across the table from him asked.

"Nobody," Jeremi replied, depressed. "I'll guess I'll watch TV in the solarium."

"That's too bad," she consoled him.

Jeremi picked at his food the rest of the meal.

As dinner finished, individuals were called one by one to the front desk as their visitors arrived. Jeremi was in his own world. He retreated to the solarium and tried to watch a movie on TV. His name was announced three times. By the third time, the nurses were all looking for him.

One finally found him. "Jeremi!" she said loud enough to get his attention over the TV.

"Huh?" he looked up.

She pointed up at the ceiling, in the direction of the closest speaker. "You should listen once in a while, they've been calling your name. You have a visitor."

"I do?"

"They've called you three times. I hope they're still here. You better hurry!"

Jeremi jumped up and followed the nurse, who took him to the place to greet the visitors. Jeremi smiled broadly when he saw Peter. Peter was somber until he saw how good Jeremi looked, then he smiled, too. They embraced.

"He does look good," William said to George and me. We had to agree.

They walked down the hallway to an empty room with couches in it. They sat down.

"So, how are you, my brother?" Peter asked enthusiastically.

"I'm pretty good."

"Just pretty good?"

"Well, I'm fine, really. Probably better than I've been in a long, long time. But I'm just . . . frankly, I'm embarrassed that it had to come to this." Peter nodded. "I'm sorry, man. I'm sorry for what happened." Peter hugged him and Jeremi broke down. After a couple of seconds, they broke apart. Jeremi wiped his eyes. "How's Jeannie? Tell me she's all right. Tell me she, the baby and the girls are all right."

Peter nodded. "She went to the doctor yesterday, I believe. He said 'Everything is okay.'" Jeremi heaved a sigh of relief. "I've seen her once since all this started, but Melinda's called her almost every day to make sure she's all right. She got a crib for the baby. I guess she and her friend won it at the slot machines." Jeremi looked at him strangely. "It sounded a little strange to me too - winning a crib on slots, I guess we'll just get the whole story later." They both shrugged their shoulders. "They got it put together, which must've been a story in itself."

"That's the truth," I told George and William.

"Do you think she'll ever talk to me again?" Jeremi asked Peter.

"Well, she's pretty hurt by everything. You know her emotions are extra strong, being pregnant and all. But I think she'll talk to you again, I think that'll happen. She's this interesting cross between mad as hell at you and worried to death about you."

Jeremi smiled slightly. "Me, too--at me, I mean."

"What's been happening since you got here?"

"Well, it's been weird. I never would've expected it to go this way. The first day is a total blur. Some people have told me I had really bad DTs. I suppose I must've because I know, I was pretty out of it." Peter nodded. "The second night, I was just plain mad. I blamed everyone and his brother," Jeremi glanced at Peter, "for my being here. That it was some big set up, like I was this innocent victim."

"Did that change?" Peter asked.

"Oh yeah," Jeremi answered. Peter sighed. "The counselor and I had this heart-to-heart. He led me down his merry path. I thought he was on my side, that it was this big conspiracy and stuff and then pow, he let me have it." He punched his hand.

"How?" Peter asked eagerly.

"By replaying all the same events but from the other person's perspective. Then he told me to get out, that I was free to leave because his time was too valuable to waste."

"So then what happened?" Peter was wide-eyed.

"I just sat here, actually." Jeremi looked around the room. "I sat over there and I thought about it. I really seriously thought about what life would be like again if I left, without getting better. What next week would look like, what next month would look like, next year. I realized that I deserved better than the life I was dooming myself to live. It felt like Dad was talking to me and telling me this was my chance. That this was where I needed to be." Jeremi got his chill bumps on his arm again. He rubbed them. "Then, you remember at his funeral? You remember the light?" Peter nodded. "I saw it again. From that moment on, it's been all right. I've just been learning and trying to figure out what to do next."

"Wow," Peter said, impressed.

Jeremi leaned back in his chair with a smile. "Yeah."

"So, what's next? When can you go home?"

"I'm hoping just a few more days. Maybe I'll be out by the weekend."

"Whatever day you get out, we'll make the best dinner you ever had. What do you want?"

"Jeannie and the girls to be there," Jeremi said after he paused to think about it.

Peter smiled, nodded and said, "I'll do everything in my power to make that happen for you, bro."

"So will I," I said softly. George patted me on the back.

They visited for about another hour. Jeremi told Peter the rest of the story of his experiences here, from the "weird guy" the second night, all about Don, all about Bill, the nurses, to the baby's name. Jeremi thanked Peter for packing the sweater, to which Peter scratched his head and dismissed it by saying "Melinda must've done that."

"I knew that was you!" I said to George.

"You did not!" he kidded back.

After they were done, Jeremi walked Peter out and they embraced again.

"I'll be here in a heartbeat, if you need anything," Peter assured Jeremi.

"Thanks."

Peter left and Jeremi went back to his room.

That night was pretty peaceful for Jeremi. He went back to his room and read some in his books and went to sleep. I went to see how Jeannie was holding up. She and the girls played a game at the kitchen table. The girls were really into it, but Jeannie was completely distracted. Carole had to tug on her mother's arm to get her attention. Jeannie answered the question at hand or took her turn, but then her look got distant again.

"It's okay if you want to stop playing, Mommy," Carole said.

"I'm fine, honey." Jeannie put her hand on Carole's cheek. "Mommy loves playing games with you girls."

After a bit, there was a knock on the door: Peter.

Jeannie opened the door and gave him a hug. Then the girls ran over to him and did the same.

After the greetings, Peter asked quietly, "Can we talk?"

Jeannie nodded and then told the girls to go to their room for a little while, which they did after they each got one more hug. They successfully stalled the inevitable sentence of going to their room until Jeannie snapped her fingers, then they both walked slowly down the hall to the bedroom. Carole stood in the doorway and tried to listen. Jeannie waited a couple of seconds, then yelled, "Close the door!" Carole turned reluctantly and closed the door behind her.

"I've just come from seeing Jeremi," Peter said.

"That's nice," Jeannie said, less than enthusiastic about it.

"He looks great. He's doing great. He says he's learned a lot."

"Good for him."

"Well, we think he'll be home in a couple of days, maybe by the weekend and Melinda and I are going to throw him a celebration dinner. But the only way it'll be complete is if you and the girls come, too."

"I see," Jeannie said curtly, then she let loose. "And I suppose I'm just supposed to sit there and smile and forget everything that happened? Forget that he cheated on me and lied to me and played me for a fool, while I'm carrying his child!"

"Jeannie, please let him in so he can tell you how sorry he is."

"I'm sorry, too. I'm sorry I ever met him. I'm sorry I ever got close to him." Tears streamed down her face. "I need to figure out what I'm going to do. To go to a dinner and sit there and pretend to be happy, are you kidding me? I've got responsibilities. I've got children to raise. I've got to get through this without having a breakdown because I'm the only one these kids can count on."

"Stop it!" Pearl got right in her face and commanded. "You're throwing a pity party and nobody's coming!"

Jeannie covered her face and cried, the tears leaking out all around her fingers.

Peter put his arm around her. "Jeannie, nobody, especially Jeremi, expects you to forget what happened. But you know as well as I do that he has a problem and that was the primary reason for what happened and he's handling that. He loves you, I know it." Jeannie shook her head and kept her face covered. "Yes, he does. And he wants so much to be part of this family. You're all he could think of--you, the baby and the girls."

Jeannie looked at Peter with a combination of hurt and anger in her eyes and in her voice. "What am I supposed to do, trust him now? Even if I wanted to take him back, I could never trust him again. What future could there be in that? I refuse to live like that! I refuse to be a mother who shows my girls that that is any way to live!" She broke down and cried again, but this time on Peter's shoulder.

"I know you're hurt and rightfully so. It'll take time. But like they're telling him, 'one day at a time.' Okay. Let's take this whole situation, one day at a time. All we can do is trust that God has this all under control - especially when it feels this out of control."

"William, he needs to go. The doctor's worried about her blood pressure getting out of control," Pearl said softly.

"Peter, let's go," William said to Peter.

"Jeannie, listen, I've got to go. I'll call you and tell you what time the dinner will be as soon as I talk to Melinda and when we know for sure what day Jeremi is coming home." Peter got up off the couch. Jeannie nodded. "So you'll come?" Peter asked hopefully.

"We'll see," Jeannie said, biting her lip in an effort to hold back more tears.

"Take care, my sister, and call us if you need us. Understand?" Jeannie reacted shocked when Peter called her his 'sister.' Then Peter helped her up off the couch and gave her another hug.

"I'll let myself out," he said and then left, closing the door behind him.

Jeannie stood there, stunned by what just happened. Pearl shined angel light on the bookmark that Jeannie had mounted in the hallway. Jeannie made her way over to it, leaned back on the opposite wall and stared at it for a moment. Then she walked down the hall and knocked on the girl's door "Ollie, ollie, in come oxen free!"

The girls bounded out of the room. "Where's Uncle Peter?" Carole asked.

"He left," Jeannie said.

Their enthusiasm turned to disappointment. "I wanted to show him my new dress," Carole whined.

"Another day, sweetie. Another day." Jeannie turned and went into her bedroom and sat on the edge of the bed. The girls followed.

"Why are you so sad, Mommy?" Carole asked and sat down on the bed beside her. "Does a baby in your tummy make you sad?"

"Sweetheart." Jeannie pulled Carole up on the bed beside her. "This baby makes me really happy, some one else is making me sad. Here, put your hand right here." She put Carole's hand on her bulging stomach. The baby responded to the pressure and moved around. Carole's eyes got really big. Jeannie groaned a little. "That was your little brother playing with you. How could I be sad, sweetheart, when I know how much I love you and Lynne and this little baby guy and how much you all love me?" Jeannie patted her stomach. Their conversation lasted a while longer. Jeannie slowly began to remember how she was so very happily mommied.

I was worried about what Pearl had said to make Peter leave. "What's wrong with her blood pressure, Pearl?"

"It's been high these past couple of visits. The doctor cautioned her to stay as calm as possible, we still have a couple weeks to go yet. Nothing serious, but we need to watch out for her," Pearl explained. We all agreed.

A little while later, Jeannie tucked the girls into bed and laid down herself. As was typical, within the hour, in waltzed Carole with Lynne close behind. They snuggled up in bed together, Mommy in the middle and baby on top. It was a sight to behold as they drifted off to sleep.

29

I checked on everyone else. Glory was asleep, as was Sarah. Peter told Melinda everything that happened. She hung on every word. I went back and sat with George, who was still at Jeremi's side.

There was a spitting-mad new arrival next to Jeremi, in Don's old bed. He woke Jeremi up a couple of times. Tony played the same part he did on the day Jeremi arrived, irritated by the noise. Jeremi played Don's role. George and I laughed every time Jeremi said something, then he'd quirk his head, as if to say "Where'd that come from?" He smiled to himself as, I'm sure, a memory of his first night here came to mind.

"What's happening out there?" George asked.

I informed him of Peter and Jeannie's talk and the status of the rest of our people. We talked between the new arrival's episodes. We'd come full circle here.

Early the next morning, the roommate was down for the count. Jeremi was on his way to breakfast, when Bill pulled him aside. He wanted to have a private talk with Jeremi. They went to the same room Bill had taken him the night he challenged him.

"Uh-oh," Jeremi said walking into this room.

"What?" Bill asked, surprised.

"The last time you took me here, you ambushed me. I hope this is different." Jeremi asked, only half joking.

"On the contrary, Jeremi, come in, sit down. I want to talk to you about your progress here." Bill Sr. sat next to Bill on his chair and we sat next to Jeremi. Bill Sr. smiled broadly.

"How do you feel about how you are progressing here, Jeremi?" Bill asked him.

Jeremi sighed and looked thoughtful. "Pretty good, I guess."

"Well, I think you're doing pretty good, too. In fact, if you think you can handle it, I want to release you into the outpatient program day after tomorrow." Bill smiled and waited for Jeremi's reaction.

"Really? Man, that's great. Thanks. I'll prove to you that I can handle it!" Jeremi stood up and shook his hand.

"I know you will," Bill said, smiling. "We need these two days here to make the transition. You'll go to a different group this morning and tomorrow morning. Then after the afternoon group on Friday, you can go home, as long as there's someone here to pick you up."

"I've already got that covered!"

Bill got up and Jeremi bounded into breakfast, got his food, sat down with a group of people and plowed right through all of it.

Jeremi was doing really well. However, Jeannie still weighed heavily on my mind--her blood pressure and the way she'd laid into Peter. I needed to get to Pearl. I needed to figure out what we could do to soften her into giving Jeremi another chance.

Jeannie was at work. She focused completely on her work and was currently free from being distracted by her personal situation.

Pearl smiled when I approached. "How's Jeremi?" she asked.

"He's doing great," I answered. "How are our charges doing here?"

"She's pretty steady this morning. Working on some conversion stuff that she's put off forever and making quite a bit of progress today," Pearl said proudly.

"That's good," I replied. There was a moment of awkward silence while I tried to phrase my next question to Pearl.

"I'm still working on it," she said.

"What?" I asked, surprised.

"How to get her to agree to see Jeremi."

"How did you know I--never mind," I said, amazed as usual, this time because it appeared that Pearl could read my mind, too. "So what do we do?"

"Well, I've been thinking about it and if we try the direct approach with her, that hard head of hers will get in the way." Pearl paused. I waited patiently for more. "She's proud, hurt and very vulnerable. What we have to do is to make going over to Peter's to see Jeremi the only option she's got and so compelling that she has to go or it'll drive her crazy."

"So how do we do that?" I completely lacked a handle on the moment.

"Well, we have to think of her well-being first. If she dwells on this, her blood pressure will go up. So, first off, we have to get her mind off it."

"How do we do that?"

"Easy, make her think she's going somewhere else, so that relieves her of her stress, then at the last minute, take that away. It'll take some cooperation from some other angels, but it'll work, sure enough."

"I see, they'll cancel and she'll be left with nothing to do but go see Jeremi. Ooo. You're slick."

"Thank you."

"Jeannie?" Judie whispered. "Jeannie," Judie said a little louder. "Jeannie," she finally said it loud enough to break through.

"Yes?" Jeannie said, with out looking up from her terminal.

"Jeannie," Judie said.

"What?" Jeannie looked over at Judie.

Judie pointed to her watch. Jeannie looked at hers.

"How'd it get so late so quick? Let me do one more thing." Jeannie typed again quickly and finished the thought. Then she rocked a couple times to get enough momentum behind her to stand up, as Judie finished putting on her walking shoes. Jeannie stretched and arched her back. She was in full profile. If the baby got much bigger, it'd pop out the front. They went outside for a walk.

"You've been into your work this morning," Judie said. "Are you getting a lot done?"

"Surprisingly, yes."

"Why are you surprised?"

"Oh, Peter came by last night and told me about Jeremi. I've been trying to keep my mind off of it."

"What happened?"

"Oh, he said Jeremi was doing great and that he was going to get out tomorrow probably and that he wanted us to come over for a big celebration dinner."

"Why has that got you so upset?"

Jeannie stopped in her tracks and gave Judie the biggest look of disbelief I think she could've mustered. "Oh, yeah, like I'm just going to go over there and fall all over him like nothing happened."

"I see. So there's zero hope for you and Jeremi ever again?"

After an awkward silence, she said quietly, "Doubtful... maybe... who knows?"

"What would have to happen for you to give him another chance?"

"What, are you on his side now?"

"No, I'm just asking. I know you've thought about it."

Jeannie stared at Judie and there was another awkward silence, then Jeannie looked down at her feet but her belly got in the way. She patted her stomach and said quietly, "Yeah. I have."

"So what would have to happen?"

Jeannie sighed. "He'd have to apologize. He'd have to apologize so big that, that . . ." Judie waited, Jeannie softened. "He'd have to stay sober for one." She paused again. "I'd have to wait and see if I could ever learn to trust him again."

"That's a good start. So could that all happen tomorrow night over at Peter's? Then you'd be able to see for yourself, instead of just worrying and fretting."

"I need more time. It's too soon." Jeannie tried to rationalize her fears about going to see Jeremi.

"You're certain, you're going to decline the invitation to go to Peter's tomorrow night, right?"

"Yes," Jeannie said, less than convincingly. Judie looked her in the eyes. "Yes," she said with a little more conviction.

"Fine, then how about I take you and the girls out to see that new cartoon movie that came out this week? I've been dying to go see it, but I wanted to take a kid.. Your girls can come too." Judie looked quickly at Jeannie, who smiled slyly.

"Okay," Jeannie conceded. "That'll be fun. I'll tell the girls tonight."

"Great!"

Judie's angel winked at Pearl and me.

"Mission accomplished: Jeannie's been diverted," I said glibly.

"Her mind is settled and her blood pressure should be all right," Pearl acknowledged.

"I need to get back to base," I said, continuing the secret-agent impression. Pearl laughed and waved at me, so I headed back to Jeremi.

He was in the outpatient group session, Don right beside him. Jeremi contributed quite a bit to the discussion.

George smiled like a proud father. "Good, I'm glad you're back, Martin. I've been called away for a while and I'll need you to stay with Jeremi until I get back."

"What's going on?" It was unusual for George to get called away like this.

"My new assignment has been decided and I need to go do some things."

My eyes got big. "Already? I thought you'd be with me until at least the baby came. Then I was hoping for a little while longer."

"I know, but once the baby comes, I'll have to go to my new charge. That's just the way it works. I'll be back soon, Martin." Then he was gone.

"But--" It was too late, he'd already left. I felt a range of emotions that I could scarcely fathom. There was apprehension that I'd be being an angel all alone. There was sadness about how much I'd miss having George teach me what he knew. There was fear that Jeremi would fall back into his old ways without an angel close enough to help him if he needed it. There was excitement that my grandson was about to arrive. There was joy about Jeremi's spiritual growth of the past few days. My emotions were all over the place. I sighed heavily. I thought: If I was this unsettled when I was alive, I'd pray. Being an angel, what better thing to do?

"God," I began.

"Yes," he replied and I was engulfed by beautiful golden light. "What's on your heart, Martin?"

I lost my train of thought.

"Tell me what's troubling you, Martin."

"I have so many worries."

"I know. I'll alleviate them all, if you just talk to me."

"There's Jeremi and Jeannie, the time for the baby is close and they're apart," I said.

"What else?"

"George is going to a new charge. He's been by my side for as long as I can remember and even before that. What if I need him? Could we have some more time together to prepare me for all of this?"

The light brightened. "Martin, you were asked to take this position because of your wisdom. You are more than ready to become your grandson's Guardian Angel. It's George you're afraid of losing, his companionship, his guidance."

"Yes, I am."

"Since you've become an angel, have you been able to see whoever you wanted, whenever you wanted, whenever they wanted you? Whether they be alive or angel?"

"Yes."

"Then George will never be long away," He assured me. "As for Jeannie and Jeremi, their child's angel will bring them back together. The strength of their bond, well, that has yet to be determined. They both still have many, many lessons to learn along the way, how well and how quickly they learn them will create the strength of their love."

I was quiet and sat there, absorbed the beauty of the light. When I finally closed my eyes, I was back at the hospital with Jeremi. Barely any time had elapsed. I felt so peaceful.

The group session ended and Jeremi went back up to his room. The new guy sat on his bed. When Jeremi walked in the new roomie said, "Hello. My name is Ken. I need to apologize for some of the things I said to you the other night."

Jeremi went over and shook his hand. "Forget about it, man. We've all been there, believe me."

"I'm still very sorry."

"Do you want to talk?"

"Yeah, I'd really like that."

So Jeremi sat on his bed, Ken on his. They told each other their life stories. The rest of the afternoon passed and it was dinnertime. After dinner, it was visiting time again. Peter came and Jeremi told him about his release the next day.

"Dinner's on!" Peter said and hugged his brother.

"Will Jeannie be there?"

Peter motioned for Jeremi to sit down, then Peter explained to him about the conversation that he and Jeannie had had the night before. Jeremi's excitement drained and he looked as if he'd been punched in the stomach.

"Listen, Jeremi, it'll be all right. Whether she comes tomorrow night or decides to stay away, so what? Big deal. You go see her the next day and you make it up to her. You find a way. You prove to her that you love her. You find a way. But I'll still try everything in my power to get her there, I promise."

Their visit lasted a little while longer. Then Peter left. Jeremi went back to his room. He stood and looked out the window. It was the first time since he'd been told that he would be released that he was quiet. "I'm going to prove to you, Jeannie, I'm going to show you how I've changed. I want you and my child and the girls in my life. We're going to make a great family! You just wait and see." A tear streamed down his face. He stared out the window a while longer, then he laid down on the top of his bed and stared at the ceiling. He worked it all out in his head. Eventually he drifted off to sleep.

George returned after Jeremi had fallen asleep and I brought him up to speed on events, then on mine.

"I'm glad you told me what happened when you talked to Jesus today. I have to admit, I feel that way, too. After all, I've known you a lot longer than you've known me," George said to me.

He had a point. We stayed there together that night. We watched over Jeremi, hoped and prayed that all our plans would come out well the next day and that Jeremi's homecoming would be joyous for him and for Jeannie.

30

As the first ray of sunlight broke through the window and across his face, Jeremi woke up. He got up, made his bed, showered, dressed, collected and organized all his personal items and prepared to go home.

The nurse came in and she and Jeremi talked alone quietly. She left and came back a bit later with a big white bag for Jeremi to put all his belongings in, which he quickly did. Then she woke his roommates.

Jeremi was fine. So I went to check on Jeannie to see how her day would start out. She was in bed still, a girl on either side, smashing the snooze alarm one more time. Pearl, Marie and Edwina chuckled at the sight. I stood there and shook my head and then they laughed at me.

"Wait 'til there's three!" Pearl said and laughed even harder. It was so funny to contemplate, I had to laugh, too.

Jeannie eventually got up and stumbled her way to the bathroom. Pearl disappeared behind the door with her and Marie and Edwina watched over their charges.

"This is going to be a big day," I said to them.

"Amen," Marie agreed.

"Promise to call if you need me," I reminded them. They nodded and I left again. I caught up with Jeremi in the dining room. He had scarfed down his breakfast and now, checked his watch. I could tell he was doing calculations in his head of how many hours it would be until Peter would come to get him and he could start his life all over again.

The morning outpatient group session went well. He and Don played around as usual, but got down to business when it was time.

Lunch came and Jeremi's excitement started to turn to nervousness. He picked at his lunch and calculated the time left remaining. At this point, he had to have been counting the minutes left. He and Ken talked quite a bit, but Jeremi was very distracted. Ken laughed really hard when Jeremi put cream and sugar in his soda.

Finally, it was time to go to the afternoon group session, his graduation. Everyone in the group wished him health, sobriety and prosperity. They wished him control over what was previously uncontrolled in his life. Then it came time for Bill to say his good-byes.

"Jeremi, I want to wish you all the same as what your fellow recovering friends have wished you. I want you to remember that this struggle is fought one day at a time. And even though you're faced with challenges in the near future, I believe you've come this far and will remain successful in doing what it is that you want to do. With that in mind, I have some gifts for you." He reached behind him and pulled out a large bag with presents inside. He handed the bag to Jeremi.

Jeremi reached in and the first thing he pulled out was a box that said, "For Jeremi." He unwrapped a coffee cup with the serenity prayer inscribed on the side. "I know, I know," Jeremi said to Bill. "This is a coffee cup!" The group laughed that Jeremi had beaten Bill to his trademark punch-line. The second thing he pulled out was a box that said, "For Marshal (with one '1')." He showed it off and muttered, "I must've said that a few times." He unwrapped a baby bottle with an inscription of the serenity prayer on the side. He held them both up to show off the set and everyone laughed.

"Now go and be a great, sober father!" Bill said.

He gave Jeremi a handshake and then they embraced, "I will," Jeremi said quietly back to Bill.

Bill Sr. and George and I said our good-byes as well. Then Jeremi hotfooted it out of the room as everyone clapped and said good-bye.

The nurse stood by the door with his belongings in a bag right beside her. He picked them up without missing a beat and she yelled after him "Good luck!"

Peter was in the waiting room, ready to go as soon as Jeremi came in.

"Excited?" Peter asked.

"Yup!"

When they got back to Peter's house, Jeremi greeted Melinda and tossed his belongings onto the bed in his room. Then he made a beeline for the phone. Peter and Melinda just watched.

He dialed and then said, "Baby, listen, I know you're at work, but I wanted to tell you that I'm home now and that I want . . . I mean, I need . . . I mean, I'd . . . I'd really like it . . . I mean, I'm sorry for what happened and I'd like to tell you that tonight over dinner here at six-thirty. Bring the girls. Please come, I have so much to tell you." Jeremi hung up the phone.

"You could've just called her directly." Melinda said.

"To call her at work, might've caused a problem."

He sat down. He crossed his legs one way, then the other. Then he shifted in his chair. Then he started to tap his fingers.

Melinda said, "Well, if we're putting on a dinner tonight, we'd better get cookin'." She smiled at Jeremi.

"Let me help." Jeremi jumped up. The three of them got to work to get ready for a family dinner.

I checked on Jeannie to make sure all our plans were still in place. They were still at work. "Make sure she listens to her answering machine when she gets home," I told Pearl.

"Okay," Pearl agreed.

Jeannie was very anxious, too. She looked just like Jeremi did. Her phone rang and she jumped a mile. Judie noticed and as soon as Jeannie hung up the phone, she asked if she was ready to take a walk. Jeannie declined, but Judie watched her carefully. Eventually Judie came to the inevitable conclusion. She whispered, "She's got it bad!"

"Did you say something, Judie?" Jeannie asked.

Judie cleared her throat and said quickly, "Uh, no, nothing, nothing at all." Judie turned her head away from Jeannie, so she could smirk freely.

Quitting time finally rolled around. Jeannie gathered her things together. "Remember, six-fifteen, my place, right? We'll grab a quick dinner before the movie," Judie said. Jeannie confirmed the deal with a nod, smiled, and left.

She picked up the girls and hurried home. She told the girls all about going out to dinner and seeing a great movie tonight. They were excited.

When Jeannie walked into the door, Pearl shined her angel light on the answering machine. Jeannie saw the light blinking, but avoided the machine like it could bite. She went down the hall to change out of her work clothes and into something more casual for a night at the movies.

Since Jeannie refused to cooperate, Marie jumped in and helped out. She shined her angel light on the answering machine and got Carole's attention focused on it. Carole ran right over to it and said, "Look, Mommy, the light is flashing; there's a message." She pressed play before Jeannie could run over and stop her. Jeannie was apprehensive and Carole was excited to hear Jeremi's voice. They stood there and listened to the message. When it was done, Jeannie's hand started to tremble and she sat down quickly.

Carole jumped up and down. "Mommy, Jeremi's all better now! Can we go see him, he said for you to bring us. Can we Mommy, pleeeeease!"

"Carole, we're going to the movies."

"Can we have dinner at Jeremi's and then go to the movies?"

"We're eating dinner with Judie and that's final!"

"Aw, Mommy!" Carole stomped out of the room. I followed Carole into her bedroom because if I really thought she'd give up that easily, they'd reassess my skills as a guardian angel.

Carole was telling Lynne all about Jeremi's invitation and then Lynne came out and begged her mommy, "Emi?" Lynne was so cute with that little baby voice and big eyes.

"Honey," she picked up Lynne. "Carole! What did you tell her?" Jeannie yelled down the hall.

Carole came out of the room sheepishly, giving her mother another dose of the puppy-dog eyes. "Nothing," she said innocently.

"I bet," Jeannie said sarcastically. "We're going over to Judie's to pick her up for dinner and then we're going to see the movie and that's that!" Jeannie commanded. She grabbed her purse, the diaper bag, the children and they left the house.

In the car, Carole nagged on at her mother. "But, why?"

"Silence!" Jeannie snapped and Carole crossed her arms in frustration.

The drive over to Judie's house was humorous. Pearl pulled out all the stops! She constantly talked to Jeannie about every place she passed and replayed a memory - any memory - that it held for her and Jeremi. Jeannie had trouble keeping it together on the road, so Edwina and Marie and I handled that part. It was clear Pearl, being the master she was, was getting through to Jeannie.

As Jeannie approached the last turn to Judie's house, Pearl went into high gear to get Jeannie's curiosity up about Jeremi now. "I know you're wondering if he really is sober. I know you're curious what he's been thinking about these past few days. You want to know if he really is sorry. You're obviously still hooked on him, feel that knot in your stomach, it's more than a baby in there! Your hands are trembling. Come on. You're just aching to know. Set aside your pride and go find out."

Jeannie shook it off. Then she looked serious and determined and drove straight up to Judie's house and into the driveway. "I'll be right back," she said to the girls, as she turned the car off and walked up to the door.

When she got to the door, she saw a note taped to the doorbell. It read, "Jeannie, I'm sorry I've got to cancel our plans for tonight. Something came up and I had to leave town suddenly. I'll be back to work on Monday, I hope. Tell you all about it then. I'm sorry again. Judie."

Jeannie heaved a heavy sigh and went back to the car. Luckily, she was oblivious to Judie as she peered out of the side window of the dark house. Judie smiled as she mouthed the words, "Good luck, Jeannie."

Judie's angel also wished us luck.

"Where's Judie?" Carole asked.

"The note says she had to leave town suddenly. I hope nothing's wrong," Jeannie said.

"So, can we go to Jeremi's now?" Carole asked.

Jeannie looked at her and tried to say no, but instead her eyes got big, she bit her bottom lip and held her stomach.

"What's happening?" I asked.

"She's having a contraction. Her blood pressure is way up about now," Pearl informed us all.

"Are you all right, Mommy?" Carole asked.

The contraction ended and so did the lip-biting. She blew out a good breath and said, "Yes, honey, Mommy's just fine."

Pearl took it from high gear to overdrive: She started to chant, "Jeremi! Jeremi!" Edwina and Marie followed her lead and got the girls to chant "Jeremi! Jeremi!"

"All right!" Jeannie yelled. The car quieted down. "We'll go see him, but just for a minute, then we're leaving!"

The girls cheered. Jeannie turned around and gave them a scolding look. The car was quiet as they drove over to Peter's house, save some light giggling in the back seat.

Pearl pointed her finger at the radio and smiled. Jeannie turned it on. The song was one of the songs that Jeremi sang frequently at the pub. Jeannie shook her head and rolled her eyes. "Okay, okay, okay!!!" she muttered. "I'm going, I'm going! Sheesh!" Jeannie snapped off the radio and the angels laughed.

I went ahead to see how Jeremi was holding up in this waiting game. He and Peter, Melinda sat around the table. It was after 6:30, barely. "Maybe she's stuck in traffic," Melinda offered.

Jeremi, looking down, shook his head.

"She's a woman, you know how they can be," Peter said. Melinda shot a look at him over her glasses of complete disbelief for saying something so stupid. Peter got very defensive. "Well, you know what I mean," he said.

"How could I know what you mean sir, I'm just a silly girl," Melinda did her best southern belle accent.

Jeremi chuckled a little at that exchange.

Their faces all perked up when they heard the car pull up.

Jeremi jumped up and knocked into the table, crushing his hand between it and his thigh. He shook out his hand and ran to the peephole in the door. "It's them!"

He opened the door just as Carole and Lynne ran up to it. They ran in. Jeremi got down on his knees and hugged them tight. Carole gave him a kiss. Jeannie appeared in the doorway. The expression on her face was neutral. She waited for him to set the tone.

Jeannie stepped inside the doorway. Jeremi went over to her and held her, just held her. He began to cry. "I'm so sorry. I'm so sorry. I just pray that some day you'll be able to forgive me those horrible things. Please, please give me a second chance."

After he said it a couple of times, her arms reached up and she hugged him back. Tears streamed down her face, too.

He let go of her and backed away a step. He patted her protruding belly and said, "Are you all right?" Jeannie nodded. Jeremi held out his hand. Jeannie looked at it, then slowly reached out hers. Then, hand-in-hand, they walked to the table. Peter, Melinda and the girls all watched and smiled.

They situated themselves around the tables. The children had their own table in the kitchen and the four adults were out in the dining room. Since Jeannie had some trouble getting up and down easily, the other three adults took turns and saw to the childrens' needs as dinner progressed.

Jeremi talked non-stop through dinner, telling them all about the experiences he'd had over the last several days. He told them about Bill cornering him. He told them about the golden light and his decision to stay. He told them about Don. He told about the group sessions. Then he showed them the good-bye presents. Peter looked at the tag on the baby's bottle.

"So you told them about Marshal, with one 'l'?" he asked.

Jeremi nodded. Jeannie was curious, so Jeremi drew it out for her. He showed her the names "Martin" and "Sheila" and drew arrows down from those letters to form the name "Marshal." Jeannie smiled and shivered.

"Do you like it?" Jeremi asked.

"Yeah, I do. It just gave me a chill."

Everyone listened to Jeremi talk on through dinner. Jeannie listened, too, but occasionally she'd lift her napkin to her mouth and clasp her hand hard on her thigh. She'd had several contractions but she did her level best to hide them from everyone.

About the fourth time this happened during dinner, I asked, "Pearl, is she all right?"

"Actually, it's time to get her some help," Pearl responded. "She's starting to have regular contractions. They're ten minutes apart right now. A couple more and we're gonna have to blow the whistle on her."

All the angels agreed.

Jeannie had stopped eating and only sipped her water.

Melinda was the first to notice something was up. Jeremi was still deep in his stories and Peter was listening intently. Melinda started to watch Jeannie. Jeannie had another contraction and as she had done before, she put her napkin over her mouth, grabbed her thigh and looked away from everyone, without making any noise. It was a feat to behold. Melinda saw this, glanced at her watch, and also kept quiet. The next time it happened, she and Jeannie made eye contact. Jeannie had a panicked look in her eye. Melinda mouthed the words "Are you all right?" Jeannie nodded. Melinda glanced at her watch again. As ten minutes approached again, Melinda looked at her watched and then waited to see if Jeannie would have another contraction. Right on schedule, up went the napkin and to her thigh went her hand. Jeannie realized that Melinda now knew, but Jeannie pleaded with her with her eyes to keep quiet. Melinda kept her secret, but looked at her watch again.

Melinda kept a watch on the time, as yet another contraction hit.

"Okay, I'm blowing the whistle on her!" Pearl announced. "Get Carole in here." Marie jiggled the table and a little water spilled on Carole's dress. Carole immediately got up and ran to her mommy. Carole stopped short when she saw the strained look on her mother's face. But before Jeannie could shake her head to keep her from saying anything, Carole announced, "Mommy, your face is all scrunchy again!"

Peter and Jeremi focused on the situation just as the contraction subsided. Jeannie looked around and realized she'd been found out. She let out a big, cleansing breath, now that her secret was out.

"That's about the sixth one I've seen. Carole, has your mom had that scrunchy-faced look before?" Melinda asked her.

"Yeah, at Judie's house just before we came here."

Melinda confronted Jeannie. "How long have you been in labor?"

"What?!" Jeremi and Peter jumped up at the same time.

"You're in labor?" Jeremi asked her directly.

"Probably," Jeannie said, then shifted in her seat.

"The ones I've seen are about ten minutes apart," Melinda said. "You're due in a couple of weeks, right?" Jeannie nodded.

"When was the last time you saw the doctor?" Jeremi asked.

"On Tuesday," Jeannie told him.

"What did he say?" They all asked in their own way.

"That I could start to have stress contractions and that I needed to work at keeping my blood pressure down."

Jeremi took that pretty hard. "Oh man, it's all my fault. I did this to you. I am so sorry."

"You did this to me, all right!" Jeannie capitalized on that confession.

They all laughed, which provided some welcomed comic relief. Jeremi's panic settled somewhat.

"What's happening, Mommy?" Carole asked.

"Well, sweetheart," Melinda got up and took Carole by the hand and led her back into the kitchen and explained, "Jeremi is going to drive your mother to the hospital. You and your sister are going to stay here with your Uncle Peter and me. How would you guys like to have a slumber party?" All the children cheered.

"I'll drive you," Jeremi offered.

"No, I'll drive. Really all this fuss is too --" Jeannie started to stand up, but another contraction hit her. After it was finished, she went to her purse and handed Jeremi the car keys. Jeremi and Peter each took an arm and helped Jeannie to the car. Melinda and all the children waved as they watched out the window.

"It's showtime!" George said. George and I sat by Jeremi and kept him driving carefully. He was carrying precious cargo.

"Is there something familiar about this scene?" Pearl whispered to Jeannie, who then chuckled to herself.

"What's so funny?" Jeremi asked her.

"I was just thinking that about nine months ago, we were doing this exact same thing." Jeannie laughed some more until a contraction interrupted it.

"That's a trip, huh?" Jeremi said and cracked a smile.

They got to the emergency room. Jeremi ran in, grabbed a wheelchair and brought it to the car. An orderly came out and assisted him. The orderly wheeled Jeannie inside, right to the check-in desk. Jeremi went to park the car. Jeannie finished checking in, when Jeremi got back to her side. The nurse pointed and Jeremi wheeled her down the hallway to the elevator.

"Wave hello to the nice doctor," Jeremi said.

Jeannie looked up and realized the man at the end of the hall was the doctor who had told her she was pregnant. They both waved and smiled and he waved back, too, but walked on. As they got on to the elevator, the doctor came back around the corner quickly to do a double-take, but Jeannie and Jeremi were already gone. The doctor scratched and shook his head, then went about his business. Even the doctor's angel laughed with us.

"Anne! I've got to call Anne," Jeannie panicked. Then she thought about it and counted on her fingers and said, "Wait, no. Anne should already be here. I think she's working tonight."

"I'll find her for you," Jeremi reassured her.

They got to the nurse's station on the labor and delivery floor. A nurse walked them down to their room and Jeannie was handed a gown and instructed to change behind some curtains. Jeremi was told to leave the room, so he did. He went to the nurse's station and asked about Anne's whereabouts. Luckily, she was already at the hospital, working only one floor up from labor and delivery. So he called her. Pearl had already contacted Robin. So Anne was right by the phone when it rang.

When Jeremi was allowed back into the room, Jeannie was hooked up to several monitors. The nurse was reading the tapes. "Ooo, that was a good one," the nurse said.

Jeannie let out a breath. "You're telling me," she said to the nurse, who turned from Jeannie and smiled to herself.

"We'll just watch you for a little while and check your progress. Just press the blue button if you need us," the nurse told her and left.

Jeremi pulled up a chair and held her hand. "Are you all right?" He asked gently. Jeannie nodded. "Thank you for letting me be here with you. I've been so worried about you." Jeannie nodded as another contraction hit her. They breathed together. He held her hand; she squeezed it. Jeremi winced.

"Ooo, that's the hand he hurt in the rush to the door," I said.

"Yup. if he knows what's good for him, he'll just keep quiet about that," George answered.

Jeremi sat back down after the contraction was over and asked her, "Do you know what?"

"What?"

"All that time in detox made me realize something," he continued. She looked at him, waiting for him to tell her. "That I love you and I love the girls and that I love this baby. Nothing's ever going to come between us ever again. I came so close to losing you all and I'm never going to risk that again for anything. I'm sorry for all the times I hurt you."

As he said that, another contraction started and she still had hold of his hand, so she squeezed. From the look on Jeremi's face, I think she squeezed a lot harder this time. They breathed together. He showed his pain to her this time. As soon as the contraction was over, she let go. He shook out his hand. and said, "Remind to keep my hands to myself if I talk about that again while you're having contactions. I really do feel your pain now."

"Did that hurt?" Jeannie asked.

"Yeah."

"Good," she said, then looked at Jeremi and they both laughed. She waited a couple of seconds and then said, "I'm sorry." Then under her breath, she added, "Kinda."

"It's okay," Jeremi replied. Then, in an act of real trust, he put his hand back in her hand again.

The contractions continued to be ten minutes apart for about another hour. In between, Jeremi told her what he'd thought about at the Hope Center about how he wanted to be a family and stay with her and the girls and the new baby forever.

As the contractions started to get more intense and closer together, there was a light knock on the door. Robin appeared when Anne opened the door. Anne hugged Jeannie and acknowledged Jeremi. She went over to the monitors to read the tape.

"They're pretty steady. This looks like the real thing," Anne said.

"I hope so," Jeannie said. "I'd hate to think somebody might be kidding me."

"Kid-ding! That's a good one," Anne said. Jeannie rolled her eyes. "Sorry, nurse humor."

Jeannie had another contraction and both Anne and Jeremi held her hands and breathed with her. Anne watched Jeremi more than Jeannie. After the contraction was over, Anne called Jeremi to the side.

"Can I talk to you in the hallway, please?" she said. It was a question, but it came out more like a command. They went out into the hallway. "Listen, Jeremi, that's my best friend in the world in there. I've known her for ten years and in all that time combined, I've never seen her cry as much as I have these past few days. If you're back, great! Go, be there for her. If you hurt her again, you will answer to me."

Jeremi looked down at his feet. "You're right, I've screwed up and I know it's been hard on her." He stared Anne down. Then he added, "But I'm different now. I swear her heart is safe with me."

They were both silent and stern during the rest of the stare-down.

Then Anne shook it off, obviously taken in by what he'd said. "Do you know what you're doing in there? I mean, being a coach?"

"Some," Jeremi admitted.

"Then get ready for a crash course." They both went back in to Jeannie.

As soon as they arrived back by Jeannie's side, she started another contraction. "Okay, keep breathing with her, he-he-who, he-he-who," Anne instructed. Jeremi and Jeannie made eye contact and breathed the way Anne instructed. When the contraction ended, Anne went on, "Okay, big cleansing breath." They all did one.

"Now, for the rest of the time, Jeremi, you just make her as comfortable as possible. Rub whatever she wants rubbed. Get her ice chips, if she wants ice chips. She's the boss, you just listen to her and the doctor."

"I got it," Jeremi said.

"Okay, I'll swing back by after I get off shift." She hugged Jeannie one more time and stared Jeremi down.

"We'll be fine," Jeremi told her.

Anne left.

"How are you holding up?" Pearl asked me.

"Yeah, you're about to graduate," George added. "From Angel-in-Training to full-fledged Guardian."

"I guess I'm doing okay," I said. "I just want these guys to be all right."

"That's what an angel does," Pearl said.

"So when do you take over for your new charge, George?" Pearl asked.

"As soon as the baby is born."

"That soon?" I asked.

"Yes. That soon."

"But what about Jeremi?" I asked. "Who's going to watch over him, if I take over for the baby and you have a new charge?"

George smiled and said, "He'll get a new angel, if and when he's proven he deserves a new angel. He's on the right track. It'll just be a matter of time now."

"How much time?" I asked.

"God knows," George answered.

"Well, if Jeremi stays close, then I'll help take care of both of them. He'll be all right. I'll just watch out for him, too. I can do that," I plotted. Then I looked at George and he was silent. "I can do that, right?"

"You must always watch over your charge first. That is your duty. If you go thinking you can save the world, Martin, you could compromise Marshal's safety. He is your primary responsibility now," George instructed.

"Then what can I do about Jeremi?"

"Let God handle it," George counseled me. "Proverbs 3:5. Remember?"

"'Trust in God with all your heart.' Yes, I remember."

The doctor was in with them now. He said Jeannie was dilated to five centimeters and that he'd break her water, if he still needed to in about an hour. This was it. The doctor gave her a pain block. She looked much better as soon as it took effect.

She and Jeremi were mostly quiet now. They just watched each other. Neither one said much.

Jeannie broke the silence and said softly, "I like the name Marshal, with one 'l'."

"You do?" Jeremi lit up.

"Yes, I really do. It's sweet the way you came up with it."

"But what if it's a girl?"

"He's a boy. He's a boy - trust me."

Jeremi talked to Jeannie's belly. "Hey, Marshal. Son, let's give your mom a break, okay? Come out and see us now." Jeremi rubbed Jeannie's stomach and leaned over and kissed it.

Jeannie's water broke right then and Jeannie commanded, "Call the nurse!"

"What did I do?" Jeremi ran around panicked and almost slipped in the puddle on the floor.

"Watch out!" I yelled at him. He spun around and got back where he belonged.

Pearl took my hand and patted it. "Your baby is almost here, Guardian," she said to me.

I patted her hand back.

We watched as the doctor came back in and took up residency. Anne had gotten off shift and helped where she could. Jeannie progressed quickly and the pushing began. Poor Jeannie, she worked so hard. Jeremi held her up from the back when she needed more strength to push. They worked together to bring the baby into the world.

"It's a boy!" the doctor announced.

"His name is Marshal," Jeannie said. Jeremi kissed Jeannie on the forehead. "With one 'l'," she added.

"Well, Dad, do you want to come and cut the cord?" the doctor asked of Jeremi.

Jeremi got in position and cut the cord. He looked so proud as he looked at his son.

"This is so amazing," I said. My new grandson was here. I was his Guardian Angel. His father was right beside him, just the way we prayed for it to be.

"Ahem, Martin," George said.

"George! This is good-bye? Really? I, ah, What can I say? What's appropriate? Thank you? Is that what you say to someone who's protected you and taught you as much as you've taught me?" We embraced. "I hope your new charge knows how lucky he is to have you as his angel."

"I loved being your angel, Martin, but that time has passed. You've been a good student and you're going to make a great Guardian. Remember, Proverbs 3:5. You need to go to your charge, Martin, and I need to go to mine."

"Good-bye," I said. George smiled, waved and disappeared.

I gathered my strength and focused on Marshal. They cleaned him up and took his measurements. He was eight pounds even and twenty-one inches long. He was the most beautiful baby I had ever seen. "You missed a spot," I told the nurse, who then cleaned a wad of goo out from behind his ear. I shined my angel light on it, as did her angel and the nurse cleaned it right up. They wrapped Marshal up in a blanket and brought him back over to Jeannie, who held him and kissed him. She smiled and cried and cried and smiled. It was wonderful.

"Let me see the baby," Naomi said. "I can only stay a minute. Aw, he's precious."

Then Sheila, my mother, father and Grandmama came to peek. So many angels came in so quickly to sneak a peek and kiss the new baby, I lost count. Jack came and some other angels from Jeannie's side of the family. There were so many things happening, I just tried to help hold on to the baby. I was lost in a blur until I heard a voice command, "Watch out for that slick spot, Jeremi!" I turned to see Jeremi jump quickly over the puddle of water still on the floor.

There was George hovering over Jeremi.

When Jeremi got back over close to the baby, I stared George down. "Jeremi's your new charge? You could've told me!" I demanded.

George said, "I told you to trust God and he'd handle it."

Jeremi was George's new charge. George laughed at me, as usual. This, now, was truly perfect.

Jeremi hovered over the baby and Jeannie. George called me over out of the way and said, "I have something for you. Close your eyes." As soon as I complied, George said, "Okay." He grinned from one ear to the other and handed me a big frosty glass--full of lemonade.

I took a sip. It was delicious and sweet. "Ahhh," I said. "We definitely made some sweet lemonade today, George."

George replied, "Why, Martin, I'd have thought you'd figured it out by now, that's how it works when you've got angels on board!"

About the Author

EJ Thornton

EJ has always been spiritual. Angel On Board 'happened to her' several years ago after some stunning events in her life. The character of Jeannie is modeled after EJ.

The writing of this book was inspired by real events in her life. During the period of the pregnancy of her son, EJ felt an extra dimension of protection around her and her unborn child. The pregnancy was unexpected and the grandfather of the baby died just a couple of weeks before the child was conceived. Even though they had never met, the connection EJ felt with the baby's grandfather was unlike anything she'd ever experienced. Almost all of the human events in the book depict real events.

EJ is dyslexic and never aspired to be a writer, but this book kept pounding on the inside of her until she let it out. Angels definitely helped her author it and she has many, many stories to tell on that score.

Originally, this book was written to an audience of one, her alcoholic (now-ex) husband. He blamed his abuse of alcohol on his grief. She was certain that his angels were angered being held up as his excuse for his addiction. Luckily, God envisioned a much larger audience.

Quite unexpectedly, EJ started receiving letters from readers who had overcome incredible grief issues, just by reading the book. She holds these most precious letters close to her heart, for from these, she's realized the true audience for the book. It can be just a fun fiction read, but when it is in the hands of one who is grieving, it is truly an incredible comfort.

EJ wrote the book, but she wants everyone to know that her angels helped every step of the way!

Now it's in your hands . . .

EJ's willing to bet that your angels put it there!

Update: August 2007

Recently, EJ's angels inspired her revisit this book. For many years, EJ has been deep in spiritual studies and realizing the power of affirmative statements. She challenged herself to rewrite *Angel On Board* completely in the affirmative, and as she did it, she realized how easy it really was to eliminate negative words from the book. Because she has *Angel On Board* now is the **Best Angel Book ever written**, it is also the **Most Positive Book Ever Written!!!**

Angel on Board
Real Life Stories
—> Now, it's your turn to tell your story <—

EJ's received so many letters detailing readers' similar experiences with angels that there is a new series of books in the process of being published.

Angel On Board, Real Life Stories, is a collection of readers' stories that are so extraordinary that the hand of the angels can clearly be seen. Some are about visions of angels, others about extraordinary people who were nothing short of angels, and others about miraculous events. If you have a "Real Life Story," please submit it for review to:

Angel On Board, Real Life Stories
c/o Profitable Publishing
17011 Lincoln Ave. #408
Parker, Colorado 80134

Stories must be 5000 words or less and must represent a real event in your life and must include your bio and the bio of the angel involved (if known).

Other Books by
EJ Thornton

Secrets to Creating
Passive Income
and becoming financially free

ISBN: 0-9801941-9-9   **$24.97**

(co authored with John Clark Craig)

I Have a Secret
Do I Keep It?
for ages 3-8, teaching child safety

ISBN: 1-932344-66-7   **$9.97**

The Basic of
Profitable Publishing

A perspective on publishing by an
author and a publisher!

ISBN: 1-932344-50-0   **$19.97**

Advanced Book Marketing

For authors who simply
want to sell more books.

ISBN: 0-9820838-6-6   **29.97**

To order copies of the book

Angel On Board - Second Edition

$19.97 + 2.50 (S&H)

online at:
http://GreatAngelBooks.com

by phone:
(303) 794-8888

by fax:
(720) 863-2013

by mail:
send check payable to:

Profitable Publishing
17011 Lincoln Ave. #408
Parker, Colorado 80134

if it is temporarily sold out at your favorite bookstore:
have them order more of ISBN: 1-932344-76-4
ISBN (first edition): 0-9670242-0-X

Name: _____
Address: _____
_____
Phone: _____
E-mail _____

Credit Card #: _____
Card Type: _____   Expiration Date: ____/ ____
Security Code: _____